KILLABLE HOURS

KILLABLE HOURS

PAMELA EDDY

Five Star • Waterville, Maine

First Edition, Second Printing.

Published in 2002 in conjunction with Tekno-Books and Ed Gorman.

The text of this edition is unabridged.

Set in 11 pt. Plantin by Elena Picard.

Printed in the United States on permanent paper.

Library of Congress Control Number: 2002107247
ISBN 0-7862-4319-8 (hc : alk. paper)

For my husband, Bill Rubin,
and in memory of M.D.E., Sr.,
the original grumpy old man.

ACKNOWLEDGMENTS

The Complete Guide to Food Allergy and Intolerance, by Jonathon Bromstoff and Linda Gamlin, was invaluable in planning the demise of Daniel Blake. The Chocolate Society's history of chocolate, Native Recipes by Paula Giese and Lucy Wing's Country Kitchen all contributed to Polly Lawrence's vast knowledge of chocolate.

With apologies to the District of Columbia Bar Association and thanks to Heidi Barron, Nicola Bearcroft, and Karen Conway for their assistance, and to everyone at Five Star.

CHAPTER 1

"You're fired!"

Daniel Benedict Blake, the meanest man in Manhattan, the terror of Tokyo, the hatchet man of Hong Kong, the most senior partner in the London office of the American law firm of Winter, Worthington & Walker, roared. His latest victim, a young woman attorney, squirmed in her seat while she waited to hear her fate. Unfortunately, that woman, the target of Blake's temper, was me.

Amy Brown. American lawyer. At least that's what my work permit, compliments of Her Majesty's Government, said. "Lion tamer" was more like it. I needed patience, finesse, nerves of steel, and a whip and a chair, maybe, but I rarely needed a law degree for my job—handling Daniel Blake.

I hadn't planned on a career based on tending to Daniel Blake's every irrational need. When I'd moved from the United States to Hong Kong with my husband, Steven Goldman, another American lawyer, I imagined the life of a glamorous expatriate attorney in the CNN global village. I quickly learned that one law firm office was just about the same as any other and that a reasonably attractive, relatively youthful, moderately ambitious but perpetually-stuck-in-the-middle, mid-level associate in a competitive market couldn't be too choosy. Five years and two continents later,

I had earned extra pages in my U.S. passport, a frequent flyer account the size of the foreign debt, and the dubious honor of being someone the extremely difficult to please Daniel Blake had actually wanted to hire. And, on more than one occasion, to fire.

I had thought that Steven's transfer to London was the escape I longed for since the first time I'd witnessed Blake erupt in the Hong Kong offices of Winter, Worthington & Walker (the usual dramatics: a little hyperventilating, some hysteria, and a lot of hurled furniture) but I'd been wrong. Like my own personal case of Swine Flu, Blake had followed me from Asia to Europe. I had been granted only time off for good behavior and I was now into my second round at the firm with the old man and finding that, other than the location, nothing had changed. In his usual fashion, Mr. Blake was screaming at me and, in my usual fashion, I was pretending to pay attention. While he fired me. Again.

In a profession filled with more than its fair share of Type A personalities, Daniel Blake—he preferred *Mister* Blake—scored an A+. Despite his successful and lucrative career, Mr. Blake went through each day like he had awakened on the wrong side of life. In a practice area not known for being contentious—his clients engaged in the bloodless battles of the redistribution of wealth and the shifting of tax liabilities—Daniel Blake always went for the jugular when a little nip at the heels, or, better yet, the art of gentle persuasion, would have sufficed.

And you hadn't really paid your dues at Winter, Worthington & Walker, not so affectionately known as DW3, short for Dead WASP, Dead WASP & Dead WASP, until you'd been fired by Daniel Blake. Senior partner status notwithstanding, he had no unilateral power to fire.

This minor detail, however, had not stopped him from firing practically everyone with whom he had come into contact: office boys, tea ladies, messengers, drivers, secretaries, paralegals, associates, other partners. He had gone so far, legend had it, as to "fire" a client. The transgressions were usually actual, albeit minor, offences. A late delivery, misspelled words. But sometimes they were merely his perceived notions of betrayal, his imagination. Mr. Blake's perceptions were not always immediately understandable and rarely if ever matched the common law standard of the reasonable man.

An opened box of chocolates on his desk provided the current distraction from Blake's typically unreasonable behavior on this Friday afternoon. My mouth watered as I tried to ignore the old man's ranting.

I'm a lot of things. Bad with numbers, hopeless with machinery and obsessed with being on time. Melodramatic, sentimental, a sucker for anything leather labeled "Made in Italy." But I'm not a chocoholic. Unlike some of my friends, I don't crave the stuff on a daily basis. Usually content with the odd Toblerone bar from Duty Free, I'll sample a truffle now and again if it's the expensive stuff. But on this particular afternoon I could have easily been mistaken for a chocolate junkie. My typical response to the man across the desk from me was to count to one thousand—Mr. Blake brought out extreme behavior even in me—but not today. Today, I was salivating.

Perhaps it was the way that the chocolates sat invitingly on the edge of his desk, pushed aside by their owner, thrust into my line of vision that made my mouth water and my stomach grumble with anticipation. Or the aroma—the top notes of dark cocoa, the hint of milky chocolates. Perhaps it was because I had had to interrupt my already very late lunch for this meeting. A half-eaten bagel from breakfast was barely a memory. Perhaps, and I suspected that this was the real reason, because the chocolates had not been offered to me. And they wouldn't be. Mr. Blake didn't share.

"I'm sorry, you were saying?" I looked away from the riveting box of chocolates back to Mr. Blake.

"I said, 'You're fired.' " He looked even angrier than usual.

We both started when the phone on the console behind his desk rang. Mr. Blake swiveled around in his chair to take the call, leaving me again to stare at the chocolates. The lid had been removed and I could see that he had already eaten a few pieces. The paper cups in which these tasty bits had rested were crinkled. I could hear in my head the rustle of the paper as his big clumsy fingers must have crawled their way through the box choosing the best piece. I could imagine him with that paper insert that companies use to identify what's what, weighing the merits of the brandied cherry filling over the coffee flavored soft-center, each equally appetizing as long as they didn't contain nuts. Mr. Blake was allergic to nuts.

Caramel was my favorite and my eyes quickly scanned the selection, wondering which piece I'd pick if I were given the chance. I recognized the brand, Darlington, an old established English company that had for years relied on a quaint ad campaign based on the word "darling" but lately had been trying to update its image. Recent commercials showed a more modern and unmistakable link between sex and chocolate. Darlington candies, noted for the distinctive swirled capital "D" that graced each piece, were not top of the line, not the luxury of Leonidas or Godiva, but were respectable blue ribbon chocolates.

My mouth continued to water as I glanced at my watch.

An hour had already passed since I had been torn from lunch—my soup was probably congealed and cold by now—and my conversation with Tony, the DW3 London office clerk. Tony'd listened patiently to my lament about broken office equipment—this time, the red light on my telephone didn't flash to indicate that I had voice mail, and every "new" message was inexplicably transformed to "old"—but he'd vanished as soon as Blake had made his presence known.

Making sure that my tormentor was still engrossed in his call, I extended my hand and, powerless from hunger, grabbed two pieces of the chocolate. They looked intact. Mr. Blake was not above biting into one and putting it back into the box if he didn't like what he'd tasted. Part of his charm.

The first piece tasted delicious, lush milk chocolate with caramel that covered my tongue, my lips and my hand. I licked my fingers and felt a rush of pleasure as I sucked on the coating and then the sweet buttery caramel center melted in my mouth. This petty theft was justifiable. A jury of my peers—I would load the panel with chocolate addicts—would not convict me. Before I could toss another piece in my mouth, the noise on the other side of the desk ebbed. I quickly tilted the box to shift pieces to disguise the appearance of the now diminished number of chocolates. I swallowed and hoped that he wouldn't notice the scent of chocolate from my direction. I sat to attention when Mr. Blake swiveled back around but he barely noticed I was there.

I swallowed again—I hoped unobtrusively—and wondered whether I'd been reprieved when he leaned on the intercom buzzer to the left of his phone, simultaneously shouting "Nikki, Nikki" and muttering, "Where is that girl?"

13

He'd probably have had more luck getting his temporary secretary's attention if he'd bothered to learn her real name. Daniel Blake, however, had, if at all possible, an even worse reputation with staff of the London office—Tony, Louise, the veteran secretary who'd helped open the office, and Lucy, the daytime receptionist—than he had among the lawyers. His attempt to treat them like coolies hadn't worked—the class system didn't apply to Americans.

And after a series of his personal secretaries had threatened litigation, DW3 had arranged for a succession of employment agencies—we were now on "M" in the alphabet—to send, in turn, a succession of temporary secretaries. It was a less than ideal solution to a permanent problem. Mr. Blake's propensity to depersonalize the person who sat at the secretary's desk by his persistence in calling them all the same name—for some unknown reason, "Nikki" was a name that stuck in his head—did not bode well for lasting relationships.

Exasperated at this Nikki's failure to instantly appear at his calling, Mr. Blake was up and at the door by the time I'd loosened the last bit of caramel from my back teeth and popped the second piece of candy into my mouth. He didn't get far. Helen Matthews-Smith, a hefty, buxom woman in her early fifties known in the office by her initials, or the less flattering title, Her Majesty's Battleship, barred his exit. Smelling of Silk Cuts poorly masked by a liberal dose of Penhaligon's—Helen believed in "buying British" regardless of the absurdity of the combination (think Camels and Johnson's Baby Powder)—she filled the doorway in her usual overbearing fashion. Helen had risen through the ranks at various offices of DW3, first as secretary, then personal assistant and paralegal, and then, six years ago, to her current job, London office manager.

H.M.S. had the one skill apparently required for all law office managers. She hated lawyers.

Helen particularly disliked Daniel Blake but not for the obvious reasons. The animosity stemmed from her failure to become the third Mrs. Blake. Thwarted in this personal battle with Mr. Blake, she took out her frustration on his one weak flank—me. H.M.S. and Blake were locked in a struggle of mythic proportions and I was the medium through which their battle was frequently fought. I could sometimes count on him to rescue me but Helen was diabolical in her scheming. It was her handiwork that resulted in my sharing in the procession of Blake's temporary secretaries.

"Why haven't you sent me your invitation list?" Helen barked. "I'm working on a very tight schedule." Today's attack, for once not aimed at me, concerned her current pet project—a gala celebration commemorating the 25th anniversary of the opening of the London office of DW3, the establishment of the firm's English partnership, and the admission of some of the American lawyers, including me, to the Law Society, the English equivalent of a state Bar (the ones without the wigs). For Her Majesty, the coincidence of these weighty events was the equivalent of Jupiter aligning with Mars on the Pope's birthday and she was devoting more time to planning the festivities than most engaged girls give their nuptials. Of course, her efforts and attention were in inverse proportion to the interest any of the rest of us showed in the celebrations and it was still several months away. The flurry of paperwork generated by application forms and invitation lists and catering menus was a new weapon in the royal arsenal. Her latest move had been to draft the Nikki of the week in this effort.

"Who decided this schedule? Why wasn't I consulted? I

want to discuss this with David." The David in question was David Knight, a DW3 partner whose reputation for coldness was exceeded only by his reputation for neatness and punctuality. He ascribed to the clean desk theory of office management and visibly blanched at the sight of paperstrewn desks. This provided the only evidence to date that something other than ice water ran through his veins. "When can we meet?" Mr. Blake growled right back as he thumbed through the pages of his diary.

Why Mr. Blake was taking such an interest in Helen's plans and invoking the name of the powerless Knight, other than to antagonize Her Majesty, which wasn't a bad reason as far as I was concerned, was unclear. A real stuffed shirt—he arrived every morning looking as though he and not his shirts had been starched—David Knight was the managing partner of the London office in name only. By the sheer force of his personality, Mr. Blake frequently called the administrative shots. Like after his heart attack. No more cheese at the monthly lawyers' luncheons. Suddenly the office had a "no smoking" policy. Another reason why Helen loathed him—she was a heavy smoker who always managed to smell like a cigarette although few of us had actually ever seen her smoke one.

"David's out of town and this can't wait. Besides, I have the approval of the partners in New York."

"I don't care." Mr. Blake was not impressed and the suggestion that he could be overruled by the home office just provoked him more. He sputtered, sending showers of spittle across the room, an unattractive personal habit that had presented itself in the last few years. Luckily for Helen, her Continental Shelf of a chest kept most of it from reaching her face.

"Excuse me." A young woman I recognized as the employment agency's latest sacrificial lamb, who had discovered that just because the job was temporary didn't mean it wasn't torture, took a step back as both Blake and Helen turned their mighty guns toward her.

"What is it?"

"Excuse me, Mrs. Matthews-Smith, but it's Ambassador Harrington's office on the phone."

Helen quickly turned from raging harridan to anxious bride-to-be. Ambassador Harrington, the guest of honor at the firm's celebrations, was the "talent" that would pull in the important clients.

"Where? Where? Which phone? I must take this." She made an exit but not without threatening to return.

"That woman." Mr. Blake wiped spit from the side of his mouth. Frustrated at not finishing his argument with Helen, he focused on me. Any thought of a stay of execution disappeared with his next words, "I had a little chat this afternoon with Ted Cunningham."

Ted Cunningham, or Robert Theodore Cunningham, III, as he was more formally known, was the head of the corporate department of the London office. With one "small" exception, Ted Cunningham was the personification of Winter, Worthington & Walker—good looks, impeccable breeding, great academic credentials combined with a judicial clerkship. An unfortunate failed first marriage to one of the secretaries at the New York office, and not his infamous womanizing, was the "small" exception. The class system was alive and well and living in the New York office.

I could not imagine Mr. Blake having had a "little chat" with Ted Cunningham. A bombastic argument was more like it. "Yes," I said warily, "we talked." Ted was, I hoped, my ticket to freedom from Daniel Blake. A steady diet of hand-holding Mr. Blake, and his banking clients, now only interested in planting their riches in real estate, had become tedious and I had jumped at the chance to get involved in something more challenging. But in so doing I had violated Mr. Blake's number one rule—keep 100% of my day available for his work and his clients. I had had my own ideas about how to break the news to Mr. Blake and they had not involved getting fired.

"He mentioned that you had offered to do some work for him on the new Declan United merger." Declan's constant merging and de-merging kept at least four Mrs. Cunninghams living in luxury in New York, Paris, Hong Kong, and Tokyo, and a dozen Cunningham children in private schools all over the world. Ted collected wives and children the way the rest of us collected artwork and carpets as souvenirs of our overseas postings. They became ex-wives and semi-abandoned children, Ted's version of excess baggage, about the time the moving van had been arranged for his next assignment. Ensconced in a huge house on the Queen's Estate in Regent's Park, Ted was currently single (with promises to stay that way).

"You cannot possibly work for Cunningham and me."

His glare and the silence made me think about turning away but I felt oddly energized. "So you'd rather fire me than let me decide how to juggle my time? That doesn't make any sense. Who else is going to do your work?" The look on Blake's face confirmed that I had compounded the unthinkable (questioning his brilliance) with the unforgivable (disloyalty) but it didn't have the desired effect. I had seen and heard it all before. Perhaps it was the first time I had really listened. Perhaps I was getting too old to continue this. I'd read somewhere that a craving for chocolate was attributable to a magnesium deficiency experienced by women just before their periods, so perhaps I was pre-menstrual. Every male lawyer I knew would have agreed. Before he could berate me—his repertoire of insults was extensive—I grabbed a piece of paper from a legal pad and started writing.

"I quit. Effective immediately," I said, as I signed "Amy Brown, Esq." on the bottom of the page.

I fully expected him to look at it and then tear it up into little pieces. But he surprised me. The old coot took the paper from me coolly, read it over briefly, signed it, and said, "Resignation accepted."

CHAPTER 2

"You're late," I said, after Steven blew in the revolving door that served as the main entrance to our favorite Italian restaurant and handed his coat over to the hostess. I'd arrived ten minutes before our 8:30 reservation and Steven had arrived twenty minutes after. It was one of those little differences that made our marriage so interesting; my obsession for being on time paired with his chronic tardiness.

"I know. I'm sorry. You know me. I'm always late." He kissed me hello and then gulped down a glass of the wine I'd already ordered. "So how was your day?"

"Very interesting." I took in a deep breath for courage and continued, "After going through another scene with Mr. Blake where he fires me and I meekly apologize for whatever imaginary indiscretion he's cooked up, this time for having the audacity to further my career, I finally stood up for myself . . ."

"and . . ."

". . . and I quit."

"You what?"

"You heard me. I said that I quit. I'm liberated. I'm a free woman."

"You what?"

Steven was clearly not as excited about my quitting as I

was or as I had hoped he would be. I thought he'd welcome an end to my complaints of how Mr. Blake had made his latest temporary secretary cry. Steven found it hard to believe that the meek, mild-mannered old man he'd met on several social occasions over the years was the same monster I described. How many times had I threatened to quit in response to Blake's latest tirade and Steven's only comment would be, "He's always been nice to me."

But even if Steven had found himself employed by a Blake clone, he would never have acted as I had. We were exact opposites when it came to decision-making. He considered everything very deliberately; never making a purchase no matter how trivial without first comparing prices, specifications, consumer reports, and respected friends' opinions. I followed the emotional weathervane of my gut.

"You what?"

I explained again how Mr. Blake had confronted me for the last time and that all I had been trying to do was secure my position at DW3 with some work with Ted Cunningham. Steven was buying it but only just and I realized I'd lost my taste for the celebratory wine.

"I wish you had discussed it with me first. I would have liked to consider how this would affect our finances. But if it makes you happy . . ."

"I'm sorry I didn't call you. Maybe it was rash, but it was the only option under the circumstances. You know how Mr. Blake is."

"Or how you say he is."

"I know, I know, 'he's always been nice to you.' You've never had to work with him. But that's ancient history, as far as I'm concerned. It's not as if I won't be able to get another job." I pushed my own doubts about my job skills—bad with numbers but always on time? caretaker to cranky

21

old men? masochistic tendencies?—aside for the moment and said, "I think the market for dual qualified attorneys is really opening up." I didn't have to remind Steven, since he'd suffered vicariously, that I had recently passed the English solicitor's exam and could claim dual qualification. The draconian rules that required a two-year apprenticeship right out of Dickens and that effectively kept most self-respecting American lawyers out of the London legal picture had been changed. All I—and three of my colleagues at DW3—had had to do in order to call ourselves "solicitors" was establish that we were active members in our state Bar associations and that we had practiced for a minimum number of years, both no-brainer requirements, and, the tough part, pass two days of exams that were similar to the Bar exams in the States. The celebrations Helen was so fervently planning would have been for me and my accomplishment but I certainly did not plan on sticking around for the party. "Besides, DW3 is a great firm. It has a great reputation."

Steven gave me a look that did not give me great confidence and we ordered our food and ate it with discussion of less weighty matters. I had the good sense not to order dessert although I could have easily managed a bowl of gelato to finish off my meal of pasta with roast chicken and tarragon. Unemployment was already making me hungry but my dress, a compulsive purchase I could attribute to the last time Blake had fired me, a little black number (emphasis on the little), was more form fitting than I remembered. Exercise and a diet would have to be added to my list of things to do now that I was unemployed.

We drove through the narrow streets back to our apartment in relative silence. Steven parked the car near Pont Street, a busy street that marked an imaginary border between expensive Knightsbridge and only slightly less expensive Chelsea. The tension from dinner long gone, we walked arm in arm through the cool night air the few steps from the street to the front door of a five-story terrace house of the type shown on greeting cards depicting scenes of Victorian England where we occupied the entire fourth floor—two bedrooms (all American expatriates have guests), two baths (for marital harmony), kitchen (where Steven did most of the cooking), dining area (a real estate agent euphemism for hallway), one reception room (we did little receiving but lots of living) and great views across the rooftops of Chelsea. We didn't know our neighbors and most of the time it felt like we had the building to ourselves.

I took in a sharp breath as we entered the pitch black hallway, and a time warp. The Victorians may have been adept at quaint but, if our building was any indication, they had apparently cared little about the fundamentals. The building boasted numerous original features like high ceilings, black and white tile floors and stained glass windows, but fell short on some things that Americans took for granted. Like light. And elevators. And heat.

When the building had been converted into apartments, the contractors had rewired the common parts to allow for electricity but had used a candle with a very short wick as their measure for adequate light. The lights, dim by even Third World standards, worked on a timer that was as unreliable and as short lived as sunshine during an English summer. We invariably had to make part of the trek up to our apartment door in complete darkness.

And a trek it was. The building had once been a private home and the floor plan left no room for modern conveniences like an elevator. There were sixty-eight stairs—we knew because my mother, after one too many sherries, had counted them. Steven and I jokingly referred to them as the sixty-eight drunken stairs, not because of my mother's inebriated counting but because the stairs themselves were unevenly spaced and, after years of use, grooves had been worn into the middle of the stone steps up to the first landing.

But it wasn't the dark or even the climb to which I objected. It was the cold. Opening the door to the building was like being assaulted by a gust of stale, frigid air from a Victorian tomb. Even on warm days, the chilled air—the electrical improvements did not extend to heating in the hallway—crept into my bones and stayed with me until I was well inside our apartment. Steven had explained that the stone tile floor and the lack of insulation kept the building a few degrees cooler than the outside temperature and the interior doors created our very own wind tunnel. Steven's explanation made sense but logic couldn't keep me from dreading that moment when I first stepped into the hallway and felt like the Little Match Girl.

Once inside, I headed towards the "dining" cum hallway and called out to Steven behind me, "I'll check for messages." The light on the answering machine blinked once and I listened to the single call from Dr. Johnson, our family doctor. His message was cryptic but was nevertheless crystal clear to me. My little black dress that I now wore with discomfort had, in fact, previously fit perfectly. My sudden loss of taste for the wine at dinner was not attributable to a bad year in Tuscany. My hunger for chocolates in Mr. Blake's office was not inexplicably uncontrollable. My one moment of clarity in my mediocre career that prompted me to stand up to Mr. Blake was probably a one-off. And I definitely was not pre-menstrual. I was pregnant.

"You're what?" Steven was beginning to sound repetitive.

"I'm pregnant!"

Steven was already dressed for bed and lay propped up against pillows and the headboard, ready for the U.S. evening news on cable. Although we'd lived abroad for years, neither of us could stand to miss our nightly half hour of murder and mayhem American style. I changed out of my little black dress and realized this was probably the first and last time I'd wear it. I threw on my flannel nightgown and said, "I thought that you'd be happy."

"Of course I'm happy. I'm thrilled. It's what we've been waiting for. But—haven't you forgotten something?" Steven, ever the practical one, asked. "You've just resigned from a job where they would *pay* you to take time off to have a baby—you can't possibly go out on interviews for new jobs while you're pregnant. This is England. Talk about a disincentive."

In my joy at the prospect of a baby I hadn't thought about the consequences of this news on the other cataclysmic event of the day—my resignation.

"You've got to go back to Blake and un-resign."

I looked at him incredulously. "Are you nuts?"

"No, I'm serious. So you have to work for Blake for a few more months, at least you know it will be for a finite period of time. How bad can it be? You can hang on until it's time to leave to have the baby, go out on maternity leave, and go back for a little while, and then resign. You can spend your time on maternity leave putting your resume together and finding another job. If you just resign now, you'll lose four paychecks. At least."

When he laid it out this way, it made sense in an un-

25

seemly way. DW3 was very generous to mothers-to-be. "But how can I face him after today? I don't think I could handle the humiliation."

"I know it will be hard, sweetheart, and I'm sorry you have to do this, but I really don't think we can continue to live in this apartment with a baby. We've always talked about buying a place but I just don't think we could afford to on one salary." Our expatriate compensation package included an attractive rent subsidy but paltry mortgage benefits.

I thought of nannies and private school. Sixty-eight stairs and a stroller.

"Look, just tell him that you lost your senses—pregnant women are over-emotional—he'll understand that. Or better yet, don't tell him at all. Leave the baby out of it— the later he learns about that the better. Just apologize. He'll enjoy seeing you grovel. And it's not as if anyone else knows that you resigned, right? Amy? Did you tell anyone else?"

"No, I didn't tell anyone." I thought back to the few hours I'd stewed in my office. Half expecting Blake to appear, contrite and asking me to reconsider, I had grown tired of waiting for a visit that the other half of me knew would never take place. It wasn't as if he had far to go. Only the minimum of space separated my office from Mr. Blake's, all the better for him to shout for me when he needed something. God forbid he'd ever pick up the phone. Who was I kidding? At the grand old age of seventy-nine, he didn't know how to use a push button phone. He'd come from the old school of pencils and erasers and dictation and legal pads and rotary dials. And shouting. But no apologizing—that was a distance he would never have traveled.

"That's good. Then you can . . ."

26

"I didn't even see anyone. . . ." But that wasn't quite true. At 6:30 p.m., I had checked the automatic urge to say goodnight to my now former boss and had instead, with head down, walked out and immediately collided with a man I recognized as one of the pack of young lawyers sent by the New York office for a six month rotation to London. "No one who matters, at least."

"Who?"

"Just one of the six monthers. And they don't count." The six monthers spent their time—just about as long as the quarantine required for pets brought in from overseas to England—milling about the reception area and the coffee room complaining about the lack of closets and hot showers. By the time they had developed a fondness for warm beer, found their way to the men's room—they were always male—and established to our satisfaction that they didn't have rabies, it was time to ship them back to New York. They were interchangeable, fresh-faced, eager, overfed and overpaid beagle pups, all taken from the same graduating litter at Harvard. I usually took the Blake approach to the short-timers—to him, they were just the male equivalent of the Nikkis except they didn't answer the phones—and, based on the exchange that followed our collision, the feeling seemed to be mutual.

"Did you talk?"

"No." I recalled the encounter. A youthful head had looked up from a legal pad and had said, "Um, sorry, Annie."

"The name's Amy," I had grumbled.

"Pardon, Mary?"

"It's Amy." I'd just resigned. Why did I care that he didn't know my name? I'd said "Never mind" to the back of a DW3 regulation pin striped suit and had continued down

27

the hall, past reception, said a quick goodnight to the night receptionist, and proceeded down a flight of stairs—DW3 had the English first floor and the basement—and out the building to hail a taxi for home.

"Did you talk to anyone else? Gideon?" Steven asked.

"No." Gideon, the newest arrival at DW3, was as close as I got to having a friend at the office. My position as Blake's assistant invoked sympathy among my colleagues but little else. Gideon was the firm's sole authentically English solicitor. Expecting an effeminate version of David Knight—I had heard all the horror stories of English public schools—I had been surprised when a massive hulking bear of a man appeared at my door one day about a year ago wanting to know how to use the telephone. More Dancing Bear than grizzly, Gideon had the requisite posh accent and Oxford First to make him desirable to the partners at DW3. His employment made possible our imminent entrance into the world of real English law firms. If Gideon was as smart as he was well educated, he would have rejoiced at my news and joined me in my departure but I had resisted the urge to tell him.

"But?"

"But, I did give Mr. Blake a resignation letter."

Steven paused for a moment. "He may not have taken you seriously. You've told me before that he can't really fire you. So there's a letter. Tendered to someone with only apparent but not actual authority to accept it. Null and void."

Leave it to another lawyer to reduce my moral dilemma into a legal problem, a simple matter of offer and acceptance. But Steven was probably right. The conversation had taken place very quickly and with all the interruptions it had been late afternoon by the time I left Blake's office. And given the lack of reaction from anyone—the temp, Helen,

New York—during the couple of hours that I had cooled my heels in my own office, it was unlikely that he'd enlisted anyone's help to broadcast the news.

And it was unlikely that he would be able to do it on his own. Mr. Blake would not have been able to distribute a copy of my letter. He didn't know how to operate the copy machines. They worked on a "forced entry" system that required knowledge beyond his ken—a four-digit identification number assigned to each lawyer as well as an eight-digit number for the charge. He would have had all night to call the firm's managing partner in New York. But that was really unlikely. Mr. Blake didn't know how to place a local call, let alone an international one, without his secretary.

"You're right. He couldn't have taken it seriously. I'll just ask for the letter back."

And so I went to sleep agreeing with Steven that, the next day, I would not go in to clear out my desk and box up my belongings as I had planned but that I would go, hat in hand, and beg my way back into servitude. I would grovel and plead and apologize and condemn myself to another few months of purgatory and, if I had to, I would use my unborn child as a bargaining tool to melt the old man's heart.

Then I remembered the drawback to this plan.

The old man had no heart.

CHAPTER 3

DW3 was located in the heart of Mayfair, an area of London that consisted of a few blocks of well-tended buildings housing private gaming clubs, foreign consulates, real estate agents and expensive gift shops. The office was a quick walk on a good day to the seamier side of the neighborhood, Shepherd Market, a tiny enclave of shops, cafes and take-aways set back from Curzon Street, one of the few areas in Central London with a pedestrian only walkway. At one time Shepherd Market had been an actual market but over the years it had become infamous for its collection of street-walkers. The hookers were recognizable from their micro mini skirts and thigh high leather boots. The staff at DW3 often joked that only the prostitutes' lascivious attire distin-guished them from the other whores in the neighborhood.

Steven dropped me off a few blocks from the office at the entrance to the Market around 9:30 a.m. The neighbor-hood I had mentally bid farewell to the night before was practically deserted except for a few ladies still in their eve-ning wear slinking back to their hiding places. I caught one's eye momentarily; I barely had time to pass the silent message that I too was back on the game. A few taxi drivers, oblivious to the women, lounged against their empty cabs savoring the last few minutes of immobility. I kicked aside an empty tin of lager and strolled into the Market Coffee

Shop. Early morning customers included a couple of Americans, recognizable from their matching white sneakers and Burberry raincoats, and a group of Japanese struggling to order scones. A plastic cup of hot tea in hand, I contemplated my confrontation with Mr. Blake as I walked to the office. I was certain he would already be there.

He was always there.

Divorced by wife number one and widowed by wife number two, he was now resolutely single. He spent most weekends in the office taking my name in vain for my absence or haranguing me when I made an appearance.

The rest of the place was usually deserted on the weekends. Unlike the New York office, the London office did not have the twenty-four hour buzz associated with round the clock word processing and secretarial staff. The other London partners and associates might come in to check their mail and faxes but they would be unlikely to linger. They worked hard but, unlike Mr. Blake, they had few local clients who demanded Saturday visits. They logged most of their billable hours on British Airways.

I fished in my briefcase for my security card as I entered the building. Why did I bother? I could have just as easily waved an expired credit card or driver's license and still gained admission. Security was notoriously lax, in spite of the efforts of DW3 to add its own improvements. I signed my initials in a tattered register and nodded at a yawning guard. I noticed that Mr. Blake had not signed in. He usually beat me to the office on the weekend but in my current state of mind, pure dread, I thought little of my earlier arrival.

I walked up the staircase to the entrance of the first floor and punched in the security numbers to DW3's immediate front door.

The reception area was still dark and I threw on some light switches and then checked the reception desk for any messages. Instead of turning right toward my office, I turned left, proceeded down the hall and walked past the offices of Walter Hughes, an excitable partner with the pedigree but not the charm to rival that of Ted Cunningham. Walter was from the Washington office and his family connections, with Ambassador Harrington and other politicians, insured that DW3 lawyers were always invited to embassy functions. I wasn't sure what kind of work Walter did, but he generated a lot of income from it and he had hatched, over the years, a small flock of young attorneys and paralegals and clerks, who labored noisily but anonymously on a hodgepodge of client matters. They resembled those plastic birds that stayed head down in the feed pan until tapped on their rears. Walter was happily married— one of the few at DW3—and his family life seemed to mirror his office life. He had a brood of boisterous children who only came up for air at mealtimes. Neither Walter nor any of his entourage was in.

Ignoring jackets on backs of chairs and lights left on overnight—all lawyers' tricks of giving the appearance of being busy without actually being there—I continued my journey confident that I was alone. I walked into the spare office that housed the communal fax machines for incoming and outgoing faxes and other assorted office equipment. No sign of Mr. Blake; his first stop was also usually the fax machine, much to everyone's dismay. He typically grabbed all the pages from the machine, shuffling the papers out of any semblance of order, taking pages that weren't his, and making a general mess of things.

I flipped through the incoming faxes—six pages of a memorandum of understanding marked "draft" to Daniel B.

Blake, a seemingly endless number of pages from Securex Bank, loan documentation for David Knight or Ted Cunningham, a take-out menu from a local restaurant, one page with numbers and Walter Hughes's name on it but without a cover page, and an urgent request that we change copiers.

I gathered the fax to Mr. Blake, marked it "Received" and left the rest for either the intended recipients to collect or in the case of the incomplete or misdirected faxes for Tony to trash or return to sender. I was betting on the trash since the latter option would have involved extra effort on Tony's part. I waited impatiently, sipping my cup of take-away tea while the copy machine warmed up. After what seemed to be an interminable amount of time—I could be impatient too—the copy machine kicked on and I fed it the pages of Mr. Blake's fax.

"Amy?"

I gasped and whirled around from the machine at the sound of my name. "Kimberly! You scared me! I didn't think anyone else was here." I exhaled and then turned back to the copying.

"Amy, I'm so sorry. I didn't mean to scare you. Are you all right?" Kimberly asked with concern. A senior associate, Kimberly Sullivan was relatively new to the London office. She'd transferred after a stint in Paris where she'd learned to speak and, more importantly to the vain and beautiful Kimberly, dress like a native. In line to become the next partner in London, Kimberly seemed to spend most of her time waiting for David Knight to get off the phone, to return from a business trip, or to sign off on a document. Careers at DW3 had been made on far less.

"I'm fine, no problem. How's it going?" I met insincerity with insincerity. Kimberly's friendliness was more in keeping with the Machiavellian principle of keeping friends close and enemies closer. I'd learned the hard way that her interest in me, my clothes, my feelings, was feigned. Thinking that we might have had more in common than our gender and slavish devotion to our bosses, I had invited Kimberly to lunch for a little bonding soon after she'd moved to London. We had spent a boozy afternoon commiserating about life in England and DW3. I discovered later that she had reported our conversation verbatim—my words only—to David Knight and others. A snake in the grass can come in all sizes; this one in a size six, preferably Chanel. She and David, if the rumors of an affair were to be believed, made a great pair. Even reptiles have sex lives.

"I'm fine. How are you doing? Hope you're not in for the entire weekend. I'm just in to check on a fax and go through my in-tray. I was out most of last week." She pushed manicured nails through her hair in a pantomime of exhaustion. "What a beautiful sweater you're wearing. Is that cashmere?" She rubbed the fabric of my sleeve between her fingers.

I stifled a surly response and the urge to swat her hand and said with a smile, *"Mais oui."*

Kimberly smiled, dropped the sweater and said, "Amy, I didn't know you could speak French. We should go to Paris together sometime for the sales." I might have been fooled into accepting her invitation if not for my earlier experience and the fact that her surprise at my language ability sounded more like, "Amy, I didn't know you could read," or "Amy, I didn't know you could walk upright."

We exchanged further banal pleasantries, Kimberly asking innocuous questions, smiling sweetly, lulling me into a welcome sense of sisterhood while in fact working to extract any nugget of information she could use to further her career, until I looked at my watch and saw that it was approaching 10:30. I had a job to do. Or to get back.

"I've got to run." I held out the documents in my hand and said, "I need to get this to Mr. Blake. See you later."

Kimberly looked up from the fax tray and smiled. "Right. Have a nice weekend."

There was still no sign of anyone else in the office as I passed back through reception to Blake's office and steeled myself to do battle. I had not decided which tack I would take with him—pregnant and repentant, or just repentant. I was hoping for a sign. I knocked timidly on his open door and then more forcefully while simultaneously crossing his threshold. He and I had long since ceased standing on ceremony. More accurately, knocking before entering wasn't in his repertoire.

I'd read somewhere that half of memory resides in the nose. As I entered his office, I had a less than aromatic recollection of changing diapers as a teenaged babysitter. I took a deep breath and marveled at the power of pregnancy to jostle such memories. But the smell, even more pungent as I stood in the doorway of Mr. Blake's office, was nothing compared to the sight beyond his desk. Within minutes of walking in, I knew that I didn't have to worry about appealing to the old man's heart. It was no longer a viable option—or organ for that matter.

He was dead.

The man I had once feared and loathed and begrudgingly admired lay sprawled, face down, on the floor at the corner of his desk. One arm was outstretched towards me. How fitting that his final posture would be with fist clenched. The other arm appeared to be underneath him, as if his hand was grasping at his throat. There was something dark and brown to the left of his head that I tried not to think about. Most of his face was obscured but the side of his head and the small area of exposed neck were the same institutional gray color of the wall-to-wall carpet on which he lay.

I hadn't ever come this close to death before and I couldn't tell if it was nascent morning sickness, the now obvious source of the odious smell, or just the normal reaction to seeing my boss dead, that brought on nausea. He was old, he'd had a minor heart attack, I told myself but then thought, no, he was fairly fit—he'd certainly been lively in our last moments together. I approached him, knelt down and reached out to touch his shoulder but thought better of it.

I looked around his desk for some sign or cause to this calamity. His desk was not neat—it never was—but it looked like a tornado had swept through. Papers were strewn towards the left of the desk as if he had, in his last moments, pushed them aside in anger. The telephone from the rear credenza was on the floor near him. It was off the hook, the buttons smashed against the panel as if someone had pressed all the numbers at once with a hammer. There was no high pitched whine of a phone off the hook that might have signaled the telephone company or even the hapless guard who I imagined had blithely turned the lights off during his evening round attributing the smell of opened bowels to the profession. I could see from my position that in his struggle to call someone, anyone, Mr. Blake must have pulled the receiver from the wall. A memory flashed in my head of the first and last time I had failed to immediately get off the phone when he wanted my attention. It hadn't been enough to press two fingers on the receiver to cut off the call. Daniel Blake had dramatically pulled the plug. I vanquished the memory and continued quickly to survey the area again for some clue as to what had happened.

A vision of his glaring face then came back to me in that moment and I remembered why I was there. I turned to go back to my office to call security and the police but not before I grabbed my resignation letter from the shambles on the desk. I was sickened by the scene but not enough to forget my purpose—to save my job and paid maternity leave.

CHAPTER 4

"And you discovered the body?"

I nodded mutely. I sat in my office with Detective Constable Lawson and my umpteenth cup of tea. As a recent arrival to England, I had been accused of believing, like most Americans, that the world ran on dollars and cents when the English knew that it really ran on cups of tea. I was definitely coming around to their world view. D.C. Lawson and another policeman, Police Constable or P.C. Ridley, had arrived soon after I had made the emergency call from my office. Although I had struggled with the proper words to convey to the dispatcher the scene in the office next door, I had had the presence of mind to shove my purloined resignation letter in my desk drawer. Minutes after his arrival, D.C. Lawson had taken out a notebook and started taking notes. P.C. Ridley had excused himself and was presumably in Mr. Blake's office doing things I could only imagine.

"We see no signs of forced entry or reason to suspect foul play. We will of course be checking with the guards downstairs. Did Mr. Blake have any enemies? Was he a well-liked sort of bloke? Did anyone wish him any harm?"

I felt my stomach begin to heave. Should I lie? They would probably learn the truth sooner or later.

"He was not very well liked." I figured that an understatement was safe.

"He was despised by one and all," came from a voice in my doorway. Both D.C. Lawson and I looked up to see David Knight whose number I had frantically dialed just after calling the police. I had been connected to an answering machine that promised to forward the call to Knight's mobile phone. D.C. Lawson glanced quickly from Knight to me and back.

"Let me introduce myself. I'm David Knight, Managing Partner of the London office of Winter, Worthington & Walker." David looked his usual cool unruffled self. A death at the office had not melted him. "Amy called me just after she called you and I came here as soon as I could. I've known Daniel Blake for over twenty years, and he was the most loathed lawyer in London." At least David stopped in the current time zone.

"Is this true?" D.C. Lawson looked at me more closely.

I nodded in agreement.

"Don't try to shelter the old man," David said.

D.C. Lawson again looked from me to the managing partner and back again. "So there might have been people who would have wanted to hurt him?"

"Every lawyer, secretary, and client who ever came into contact with him. I don't intend to be disrespectful to the dead but, at one time or another, I suspect we all wished him dead," Knight said.

"Do you think someone really meant to kill him?" I looked shamefacedly at the officer and David.

"I'm not suggesting that. Until there is a cause of death, we must ask these questions. It's routine police procedure when there's a suspicious death in the workplace. I'm just trying to get a feel for the deceased, what type of person he was, who he had been in life. Did you say he was over 75 years old?"

"Yes. Eighty at his next birthday."

"Did he seem in good health to you? It may well be that the coroner can establish a cause of death that will make an official investigation unnecessary." The officer said this re-assuringly but I did not feel reassured.

"Yes, he'd had a minor heart attack but he watched his diet, took good care of himself. No other problems." David said this with authority.

But then I stirred from the daze that I'd found myself in since walking into Mr. Blake's office. Something important struggled to bubble up from my subconscious. "No other problems," I heard David saying. No other problems.

"Except," I realized that I was speaking.

"Yes, Miss Brown?"

"Except for the nut allergy." Daniel Blake, as I knew and as anyone who had ever had the pleasure (using the term loosely) of dining with him knew, had been allergic to nuts. Highly allergic. Apparently deathly allergic.

"Was everyone generally aware of this allergy?"

"All of us were." David spoke my sentiments exactly.

"Well, we'll be looking into that possibility. Perhaps if one of you could refer us to his family doctor. I take it he wasn't living with any family here?"

"No, he lived alone. Well, that's not exactly right. He has, sorry, had a Chinese housekeeper, Mei. She's been with him since Hong Kong."

While David and D.C. Lawson discussed the details of Mr. Blake's domestic arrangements, I pictured Mr. Blake giving in to the same temptation I had fallen to just a few hours before. Mr. Blake digging into the box of chocolates.

"There was a box of chocolates on his desk." My mind flew to the brown globs I had glimpsed next to Mr. Blake's body. What horrors I had imagined them to be, blood, or worse. Could the dark stains have been something as innocuous as Darlington's truffles supreme? "He must have eaten some of the candy."

"Wouldn't that have been risky for someone with this susceptibility?"

How to describe to this stranger the child-like greediness that possessed Mr. Blake when presented with a desirable treat—how to convey the glee, the gluttony, the selfish desire to consume? My mind flashed on the candy that I had secretly enjoyed. "He could be pretty impatient."

"So it would not have been unlike him to open the box and dig in, so to speak?"

"It would have been exactly like him," David said.

"But not," I insisted, "without checking the contents for nuts. He wouldn't have gone that far." I had dined too many times with Mr. Blake not to know that he would have scrutinized any candy.

P.C. Ridley stepped into my office at that moment and coughed politely to get our attention. He wore latex gloves and I tried not to think too hard about where his hands had been. "We've taken photos of the scene, and the ambulance men are here to remove the body." He stepped mercifully back into the hallway.

"We will need to notify the next of kin." D.C. Lawson looked at David.

"That would be James, his son. He's a banker in Los Angeles. I can give you those details, or one of us can call him," David offered. D.C. Lawson made a note of this information on his pad, and, as if satisfied by our answers, stood to leave.

"I'm sure we'll have some more questions for you but at this point I think you've provided sufficient information for us to go forward."

"Do you really think someone . . . ?" I asked again as I stood up to extend my hand to D.C. Lawson who had moved to the door.

"I can't, and actually it's not for me to, say. Hopefully, a medical examination will provide details of cause and time of death. In the meantime, Mr. Knight, we'll need continued access to the deceased's office, to consider the scene again, see if anything is missing or has been tampered with."

The unborn Brown-Goldman baby reared its ugly head at the mention of missing papers and chose that moment to announce its presence at Winter, Worthington & Walker.

I lost all those cups of tea onto D.C. Lawson's shoes.

"I'm terribly sorry." I had already made this apology as many times as D.C. Lawson had assured me that I was not to worry. I was sure that I had confirmed every stereotype he had ever held about Americans, women, and lawyers. "I'm pregnant." At this announcement, both D.C. Lawson and David Knight took a noticeable step back, as if a leper had entered the room. "I guess all of this has been just a bit too much for me."

"It's perfectly understandable." David crossed the divide and came over to me and placed his hand on my shoulder. I expected an icicle to form at the point of contact, but his hand was surprisingly warm. "Is there anything more you need from us now, Officer? It's clear that Miss, er, Ms. Brown should be going home and getting some rest."

"No, no, I'm fine." I still wanted to explain to D.C. Lawson and P.C. Ridley that Mr. Blake would have been scrupulous about the candy. That he would have checked the box for ingredients. He would have asked someone twenty questions. He would have had some poor schmo do a blind taste test before he bit into one of those chocolates. But every time I lifted my head to begin to explain, nausea returned and my office, D.C. Lawson and David Knight swam before my eyes. I couldn't, or rather didn't, want to see P.C. Ridley who had magically appeared and was on his hands and knees cleaning up the remains of my breakfast. This must have been just another day at the office for him. And I had thought my job was bad.

"We'll be reporting this to the coroner who'll undoubtedly want to make his own inquiries, perhaps order a postmortem examination in order to determine cause of death. We'll probably want to have a chat with the rest of your office staff, the security guards, have a look around the office."

"Of course."

"If you'll just let us carry on our business then Mrs. Brown is free to go home. We may need to contact you later." He turned from David to me. "I hope you're feeling better soon."

"Thank you." I managed a meek goodbye.

I sat alone in my office with David Knight, a man with whom I had probably only ever spoken to on the rare occasions the entire office got together for administrative meetings and lawyer lunches. I thought about raising the temperature on my office thermostat but remembered that he'd seemed almost human a few minutes ago. We had made tremendous progress in bonding this morning over death and pregnancy.

"What do we do now?"

"We cooperate with the police, show them we have nothing to hide, and hope this goes away as quietly and as quickly as possible."

I was surprised by his tone of voice. He did, however,

have an office to worry about and death on the job was not an effective recruiting policy. On the other hand, it would probably impress the clients.

"Look, I've just returned this morning so would you mind getting in touch with James? I'll contact the partners here and in New York, and Helen, of course. I'll have to make a brief statement for the press."

I agreed to call Mr. Blake's only child, James, whom I'd known for years. James had always seemed relieved to see me on his infrequent visits with his father. I reached for my telephone to call James but stopped. It would still be hours before it would make sense to call Los Angeles.

"I'll walk out with you." I tried to ignore the sight of latex-gloved men and a stretcher to my left as David and I walked down the corridor and instead concentrated on making an exit. We ran into Kimberly and one of the young associates on rotation from the New York office in the reception area. In all the confusion, I had forgotten that other people may have been in the office for reasons not having to do with discovering a dead body, or, for that matter, playing Indian giver with a resignation letter. Kimberly mumbled something in my general direction that sounded like "I'm sorry, Amy. Let me know if there's anything I can do" and I almost believed her. The anonymous associate looked at David but didn't glance my way. He held the security door while David and I passed through.

David turned and said, "It's been a tough morning. Let me know when you've reached James. If you want to take a few days off in light of your condition, that would be fine. Just let me know what your plans are. You can deal with the fall-out from all of this later." He looked over my shoulder and shouted to a man entering our building, "Walter, good, you're here."

"David! I just heard. Kimberly called me at home. What happened? Do the police know what happened? What will we tell the papers? God, what will we tell New York? Have you called New York? No, no one will be in New York yet. What are we going to do? We should convene a partners' meeting. A conference call. A press briefing. And someone will have to call the firm's insurers. Have you thought of those things?" Walter's enthusiasm for solving problems aloud while rocking on the balls of his feet and focusing on a point in the middle distance could be disconcerting. But his behavior with David meant he was handling the news of Blake's unexpected demise well.

David took Walter by the arm, and turned back to me and said, "Amy, I'll talk to you later," and then launched into an animated conversation with Walter (all conversations with Walter seemed animated even in the absence of direct eye contact). Minutes later, Walter made his delayed entrance into the office as Kimberly and the young associate, Jonathan or Josh, one of those trendy J names from the '70s, came out. I was hailing my cab to take me back to Pont Street when I noticed the two of them join David and, after a bit of a huddle, climb into the taxi behind mine.

David Knight was presumably headed north. He and his wife Dorthea, a hypochondriac for whom London was the perfect posting since the damp weather brought out the best in her consumptive nature, had already started the progression north—they lived in St. John's Wood—but I'd heard a move to Hampstead was in the works. It was an axiom of American law firms in London that lawyers moved increasingly north just about the time their marriages went south. David's anemic wife had better be on guard. Perhaps Kimberly was going to kill two birds—

45

social and professional—with one stone.

I drifted while yet another taxi ferried me home. I surprised Steven on the landing at the first floor of the building. I told him briefly how my morning had gone and, for the first time since my devastating discovery, I started to cry. Once inside the apartment, he tried to comfort me and, convinced that I was fine and the baby was fine, he asked wearily, "Amy, I know it must have been horrible finding a dead body, but honey, you've got to calm down, take care of yourself and the baby, put this out of your mind. Besides, I know it's little consolation, but Amy, you hated this guy."

"Hate is really too strong a word."

"Okay, so you couldn't stand him. He made you crazy."

"Not exactly crazy."

"You've got to admit it, Amy. He was extremely difficult to work for."

"He had his moments."

"You said he was a maniac."

"He was a good lawyer."

"Everyone hated him."

"His clients loved him."

"You told me a thousand times that he was cruel to family and friends and staff."

"But he was devoted to his career."

"Well, you've just beat the Soviets in rewriting history." Steven threw up his hands in defeat.

"I know. I said all those things. I guess I didn't know you'd been listening. I can't believe he's dead. It's so, so anticlimactic. I guess I thought that he'd live forever. Or die at his desk. Not under it."

"Just yesterday you were ready to resign, Amy. He was going to be out of your life one way or another. I'm sorry it had to be this way. What are you going to do about that now?"

"Do about what?"

"Resigning."

"I took it back."

"You took what back?"

"The resignation letter. It's in my office. Mr. Blake didn't need it, and it was just lying on his desk, so I took it." I winced then at the memory of my snatching it from Mr. Blake's desk.

Steven pulled back a bit and said uneasily, "Do you think that's such a good idea? This is the police we're dealing with."

"But I didn't commit a crime or anything."

"Probably not. But you may have removed something from a potential crime scene. I'm not a criminal lawyer but even I know you shouldn't just take something away." He stopped talking when my tears started again. "Look," he said, "you're tired. We can talk about this later."

"No," I sniffed, "you're right." I agreed with Steven to return to the office Sunday morning in order to retrieve the resignation letter after a good night's sleep. But for the second time that day, baby-to-be Brown-Goldman took over the spotlight. Thinking I was waterlogged from all the tea, I didn't immediately notice that I had sprung a leak. A sure sign that I was losing the baby.

CHAPTER 5

"You poor thing! First, you find a dead body, then you find out you're pregnant, then you almost lose the baby. . . ."

"The doctor said the baby was never really in danger. I'm fine, we're fine, now."

". . . or was it that you found out you were pregnant and then you found the dead body?"

"Kimberly . . ."

"I suppose the order doesn't matter. Where was I? Oh, right," she ticked off the list of familiar events, "Pregnancy, dead body, threatened miscarriage, hospital, autopsy, police investigation, that was all so horrible, and now, if all that wasn't enough, *that, that thing!*"

"That thing," the latest in the string of catastrophes and near catastrophes that Kimberly had so lovingly catalogued, had not made its appearance until moments before her arrival at my office with coos of condolences: the woman had radar for incoming aimed at my direction. "Congratulations" was a definite afterthought.

It was hard to believe that almost five months had passed since the Saturday morning that found Mr. Blake and me in our last one-sided conversation. During my extended "pre-maternity post-mortality *paid* leave," late spring had turned to early fall without a noticeable change in the weather. Other than my waistline—my stomach preceded me in my return to the office by four inches—and my attire—I'd swapped sleek Italian pumps for sensible flats and an orthopedic back support—things seemed about the same. Helen Matthews-Smith was still ignoring my pleas for a permanent secretary. Ted Cunningham was still holding out the promise of a piece of the Declan merger without actually delivering on it. Tony was still claiming that the red message light on my voice mail was working when it hadn't blinked all morning. Kimberly was still faking concern over my welfare while really trying to wheedle information from me about the meeting I'd just had with David Knight.

And, despite an end to the investigation—an autopsy had established the official cause of Mr. Blake's death as anaphylactic shock after he'd eaten nuts, as I expected, in the chocolate candy I'd seen on his desk—Mr. Blake, the person responsible for "that thing," was still making my life miserable.

The day had started off innocently, but disappointingly, enough. Steven had brought me breakfast in bed and once I'd finished had said, "I bought you something. A 'going back to work, the baby's fine and I want to cheer you up' present."

"Steven, you're so sweet. Where is it? What is it?"

"Come, get out of bed."

I had pulled on a dressing robe and, rubbing my eyes, followed him down the hall.

He had pointed to our desk and chair in the hallway and had said, "Sit down and close your eyes!"

I had sat down as instructed.

"I picked it up that last time I was in Paris."

I had felt something being placed between me and the

chair back—definitely not a bottle of Duty Free perfume or a silk scarf.

"What is it?"

"It's a pillow. To use at your desk. For lower backache. I found this great store near my hotel, full of wonderful things, you know, time savers, gadgets. You haven't been complaining about backache, but the lady in the store thought it would only be a matter of time."

"Something to really look forward to."

"Isn't it great?"

"Yes. It's wonderful." The pillow was a step away—in the wrong direction—from an electrical appliance. I had hoped for a romantic present from Paris but my sarcasm was lost on Steven, and so I had hid my lack of enthusiasm during the trip to Mayfair. Waving at Lucy, I'd gone straight to my desk and plopped the pillow down on my chair and looked around.

My office had looked pretty much just like I had left it. Fortunately, the cleaning people had done a good job of tidying up the spots on the carpet where I had tossed my tea on D.C. Lawson's shoes. The files that I had been working on before my fateful resignation and Blake's unexpected demise were still spaced evenly along the front of the desk, with an empty space where the Declan United file had been. My in-tray looked like the Leaning Tower of Pisa but I had taken a deep breath and begun the meaningless process of picking away at the monument of mail until David Knight had called and asked that I drop by his office, where, in his most oblique lawyerly way, he had explained that Blake's client work had been dispersed in my absence to Gideon, Ted, and Kimberly, to everyone, that was, but me. David had assured me that my "valuable assistance" would, of course, still be needed for "various other matters" but at this point he had become even more vague. He had mumbled something about someone being by to fill me in on these mysterious other matters and he had looked relieved when I had stood up to leave.

When I had returned from lunch with Gideon, who, in the period I'd been gone, appeared to have lost all the weight I'd gained, my desk had been taken over by a box, a banker's box to be more precise, although why it bore that name was a mystery. No bankers I knew would be caught dead with a cardboard box. I had noticed next and more disturbingly that my office had also been taken over, which was much more ominous, by Helen Matthews-Smith.

That David Knight had sent Helen as his envoy had been a very bad sign. She had stood next to my windows, moored to my sofa, hands on hips indicating her displeasure at my impertinent absence. "There you are. I've been waiting." She had made no effort to hide her annoyance and had pointedly looked at her watch. She had waited for an apology but I had not obliged.

"What's with the box?"

We had then proceeded to have one of those conversations where she had assumed that I had knowledge that I did not possess. David Knight had a lot to answer for. After several minutes of her talking and my unsuccessful attempts to interrupt her, she had finished with a smug "I'll leave you to get on with it then" and had pointed to the box. I had taken delight in saying, "I haven't the faintest idea of what you are talking about."

"Didn't David tell you about the, um, box?"

"You mean this box?"

"Yes, this box. Daniel's box." She had pointed at, but I noticed did not touch, the package on my desk.

I had lifted the lid wondering from her demeanor

whether I had been mistaken about Mr. Blake's funeral arrangements, fearing that he'd not been laid to rest in a cemetery in Cambridge, that instead he'd been cremated, and that in some cruel twist of fate it had been decided that I would be, as I'd been in the past, his keeper. But the contents had been far less dramatic I had realized as soon as I had ripped the tape with a letter opener and removed the top. Just the detritus of office life, for someone, probably P.C. Ridley of the gloved hands, had taken the items on Mr. Blake's desk that Saturday morning—items that I recalled had been swept aside in Mr. Blake's desperate effort to breathe—and had placed them in this tidy banker's box, where the torn address label indicated they had traveled from the Mayfair police station to Mr. Blake's home in Hampstead to DW3's offices. And to its permanent resting place, my office.

"Shouldn't James be going through these? They are, after all, Mr. Blake's belongings." I had shied away from using the term the police had scrawled on the special delivery form. "Personal Effects" seemed so, well, impersonal.

"He doesn't want them. Besides, technically, they're still the firm's."

With visions of an administrative nightmare where you couldn't leave DW3 even at death's door before you'd accounted for every stapler, paper clip, and litigation bag, I had asked, "Why does the firm want this stuff?"

"There may be client files or confidential documents." She had been very bad at dissembling. Unlike Kimberly, Helen was more adept at direct hostility. "And, er um, there is one other matter. I thought that David told you about all of this."

"No." But as I had shifted the box, less sinister once I knew it contained Mr. Blake's things and not Mr. Blake, to the corner of my desk, I had realized the importance of the contents and the ghoulish task that neither David nor Helen could bring themselves to articulate. The client matters were just a pretext. If a client hadn't screamed for attention sometime since its lawyer's death over a matter lost on his desk, then it could hardly be that important. No, I had no illusions. This was all about money and the firm's unlimited capacity to squeeze blood from a stone. "You want me to do his timesheets."

"Well, yes."

I didn't say anything.

"It's not as if you haven't done them before."

As if that would be why I would protest.

"With a billing rate of $400 an hour, with even a modest number of billable hours and I'm sure there's a month's worth of time here, well, you've got to admit . . ."

She had been right, of course. The box, or more specifically, the record of Mr. Blake's time enclosed in it, amounted to a $64,000 prize that even a firm as profitable as DW3 would have been foolish to throw away.

"You are the logical person to do this." She had stated this as a fact and not as a question. "You're familiar with his clients. You knew what he was working on. There may be important client documents buried in there." Even she had cringed at the poor word choice. "Besides, no one else can read his handwriting."

Helen had left my office undoubtedly considering herself the victor in this latest office battle but not before adding her own request to the assignment. "Could you please keep an eye out for Blake's invitation list for the anniversary party? I'm certain that he prepared one." She had waited until she was nearly out of sight before she had added, "He may be dead, but his clients aren't."

53

"Poor, poor Amy." Kimberly shuddered in mock sympathy.

"I'll be fine." I ushered her out of the door of my office, thanked her profusely for her sympathy, and wondered why I felt that, on my first day back in the office, I was comforting her and not the other way around.

With Kimberly gone, and only a trace of lavender laced with nicotine in the air to remind me of Helen, I cleared an area on my desk on which I could unpack the object of Kimberly's morbid curiosity and Helen's impatience. The police had prepared an inventory identifying the contents taken from the scene and I reviewed the contents against the inventory as I pulled items from "that thing." The box.

It was a topographic map of a day in the life of Daniel Benedict Blake. Top layer—loose pieces of paper that carried whatever was the current crisis up to the surface. Random notes of telephone conversations, the date and time the only immediately decipherable words. Used and unused tissues crammed in unexpected places.

The next layer, important but not as urgent, client files. An annual report from a prospective client that had never materialized. A letter from one of Blake's Hong Kong clients requesting theater tickets. He'd penciled Kimberly's name across the top—an assignment that would not amuse her. A partnership evaluation form on Kimberly. On first reading, Mr. Blake's recommendation was favorable. But, in between the qualifications and suppositions, the message was clear that Mr. Blake hadn't thought that the London office could support a fifth partner. No wonder Kimberly had been eager to commiserate over the box.

Contact details for Declan United management. Blake's interest in the Declan United merger must have extended beyond keeping me uninvolved. A request to the New York office to approve a new client in the Cayman Islands, details such as name and billing partner missing.

Mr. Blake's invitation list, a single sheet of paper with a few names on it. I recognized the name of a district court judge and some titled Englishman. Lawrence Worthington must have been second or third generation DW3 royalty. I drew a blank on the others, Charles Kent and Paige something. Helen would not be happy trying to read these. In usual Blake fashion, he had fastened the list with a paper clip to a file marked "Anniversary Celebrations." The file, clearly Helen's and not Mr. Blake's, contained application forms for those of us who had passed the English solicitor's exam, grouped by state Bar membership: Walter Hughes—D.C. Bar, David Knight—New York Bar, and Kimberly Sullivan and me—California Bar.

Next, the fixtures, the firmament of Mr. Blake's desk. Tombstones, Plexiglas mementos of corporate deals, paperweights, a desk clock permanently stopped at 3:00—Mr. Blake had thrown it at the back of a departing attorney who had somehow displeased him—an assortment of pencils, erasers, business cards, a pencil sharpener, the *Concise Oxford Dictionary*, and blank legal pads.

I set the partnership evaluation form and the Declan file aside. I reluctantly removed the invitation list and Helen's file from the pile and considered whether to take them to her directly, or to call her so she could come pick them up herself. I happily placed them in an interoffice envelope in my out-tray, guaranteeing delivery sometime before the next Millennium.

I set the inventory list aside, certain that I had reached the bottom of the box, except perhaps for just a few pieces of stray paper and legal pads, when my hands came across a not immediately identifiable package. I closed my eyes, lifting it from the box with distaste. Along with the paraphernalia of Mr. Blake's professional life, the police had also returned Item Number 47, the chocolates neither Mr. Blake nor I had eaten that Friday afternoon. White with age or fingerprint dust—I couldn't tell which—they lay unappetizingly in a transparent plastic evidence bag. And resting at the bottom of the returned box, my fingers came across the tattered and empty Darlington container.

Every crumpled paper, gnawed pencil and used tissue had been documented—and from a quick scan of the inventory it had all been returned. The only thing missing was a resignation letter—that only I knew to miss—taken in haste and regretted in horrified silence when I'd been questioned by D.C. Lawson. Steven had been too worried about my health and our baby during the weeks following the miscarriage scare to concern himself with the return of the resignation letter. The official verdict, that Blake had died of natural causes, convinced both of us that it was a moot point.

I don't know what motivated me to rise, close the door, and rummage through the top drawer of my desk. I tossed out handfuls of paper while still keeping an ear cocked for an inquisitive Kimberly or a dour Gideon. Past loose change and paper clips, my fingers fell on a piece of paper lodged in a corner, which, as I tugged it from its resting place, I recognized as the resignation letter I'd foolishly thrust at Mr. Blake in a hormone- and chocolate-fuelled fit and had foolishly snatched from his desk the next day.

Helen had implied that once valuable client files had been salvaged and billable hours tallied, the box would be sent back to Blake's family for posterity, or, if I knew James, the rubbish heap. Wasn't this the perfect opportunity to set the record straight, ease my conscience, and return the letter to its rightful place as if nothing had ever happened? Even I wasn't that stupid. I decided to rip the letter in two, relieved that some secrets really do go to the grave, but stopped when I felt the flutter of something else on the back of the page.

It was a tiny yellow sticker. A post-it note. For a generation of conscientious students that had been admonished not to write in books, yellow post-it notes were a godsend and the bane of librarians. They marked the spot all right but like rabbits seemed to multiply until the written page became a sea of yellow. No more excuses for messages slipping off into the great unknown. The adhesive guaranteed that no nagging point was left unnoticed. This caution-colored reminder had apparently gone astray from Mr. Blake's desk and become attached to my resignation letter.

A brief message had been printed on it in bold, upper case letters with a black felt tip pen. Punctuated with several exclamation points, the message would have been as enticing to Mr. Blake as a siren luring a sailor into the bottomless sea. There on the yellow sticker were three seemingly innocent but deadly words—"NO NUTS—ENJOY!!!!"

I knew that Mr. Blake would not have just dug into those chocolates without knowing if they contained nuts. But the satisfaction I had from knowing that my knowledge of his behavior was right was outweighed by the troubling thought that someone had mislabeled the candy and indeed invited him to feast upon it. The invitation had been to disaster and this yellow sticker was proof of a crime that in my panic I had stolen. What should I do with it now?

CHAPTER 6

Whatever emotion had prompted me before—curiosity? bemusement? self-preservation?—vanished. Even vindication was gone, replaced by an overwhelming sense of guilt. And when standing outside a police station, guilt was not good. I knew D.C. Lawson sat at a desk somewhere on the inside waiting for me to arrive and confess. Bobbies strode off to their waiting panda cars. I was certain that they saw me exactly for what I was. Guilty. I might as well have had "guilty as charged" branded across my forehead. Guilty as not even charged. At least not yet.

Summoning up my courage and walking unsteadily to the front desk for inquiries, I asked for D.C. Lawson who, no, was not expecting me (not unless his guilt antenna was fine-tuned) but who, yes, would recognize my name. After a few moments, a genial officer directed me to a bank of elevators to my right and told me to follow the signs to the second floor, Detectives—Serious Crimes Section.

As the grilled elevator pulled me up to my destination, I fingered the incriminating evidence in my briefcase, my resignation letter that I had swiped from Mr. Blake's office and the yellow "no nuts" sticker. I'd stashed both in my briefcase along with the empty Darlington box. The chocolates, unimaginably unsavory, remained in the plastic bag among the "Personal Effects," safe in my desk.

Steven, whom I'd called from a pay phone around the corner from my office, had insisted that my only option was to hand it all over to the police. I walked down the aisle to D.C. Lawson's desk and put out my hand, expecting him to begin chanting the English equivalent of the Miranda warning but he only said hello and offered me a seat.

"I trust you're well, Mrs. Brown." He moved his shoes behind his desk.

"It's 'Ms.', but, yes, yes, I'm fine. Much better." I cringed.

"How can I help you?"

"It's—it's about Daniel Blake."

"Yes, I assumed that was the case since I hadn't heard of any further deaths at Winter, Worthington & Walker. Am I right?"

"Yes, you're absolutely right."

He waited for me to speak.

"I've found something. Well, I didn't exactly find it—I mean I had it all along—I mean not all along—I mean I took it but it was sort of mine in the first place. I realize I'm not making sense. Let me start over. I have some things for you. I wasn't entirely truthful at our first interview. I took something from Mr. Blake's office—it had nothing to do with his death, believe me—and it wasn't until later, that is, today, that I found the other thing and realized that it could be important."

His look did not lead me to believe that I was making myself any clearer. I stuck my hand in my briefcase and pulled out the two pieces of paper.

"Mr. Blake and I had an argument that Friday, I got really pissed, pardon, annoyed at him and submitted a resignation letter on the spot that he accepted." I pushed the piece of paper towards the officer on the gray metal desk. "See—it's dated that Friday and those are our signatures. Well, I thought better of it overnight—I had just got the news about the baby—and decided on Saturday that I'd undo it—but when I went into his office to discuss it with him—he, he was dead—I just panicked and grabbed my resignation letter and took it back to my office where I called you."

"And are you here to confess to killing Mr. Blake in the course of your argument on Friday?"

"NO!" I screeched. "I didn't *kill* him! I only *resigned*. It's just that I did take something out of his office."

"Your resignation letter."

"Yes."

"And you think this is important to a closed investigation?"

"No, no." I was getting frustrated with his interruptions and patronizing air.

"The resignation letter wasn't all I took. I didn't realize until later that this was stuck to the back of it." I pushed forward the letter and the yellow sticker. He looked at it and read aloud in a monotone, " 'No nuts enjoy.' Yes, I see."

"No, it's 'ENJOY!' " I exclaimed and waved my hand in a gesture of invitation. "You see—it's just as I thought— Mr. Blake would never have eaten that candy if someone hadn't told him it was okay to do so. He was very careful. This is proof someone wanted him to eat nuts and, and, well, to die." I was nearing the end of having any control over the ocean of remorse and felt myself drowning. "I'm so sorry—I didn't mean to cover-up something or to interfere with your investigation."

The dispensation from my guilt I hoped for did not

come. Instead, D.C. Lawson looked over the sticker and turned it over several times with tweezers-like pincers he had removed from his desk drawer.

"And you think this little note makes it murder?"

"I'm not sure. But I took something from his desk without raising suspicions. Doesn't that mean that someone else could have also? Doesn't the yellow sticker mean that the nuts in the candy were intentional?"

He pulled out a file from a cabinet behind him and read for a few minutes. He looked up and said, "Just reminding myself of some details. It is conceivable that whoever gave the candy to Blake honestly believed it was all nut-free—that it was an honest mistake that turned out horribly wrong, Miss Brown."

"It's 'Ms.' But has anyone come forward to admit that?"

"No, but I don't think that they would."

Not unless they had a tremendously guilty conscience like mine, I thought. "But doesn't the fact that there was a note and that no one has come forward make it all the more likely that it was a deliberate act?"

"Except that the note was still there when you went in that morning. Anyone who had deliberately put the note on the chocolates with a malicious intent would have just as deliberately made sure to remove it from the scene."

"And I did that for them."

"Yes, unfortunately, you did. Perhaps all you did was muddy the waters a bit."

This was the most benign description of my activities that I could have imagined.

"It was extremely inappropriate of you to have taken your letter and not to have told us. Now that you have—I'll admit, the new information does give me pause. I would be overstepping my duties if I made any particular comment either way. I should first show this new piece of information to my superiors."

"But won't you have to look further into how those chocolates got to Mr. Blake, where they came from, who gave them to him? Can't you run a fingerprint check on the yellow sticker? Do a hand-writing analysis?" I was grasping at all the criminal evidence straws I could remember from a lifetime of TV police shows and detective novels.

"I will run the usual tests but on something like this, which has already passed through at a minimum one set of hands that we know of"—my guilty look was for once justified—"and of which millions are sold and left lying around on every desk and table top—there's little hope of finding anything crucial. As for the handwriting, this looks like the ink of a generic felt tip pen—of which there are probably thousands sold daily across London—and block printing is invariably more difficult to match than hooked-up letters or script. We looked at the candy and the box in the course of our initial investigation to confirm the presence of nuts. Nothing suspicious there."

Eyeing the eagerness in my face, he was quick to dispel any notion that now, with the pivotal piece of evidence that I, like some prized Springer Spaniel, had put at his feet, a solution was obvious.

"Don't think that this will be over and done with now that your conscience is clear. The course of the investigation may have gone differently had we known of this note before but certain circumstances have not and will not change. Here was an elderly man with a heart condition and a deathly allergy to a food that was widely available. He was a millionaire whose only child lived a continent and an ocean away. He worked for a prestigious and financially prosperous law firm with impeccable political connections in both Washington and Whitehall, none of whose partners stood to gain directly from his demise but who did have a lot to lose from too much adverse publicity. His personal finances were in order, he had no obvious romantic entanglements, no organized crime connections. The only person who seems to have been affected by his demise was his elderly housekeeper who's had to move from her palatial surroundings in Hampstead to a Council flat in Chinatown." He paused. "And you, Ms. Brown."

Why did he choose this moment to finally get my name right?

"With respect, your Mr. Blake was, from your own description, greedy, egotistical, a glutton even, detested universally but, from all appearances, not to a level that could have led to his murder. Don't be too surprised when, or if, subsequent inquiries are relatively perfunctory and that, after a reasonable amount of time, the verdict continues to be accidental death by ingestion of a natural toxin from an otherwise innocent box of chocolates. Look." He paused a moment before continuing. "I've already said too much. I need you to sign this receipt form, indicating your release of these two pieces of paper."

I signed.

"If you'll excuse me, I'll take a photocopy of the form for your files." He stood up, pushed his chair away and disappeared around a corner. I jumped when he appeared back at the desk but his tone was more forgiving.

"Given a box of inviting chocolates, it was just the bad luck of the draw that your late Mr. Blake ate one with nuts. Now, if he had been the type to share, the chances of his eating the ones with nuts may have been decreased dramatically. A rather inefficient method of murder though, wouldn't you agree, Ms. Brown?"

Inefficient. I thought over D.C. Lawson's words outside the police station. Mr. Blake had also been accused of being inefficient, a dinosaur, even. He had never thought much of modern technology. He wouldn't even use a mechanical pencil. He would labor over a document, flourishing his Number 2 pencil, running it across his tongue for inspiration, while I impatiently tapped my fingers and surreptitiously checked my watch. I would mentally prime the pump, hoping for a torrent of words to carry me from the room. But in a variation on Chinese water torture, he would read aloud as he wrote, syllable by excruciating syllable, each word drawn out until a complete sentence finally dribbled onto the page. And invariably his contribution would be worthwhile. Inefficient, like murder by chocolates, but no less effective.

It would be difficult, juggling a full-time job, husband, apartment, preparing for a baby, and solving a crime that D.C. Lawson had dismissed as unlikely and that I was convinced was murder. I didn't have much time, less than two months before I left on maternity leave. I was still required to bill the requisite eight hours a day required from attorneys at Winter, Worthington & Walker. And once I had the baby, well, no new mother I'd ever met had the luxury of free time. But I'd had difficult assignments and tight deadlines before. Unlike Mr. Blake and his murderer, Amy Brown, novice detective, undercover work in a maternity dress a specialty, would just have to be both efficient *and* effective.

I would start with a box of chocolates.

CHAPTER 7

Who had bought Mr. Blake a box of chocolates? Who had left the yellow "no nuts" sticker? And what if it wasn't a "who" to blame, but a "what?" What if Darlington had screwed up, and, as D.C. Lawson had suggested, the note on the yellow sticker wasn't a deliberate lie but an unfortunate mistake? Before I could answer any of those questions, I needed to know "how?"

Which was why, less than an hour after leaving the Mayfair police station, I found myself ringing the bell at the front door of a Georgian townhouse that had been converted into offices on a side street just blocks from St. James's Park Underground station. The door bore a small brass nameplate that read, "Law Offices of Polly Lawrence, Esq." I rang a second time and the door clicked open. I walked into a small lobby with a reception room on the right and greeted Ms. Lawrence, my unwitting accomplice in crime detection.

After many years of so-called "higher" education, I am convinced that each class produces its quota of characters that, upon graduation, take their places in the world for the sole purpose of perpetuating certain stereotypes—thinkers, cynics, loafers, beauty queens, party girls, but worst of all, the know-it-all. The type that correctly answers rhetorical questions the first day of school, oblivious to murderous looks from fellow classmates. The one who always knows the answer when no one else does and who through guile or egotism or a mixture of both must show others that she knows the answer. And knows the answer regardless of how obscure the subject matter. Eighteenth-century paintings? Took a course at the Smithsonian one summer. Architectural design? Subscribes to *Architecture Today* and not just for the pictures. Wines? Certified oenologist, just as a hobby, of course. Food? Cordon Bleu training. Supreme Court rulings? Wrote thesis on the Rehnquist Court. The one who never admits to watching something as plebian as television or has time for popular culture but who still knows all the answers on Jeopardy. A smarty pants.

Unfortunately, the legal profession seems to produce more than its fair share of smarty pants. Before me stood a perfect example of the phenomenon. Polly's life seemed to be an exercise in staying a step ahead of all other potential know-it-alls. In addition to having an astounding knowledge of miniature Mogul paintings and other esoteric facts about the Indian subcontinent, her birthplace, Polly knew everything there was to know about Japanese food, French wines, and the English monarchy, and she was not shy in sharing her knowledge. This annoying quality alone may have been enough to make her merely boring, but her legal expertise and her tendency to flaunt it at the most inopportune times was what cemented her role as social pariah.

Polly's practice was rather unique. She was a product liability and safety expert. She represented clients whose products were objects that most people used in their daily lives—drugs, cosmetics, food, drinks, appliances, toys, furniture. But her title did little to convey the excruciating minutia of the rules she reported on or the "cradle-to-grave" advice she rendered on all aspects of product development, testing and marketing. Clients actually paid her to advise them on the permitted ingredients in paper plates, the placement of the expiration date on cartons of milk, the proper sterilization method for bandages, the differences between Red Dye Numbers 1 and 7. She spent her free time trolling through the aisles of pharmacies and grocery stores reading labels and ingredient listings. And she never hesitated to impart the less than appetizing details of her latest research—usually just about the time her audience bit into the offensive product.

Smarty pants extraordinaire.

"Thanks for seeing me at such short notice."

"No problem. This way. My office is upstairs." Polly, striking in appearance but not conventionally beautiful, had long, red hair she swept back from her broad forehead with a pencil and a bulldog clip. On the far side of forty, she'd lived in London longer than any other American expat I knew and had qualified as an English solicitor by the traditional method and not the easy streamlined way that I had. Limping slightly from the polio she'd contracted as the only child of diplomats stationed in some foreign outpost, she led me to her office on the first floor of the town house.

"Watch your step."

I stepped over a disassembled vacuum cleaner. I knew she was a one-man band, as unlike the vast bureaucracy of DW3 as possible, but I hadn't realized that meant she did her own cleaning.

"Sorry. Just ignore that. But be careful. More than a thousand people are injured falling down the stairs over these things every year. A thousand stupid, clumsy people. I'm in here." She opened a door and said, "You'll have to excuse the mess. I'm used to it."

Stepping inside was like entering a warehouse of the

Home Shopping Network. In a scene that would have made David Knight apoplectic, every available space was occupied. Aspirin, shampoo, razor blades, lemonade coolers, vitamins, suntan lotion, toys and dozens of bottles and jars and packets, most bare of labels, lay scattered about the room. I hesitated to take the seat that had been offered to me. Was it just another faulty product sample?

"As you can see, I'm pretty busy. So how are things over at Winter, Worthington & Walker?"

"Fine. Busy."

"Is Walter Hughes still over there?"

"Yes, he is. I didn't know you knew Walter."

"From D.C. My parents retired there. We're both Foreign Service brats." Six was double the number of degrees of separation needed for a connection among American expatriates in London, and the number grew even smaller among lawyers, and became downright incestuous when it came to Washington connections.

"I see."

"I was sorry to hear about your colleague. Daniel Blake. Never met him but. . . ."

"Oh, yes, thank you." I hoped to avoid the usual slurs.

"And congratulations on the baby. Have you read the Penelope Leach book on parenting? She says. . . ."

Disappointed to learn that never (to my knowledge) having had a baby had not kept Polly from becoming an expert on maternity and impatient to move on to the purpose of my visit, I lied easily and said that I had. I moved stuffed plush toys from the chair while she moved several bottles of perfume, deodorant, hair spray, household cleansers and furniture polish from her desk.

"I'm looking into the labeling—it's kind of my subspecialty—and packaging requirements for aerosols.

'When is an aerosol not really an aerosol? That is the question.' "

I stared at her blankly. This was going to be more painful than I thought.

"Do you see this warning?" She pointed a ruler at one of the cans she had just swept aside. " 'DO NOT SPRAY DIRECTLY INTO FLAME.' Those letters are exactly 5cm high. I know. I measured them. There's a reason they're that height. So consumers can see them. But do you know how many consumers do just that? Spray directly into a flame?"

I didn't know but I was sure that I was going to find out. Here was a smarty pants who answered her own rhetorical questions.

"Hundreds. Virtual flame throwers." She slapped the ruler in her hand as she shared with me her contempt for the lowly consumer, which included just about every one I knew. Including me.

"I can't tell you how many times I've reviewed and revised the warning panels on these things. Consumers are idiots. They climb on ladders with high heels. They trim their hedges with lawn mowers. They let children play with toys that have small pieces and then they sue when their little darlings swallow them. Take this label for example," she pointed to a giant mockup of the label for a well-known cold medicine. " 'DO NOT TAKE THIS PRODUCT WITH CAFFEINE.' So what does some moron do?"

"Take it with caffeine?" I asked meekly.

"Exactly."

I banished thoughts of washing down this very cold medicine with a Coke just a few months ago. I wasn't about to confess my sin to Polly.

"And do you know how many fatalities are attributable

to accidents in the home?"

I didn't hear her answer because I was staring at what appeared to be a silicone breast implant, now being used as a paperweight.

"And that's not even counting the vacuum cleaners. Don't let anyone tell you otherwise. Housekeeping kills."

That excuse certainly explained the state of Polly's office.

"It's because consumers are just so stupid. I could go on and on. But that's not why you're here. How can I help you?"

"Well, as I explained on the phone, I'm interested in paying for a few hours of your time to bring me up to speed on an area about which I know very little. It's in preparation for a major acquisition by one of our clients of a U.K. company. The potential acquisition sells consumer products that are outside of the client's usual line of business. Is this something you would be able to do?"

"I imagine so. Other law firms hire me from time to time for my expertise, to pick my brain."

An unpleasant image of the contents of Polly's brain, all flash cards, *Black's Law Dictionary* and a couple of volumes of the *Encyclopedia Britannica* appeared in my head. "I'm sorry, you were saying?"

"I said, 'it depends on the product.' Can you be more specific?"

"Well, yes. Our client, a non-food company, is interested in acquiring the assets of a food company, or perhaps reaching a commercial arrangement for the production and distribution rights to the food company's principal product."

"Which is?"

"Chocolate." I began again. "Our dilemma, both

Winter, Worthington's and our client's, is that we know very little about the market for chocolate from a regulatory or commercial perspective. We have only the target's published figures. Before we take negotiations further, as you can imagine, we want, that is, the client wants to know a bit more about, um, chocolate. Specifically, boxed chocolates."

Her eyes grew round like Junior Mints. I had come to the right place.

CHAPTER 8

Polly drew her hand in the direction of her bulletin board. Pinned to the wall like butterfly specimens were discarded candy bar wrappers of brands that I immediately recognized. "As you can see," she said, "I've been personally responsible for bringing all the well known brands to market here."

It wasn't a cure for cancer but even I had to admit it was impressive.

"Well, first, let's think about the commercial setting. There are about half a dozen major players in the chocolate industry. Nestlé, Jacob Suchard, Mars, Cadbury, Ferrero. These are most well known in Europe and the U.K. There's a tremendous market for chocolate. Here in Britain, we each eat about eight kilograms of chocolate a year."

"What's that in pounds?"

"About seventeen pounds. Put another way, that's about 540,000 tons of chocolate a year. But that's all kinds of chocolate. Will your client be getting into local or international distribution outlets?"

"Well, we're keeping an open mind." I nodded to the possibility. Why not? I thought. The client was a figment of my imagination.

"In that case, there are hundreds of stores in England

selling what is known in the trade as boxed confectionery, or filled chocolates. You know, assorted chocolates where the customer can hand pick his selection or buy a ready-made one. The real market leaders for the luxury brands are the Belgian and French producers. The Swiss like to consider themselves competitors." She paused and looked at me. "How much do you already know about chocolate?"

My plea of ignorance was the encouragement Polly needed. She then proceeded—with occasional pauses to make sure that I was taking notes—to tell me more about chocolate than Willy Wonka would have wanted to know.

"The history of chocolate is a long and interesting one. Chocolate, as we know it, is the result of the fermentation and processing of the fruit pods of the cacao plant. The cacao beans are fermented, roasted, and shelled in order to get to the heart, or the nib, of each bean. The nibs are then ground and heated to produce the essence of chocolate. The technical term is liquor. Chocolate liquor—it's generally more than half cocoa butter—is the starting point for the multitude of chocolate products we consume.

"The Mayans and the Aztecs cultivated cacao plants long before the Spanish conquistadors sailed for the New World. Cacao beans were used by the Aztecs as food but also as a form of currency. A good slave went for about 100 beans. The Aztecs drank xocatl—that's spelled 'x-o-c-a-t-l'—the precursor, I suppose, to what we call hot chocolate, a mixture of ground cacao beans and water and other vegetables—I've seen reports that peppers or corn were used. That beverage must have been very bitter for it wasn't until the early 16th century, after the Spanish arrived in the New World, that sugar and vanilla were added to the mix.

"The first factories for the cacao bean production opened sometime later in, as you might have guessed,

Spain, and by the next century, cocoa drinks became popular throughout Europe and the thirteen colonies. Following on from the invention of the steam engine, a Dutch manufacturer perfected the method of extracting the liquor, separating the wheat from the chaff, if you will, from the rest of the beans . . ."

I lost interest just after the Industrial Revolution and sat up in my seat only at the mention of another food group.

". . . since chocolate is something of a political hot potato."

Had I missed something? I looked at Polly and asked, "What?"

"Would you like me to put this down in writing?"

"No, no. I'm getting it all down." I shifted my pad and paper and wondered where the last two hundred years had gone.

". . . compositional requirements established by the European Union. Back in the early 1960s and '70s, the European Community—it hadn't become the Union yet—determined that certain foods—chocolate, honey, coffee, jam, wines—of course, alcohol is a whole other specialty, don't get me started on alcohol—shouldn't be entitled to bear the name of that food unless they met certain compositional requirements. The rules came up again for discussion just a couple of years ago with the admission of the Nordic countries and, more recently, the European Parliament wanted to ban English chocolates, but the situation essentially has remained the same since 1974.

"Agreement on compositional requirements was intended to promote the free movement of products across borders. The resulting rules—the Chocolate Directive—led to definitions and compositional requirements for every type of chocolate—plain chocolate, milk chocolate, white chocolate, filled chocolates—and their ingredients. How much dry cocoa solids, how much milk solids, how much sucrose, permitted cocoa butter substitutes—the required percentages are all spelled out in the rules. In order to label a product 'chocolate,' it has to contain a minimum of 35% dry cocoa solids, for example. Or the chocolate coating of a piece of chocolate in a box of candy with a caramel center—filled chocolate—must be, at a minimum, a quarter of the entire piece, or it can't be called 'filled chocolate.' Those are just a couple of examples. And believe me, it would be death to be considered not 'chocolate.' "

"Hot chocolate?" The baby, who'd apparently not been turned off by its mother's disastrous encounters with chocolate, kicked.

"No, not *hot* chocolate." Polly looked at me with exasperation. "*Not* chocolate. If a product doesn't meet the compositional requirements, it's not chocolate, or more accurately, it can't be packaged and sold in Europe as chocolate. Your product may be 'chocolate' "—she formed imaginary quotation marks around the words—"in the United States, or Mexico, or Malaysia, or Timbuktu—other countries have their own rules—but if your product is not 'chocolate' as the Europeans define it, then it can't be called 'chocolate.' And if you're not 'chocolate,' you're nowhere. The alternatives are commercial disaster—'fantasy chocolate,' 'pretend chocolate,' or, I like this one, 'chocolatey.' "

"I see." Her hand motions made me dizzy and I feigned interest that I did not feel. It was time to bring the discussion back to my interests. "You mentioned labeling—would the labeling be any different for a candy bar as opposed to, say, a box of chocolates?"

"Well, that's a little more complicated. Special rules

apply to things like a bar of chocolate and a box of candy."

"So it's conceivable that if a box of chocolates had, say, fruit centers, the label wouldn't necessarily mention fruit? Or say something slightly less innocuous like, for instance, peanuts?"

"Now, that's an interesting point. Because of recent reports of fatal cases of allergic reaction, particularly to peanuts, some companies have, at the invitation of the government, started voluntarily to label their products to warn about the possibility of certain ingredients. For product liability reasons. Just what did you have in mind?"

"As I mentioned earlier, we—that is—my client currently has no independent means of judging the performance record of its potential partner or, um, acquisition—but on the basis of the public information we could give you and using your knowledge of the industry and your contacts, could you find out whether there had been any reports of safety problems, or issues of quality control that might make my, or the firm's, client rethink its investment?"

"I suppose that I could make a few phone calls, check on enforcement actions under the food safety laws, see if any claims have been filed against the company. Is that what you had in mind?"

"Something like that. The client is also interested in the target's product as well and not just its production facilities. Let's say that I gave you a sample of its product, could you give us information on composition, something that might give me, er us, a clue as to the characteristics and quality of the target's product compared, to say, its closest competitors?"

I was thinking as fast as I could since I wasn't even sure exactly what I was looking for, other than whether the remains of the box of chocolates contained nuts.

She drew back as my questions took a slightly different direction. "Food samples can be analyzed. There's a lab that my clients use from time to time."

"What if we wanted to find out whether the company had ever experienced contamination of its production process?"

"There are probably reports of inspections, safety citations, that sort of thing. What's the name of the target company?"

I pulled the empty box from my briefcase and said, "Darlington."

She looked me straight in the eye and said, "And is that the company whose chocolates killed Dan Blake?"

Like I said, she was a smarty pants.

CHAPTER 9

"I'm sorry." The situation had changed quickly from prospective client to supplicant.

"There is no client?"

"No, no client, but I didn't think that you'd help me if I didn't come to you with a real commercial interest."

"I have to admit that you really had me going until the labeling for peanuts. Then something clicked. Maybe my recollection of the newspaper accounts of your partner's death."

"Look, I know I've been a jerk to come to you with this story."

"No kidding."

"But I didn't know what else to do. You see, I'm convinced that either Darlington has something to hide or that someone deliberately gave chocolates with nuts to Mr. Blake, knowing that he would eat them."

"You mean . . . murder him? With *candy?*"

Even I knew it sounded crazy and if Polly, who obviously believed consumers were doomed, thought the idea was preposterous, I was in real trouble. "Yes. It could have just as easily been a mistake—the chocolate with the nuts, I mean." I sensed smarty pants was a stickler for ethics, morals and proper police procedure. And I knew that if I revealed my intentions then this meeting would be over. But if she was going to become my accomplice, however reluctant, I needed to give her full information, or at least what passed as full information between lawyer and client. "There was a note on the candy—someone had written 'No Nuts' on it. That effectively told Mr. Blake that it was okay to eat them. And, in fact, maybe not all of the candy had nuts. I don't think that they did. But for my own purposes I'd like to know if the candy did. And whether they were really supposed to have nuts. Or if something had gone wrong at Darlington."

She continued to look at me in disbelief.

"The bottom line is that I think that this company's chocolates killed someone. And I need to know how that happened."

"Why can't the police do that? Didn't they test the candy? Didn't they have the box? The wrappings?"

"Well, yes, they do or they did."

"Then let them do their job."

"But I'm not sure they will do their job. If you're worried about the police, don't. No one knows I'm here. I don't think anyone knows, or even cares, that I have this," I pointed to the box, "or the candy."

"So you do have the candy?"

"Well, yes, just not with me."

"Uh huh."

"If you ship the candy off to the lab then there will be no suspicions raised about my firm's involvement. It makes sense coming from you."

"And just what are you hoping to find besides whether the candy contains nuts?"

"Well, anything you can tell me really. About the candy. And anything you can tell me about the company that produced them. Darlington." I pointed to the capital "D" on the box that I had pulled from my briefcase.

She sat back in her chair and fingered the ruler some more and then spoke. "I suppose there could be ways to contaminate a production process. Were you thinking of a product liability problem, something along those lines?"

"I'm not sure, you're the expert."

"Let me see that box again."

I handed it over. "There isn't an ingredient panel."

"Doesn't need one. Boxed at the source." She turned the box over. "Do you know where it was bought?"

"No, well, not what store or anything specific but doesn't it say 'Made in England'?"

"Yes. It's right here. Means we know at least one ingredient."

"You mean nuts?"

"No. Vegetable fat."

"What do you mean?"

"Like I said before, there's a derogation to the chocolate rules for England and Ireland. It also applies to Denmark and the other Nordic countries."

"Right." I pretended to look at my notes but had no idea what she was talking about.

"It's all part of the compositional requirements. The traditional chocolate making in England was considered scandalous by the purists on the Continent—the Brits and others use vegetable fat and not 100% cocoa butter in their chocolate. The higher the cocoa butter content, the dearer the product. After some political wrangling, the rules were written to allow U.K. companies, and others, to continue using vegetable fat. You know how when you eat some chocolate here it leaves a coating in your mouth?"

"I guess so."

"Vegetable fat. Not all U.K. companies use vegetable fat

but they can if they want to. It's a cheaper method of manufacture. The luxury end of the market doesn't use it. Darlington may like to market itself as luxury but it's a sure thing their candy contains vegetable fat. A food analysis by a lab could figure that out. Let me think. Give me a minute, won't you?"

"Sure." While Polly leafed through a book she took from the monstrous shelves behind her, I looked at the papers on her desk. *The Viagra Newsletter*, Polly's idea of light reading, was too technical to be entertaining. I replaced it when she cleared her throat to signal that she was finished.

"I'm not saying I'll do anything. I'm just thinking more or less out loud."

"I understand."

"As an intellectual exercise."

"Right."

"As long as we're clear on that."

"Of course."

"And I'm certainly in no position to give any advice without the candy."

"I understand."

"The candy would have to be analyzed, sent to a lab, I'd have to consult with some specialist . . ."

"Of course. I'm happy to hear whatever you can tell me."

"Good. As long as you understand the nature of what I'm about to tell you." She set the tome she'd been looking through aside. "Let's assume, for the moment, that whoever wrote that note truly believed that the candy was nut free."

"All right."

"That would leave the manufacturer the responsible party. I can envision two possible scenarios. Three really,

81

but the third doesn't bear thinking about and we'd have to change our assumptions about the note, and there could be more, but these two occur to me right now."

I nodded, confused, but said, "Go on."

"The first, let's call it the 'lip service' hypothetical."

"Okay." I wrote on my tablet the first two words that Polly had spoken that I understood.

"I did some research some time ago on how companies have addressed the problem of cross-contamination with nuts and other allergens in connection with a case for a kosher food company. Thought it would make an interesting analogy. In the U.S., companies have invested tremendous amounts of money to ensure that products with known allergens—nuts, peanuts, that kind of thing—don't come into contact with allergen-free products. They use various methods, usually separate production or packaging facilities. When a company learns that, despite all its efforts, allergen-containing products have come into contact with other products, there's usually only one remedy—shut down the production line until it can be cleaned and made contaminant-free—expensive and time consuming for a company whose product sales are subject to seasonal demands."

I thought of Christmas and Valentine's Day.

"This box is labeled 'May contain nuts.' " She pointed to words on the inner lid that I hadn't noticed. "A very savvy move for product liability purposes. Darlington—good lawyers, probably—can consider itself shielded from liability for the occasional bad reaction to nuts. But this awareness raises a troubling possibility. What if the company actually pays little attention to cross-contamination with nuts during the production process and, rarely if ever, undertakes the expensive and time consuming production precautions?"

"What are you suggesting?"

"What if it's more than the occasional nut? At what point does Darlington's warning 'May contain nuts' become meaningless?"

"Because the warning really means '*Always* contains nuts.' "

"Exactly. That's the first possibility. The second idea goes back to the compositional requirements, the derogation for England."

"The vegetable fat." I wrote the word "fat" and resisted writing the word "Amy" next to it.

"Right. Let's assume the company is not at fault when it comes to nuts. But what if, and this is a big if, Darlington produces a product that's labeled, marketed and priced as a luxury brand but uses the cheaper ingredients . . ."

"Like vegetable fat."

"Or others. It takes advantage of the derogation. It just doesn't tell anybody about it."

"Wouldn't people taste the difference?"

"Amy. This is England. Think about it."

England. Toad in the hole. Spotted Dick. Beans on toast. Kippers. Mushy peas. Ice cream without cream. The ominous vegetable fat. "You're right."

"Darlington might have been willing to take it on the chin for the one safety problem experienced by your boss, apologies all around and a quick settlement, in order to hide its gross non-compliance on labeling, quality and composition. Call it the 'vegetable fat derogation deception.' Darlington sells cheaper, inferior candy at inflated luxury prices. Depending on the scale of the operation, that could be very lucrative for them. And fines for an entire inventory of candy could end up being very expensive. Non-compliance brings a fine for every non-conforming piece. Much more expensive than the going rate on one dead old man."

Polly's theories were interesting, to the extent I actually understood them—the rules on chocolate were a far cry from corporate restructuring. "Aren't candy companies inspected? Isn't there a risk with both of these hypotheticals that, I don't know, the chocolate police could take the offenders away in chains?"

"Safety and hygiene inspectors are notoriously overworked and unless many members of the public are actually injured—and we don't know if your late boss was part of a larger problem—or complain, the risk of enforcement is rather low."

"So Darlington could be hiding something."

"I didn't say that. I'm just willing to admit to the possibilities."

"Then you'll look into it for me?"

"Let me put this to you as bluntly as I can, Amy. Historically, and as a general rule, food companies are not likely to hide problems, contamination or otherwise. It's not like an auto manufacturer who can point the finger at the designer, or the production team, or the assembly line worker, or even the driver, in an attempt to avoid blame. It's extremely bad for business to have your product—and food is one of life's necessities—kill someone just by eating it. Believe me, the public expects its food to be absolutely safe or as near to absolute as possible. That public trust— food safety is something most people have taken for granted, until very recently—means that food companies are usually the first to announce recalls and usually the last to deny responsibility, Mad Cow Disease being the exception to the rule, although that seems to be more of a political problem. Real problems are typically handled quickly in order to quell bad publicity. The Perrier case is still discussed as a model for handling public relations."

She looked at me to make sure I was paying attention. "I could make all the inquiries you want, spin out the hypotheticals, review files and case law—food safety issues hardly ever make it to court—but at the end of the day, I doubt that you'll be any closer to laying the blame on Darlington than you are right now. The most you can hope for is an analysis of one thing."

"And that is?"

"Whether the candy has nuts." She handed me the empty box back. "But you don't need a lawyer for that."

Chapter 10

I thanked Polly for her time and left thinking that I had to start thinking less like a lawyer if I wanted to prove the third, more sinister—and based on Polly's advice, most likely—explanation for the nuts in Blake's chocolates. That somehow, someone had made sure that the box of chocolates on Mr. Blake's desk had been full of nuts and that, by leaving the yellow sticker, he would eat them, and that that someone could be found at the London office of Winter, Worthington & Walker.

And could be found quite easily, I believed, for DW3 London may have been only five hours ahead of New York, but it was more than a decade behind when it came to insuring the level of confidentiality expected from the legal profession. The mailroom was an open book. Deep in the bowels of DW3 London, each lawyer had a pigeonhole for his or her mail. Interoffice mail was hardly ever sealed. Secretaries wantonly opened confidential and personal interoffice envelopes from the New York office. They knew from experience that the envelopes only contained the latest L.L. Bean catalogue for their homesick bosses. Marking something "confidential" was, at best, a fig leaf for our consciences.

Delivery of mail and faxes was entrusted to the least capable person on staff—who else would take such mind-numbing work?—and, not infrequently, correspondence did not reach its intended recipient until it had passed through the hands of other lawyers. Pink phone messages lay on the front reception desk to be read by anyone. Incoming faxes lay unattended on the fax machines in the late evening and into the early hours of the morning. E-mails, when the system was working, which was hardly ever, could be accessed by anyone with some knowledge of computers and Tony could override passwords by creating new ones. Voice mail was also not sacrosanct. Anyone could listen to anyone else's voice mail by punching in an internal extension, the absence of the red flashing light and the designation of "new" messages as "old" the only evidence that a message may have been accessed. Speakerphones were so faulty that even closed doors could not block out the sounds of lawyers huddled around the desk shouting to make themselves heard.

Except for Helen's office, where petty cash and payroll records were kept, office and file cabinet doors were left unlocked. An earlier attempt by David Knight to change that situation had been unsuccessful. Fees for the locksmiths, called out at all hours to let in some hapless lawyer who'd forgotten his or her keys—Mr. Blake had been the worst offender—had exceeded a first year associate's salary and the New York office had drawn the line at that expense. As an alternative to keys, Helen had installed keypads on the internal doors on David's orders. After several embarrassing false alarms, Helen had changed the entry code to "1-2-3-4." Easy enough for any would-be thief, but, more importantly, easy for Mr. Blake, to remember. That was as sophisticated as we got.

But the low-tech nature of our frequently malfunctioning office equipment wasn't the only explanation for DW3 London's lax attitude toward confidentiality. Headquarters may have only been a phone call and a time zone away but, in terms of corporate culture, the London satellite was light years from the mother ship. DW3 had had no trouble supplying the manpower, the letterhead, and the other symbols of its identity, but capturing and transferring something as elusive as tradition and reputation had been as challenging as finding a decent bagel in Mayfair or a proper cup of tea in Manhattan. Those who had tried to instill the intangible values of Winter, Worthington & Walker in the likes of Tony, Lucy, and Louise ultimately became convinced that the magic really was in the water.

With lawyer-hating H.M.S. at its helm, DW3 London had developed its own unique, sometimes surreal, sometimes combative, atmosphere in which a succession of lawyers with short memories audibly pined for an America where no computer ever broke down, no secretary ever called in sick, no copy machine ever ran out of paper, no taxi ever got stuck in traffic, no fax operator ever dialed the wrong number, no important file ever got mislaid, no client ever got put on hold, no staff member ever refused to work overtime, why, such a Utopia that one wondered why anyone in his right mind had ever left. These amnesia victims co-existed with a staff that resented the implications in the mantra "This is how we do it in the States" but that nevertheless lived up to the lowest of expectations.

It wasn't always a hostile environment. In some ways, it was probably a more pleasant place to work than DW3 New York. Whether because of its small size or just sheer stubbornness, DW3 London had resisted all efforts to be molded in the image of its parent office. Not for it the hushed corridors and oak paneled boardrooms where running in the hall was frowned upon. But this combination of characters—anal, self-important and ultimately self-centered lawyers who refused to be inconvenienced, an overbearing office manager who believed that expensive time saving and security measures were for her to know and for the lawyers to find out, and a bored staff not above losing a file for the sheer entertainment value and for whom a slowdown would have meant a noticeable improvement in job performance—and atmosphere—an informality bordering on the raucous—meant that invariably corners were cut, standards slipped, lawyers resorted to self-help, and "information control" became an oxymoron.

Not that I wouldn't experience some difficulties. Direct questioning of my colleagues was out of the question. They weren't sentimental. "Do you remember what you were doing the day Mr. Blake died?" was unlikely to invoke any memories, and certainly not fond ones. They weren't stupid. Like most hard working ambitious professionals, they were paranoid and looked for the meaning behind any query that strayed outside the realm of business. "How well did you know Daniel Blake?" would most assuredly be met with an immediately suspicious "What's your point?" or "Who wants to know?" And they weren't, by nature, social. Although life in a small overseas office meant that I occasionally knew more details of my colleagues' personal life—spousal arrangements, private school choices, nanny nationalities—than I might have known had I been just another anonymous associate in the New York office, the forced intimacy was just that—forced. Kimberly's comments on my wardrobe, Ted Cunningham's mild flirtations, even Gideon's inquiries into my state of health, might have been mistaken for social niceties, but I recognized them for what they were. Office guerrilla warfare.

E-mail would be off limits. One of the young lawyers—all

techies—would notice that I'd entered a computer other than my own. But I wasn't too concerned about missing anything important. DW3 had learned a painful and expensive lesson at the hands of a savvy lawyer who'd represented a disgruntled secretary claiming sexual harassment in the New York office: "delete" didn't really mean "delete" when it came to computers. Just as lost files could almost always be retrieved, so could off-color jokes making the rounds of e-mail. I didn't have to access my colleagues' e-mail. Big Brother was already watching and he would not be made to pay again.

And if I really wanted to know what was on my colleagues' minds, I had two choices. First, I had Lucy. Not just decorative, Lucy had everything called for in a great receptionist—posh accent, a talent for matching faces and voices with names, and an easygoing manner. As a captive audience near the newspapers and the only comfortable sofa in the office, Lucy heard every bit of gossip—from the disgruntled mail room staff, the lonely six-monthers to whom Lucy seemed maternal, and the egotistical clients who flattered themselves by thinking that Lucy's special greeting was reserved solely for them, to the needy lawyers for whom Lucy worked wonders on flight bookings, dinner reservations and last minute flowers for the wife, girlfriend, or mistress. Lucy gave, as well as received, good information and although everyone knew that once Lucy knew something, it was the equivalent of pressing the broadcast button on the intercom, no one ever stopped talking to her.

And I had voice mail. DW3 vigilance stopped short of tape recordings. In a stroke of brilliance, self-proclaimed, of course, I called Tony the morning after my meeting with Polly and complained that once again the tell tale blinking red light on my voice mail wasn't working. Conscientious colleague that I'd become, I sent my own e-mail to staff and

lawyers at DW3 warning them of this fault in the system—
not knowing if I had new messages because the red light
didn't flash—and advising them, as I'd learned, that the
only way to be absolutely sure was to check the phone from
time to time. I pushed the button for "SEND" and smiled
as I gave myself the license to eavesdrop.

Polly was probably right. I already had what I needed to
find a killer—an office where chaos reigned and the skills
I'd acquired during my tenure with Daniel Blake but had
never been taught in law school. Reading correspondence
upside down, distracting delivery men, repairing and sabo-
taging office machinery, dropping well placed nuggets of
misinformation, perpetuating rumors, dissembling to op-
posing counsel, listening in on other people's conversations.
I didn't need a lawyer. I just needed to start thinking more
like a suspicious spouse searching through the pockets of
my wayward colleagues.

*"Welcome to the Winter, Worthington & Walker voice
mail system. The party you are calling is not available.
Please leave a message after the tone or press the star key
for more options."*

I pressed the star key and, pregnant and above reproach,
I welcomed myself to my colleagues' voice mail:

*"David. It's Dorthea. Your wife. I'll be in Baden
until sometime next week. I've left the details with the
maid. If you care."*

*"David. Kimberly. Blake's office is still empty and
I'm stuck in this closet. Even Amy's office is bigger than
mine. Can't you do something?"*

"This is Harrods Men's Department calling for Mr. Knight. The waxed jacket you ordered is in. You can pick it up anytime."

"This is a message for Kimberly Sullivan. I'm calling from Harrods. The credit card number you gave for payment for the furniture you ordered from our catalog has been rejected. Could you please call me to provide other details?"

"Kimberly. David. Please call me as soon as you get in. I want to change our schedule for next week. Dorthea's going to be away."

"I'm calling for Kimberly Sullivan. I'm not sure what number I've reached. Is this an overseas number? I'm calling from Easy Housing Association. John Sullivan has given us your name as a credit reference. I'm assuming he's a relative. Could you please call me on our toll free number in the United States?"

"This is a message for Walter Hughes. Is this an office phone? It sounds like an office phone. I don't want to leave a message. Just call me on my mobile. It's the same number as the office, plus the usual access code."

"Walter. You left so early this morning we didn't have a chance to talk. Harrods called and Chewy Harrington's office called but that's not why I'm calling. It's about Robbie. His school called. They found—I don't know what else to call them—porno magazines in his locker. He's only twelve. I'm beside myself. How would he have gotten them? Call me as soon as you can. Does anyone

check these messages? Maybe I shouldn't. . . ."

"Mr. Hughes. Your receptionist suggested that I leave this message on your voice mail. I'm calling from the credit department of Trustees Bank about the credit card we issued on June 30th of last year. Your card shows a considerable amount of activity over the last few days, put quite bluntly, to calls to a sex chat line. Perhaps this is an error. If you could just call me at the number on your card. Thank you."

"Gideon. It's Hugh. You asked that I call when I had a chance. How are things amongst the colonials? You know the number."

"Gideon. It's Alice. I'm really worried about you. You didn't get any sleep last night at all. I've made you an appointment to see a doctor. Things can't go on like this. Call me at home."

"Mr. Chapman. This is Harrods charge account department calling. Your application has been approved. You should be receiving your new card in the post shortly, along with a description of membership benefits, including special presale viewing and free admission to the toilet facilities."

"Teddy. It's me. Ex-wife Number 1. I've tried leaving messages at your home but I get the feeling that I'm speaking into a black hole. Like our marriage. I'll make this quick. Where's my money? And none of this 'the check's in the mail' crap. I'm not one of your little girlfriends who'll believe . . ." *"Where was I? Oh, yes, not be-*

lieving your every word. So don't get any ideas that we're even. Just send the money. Give my love to Aischa or is she already ancient history?"

"This is a message for Mr. Cunningham. This is Harrods Food Hall calling. The champagne and caviar that you ordered is in. Can you just call to confirm the delivery details?"

Expensive tastes, money problems, dysfunctional families. What had I expected from my colleagues? A confession? A volume discount at Harrods? Hughes' minions used the voice mail to complain to each other about Hughes. A revolution seemed to be brewing among the ranks. The six-monthers—Jonathan, Jason, Jeremy, Josh, their voices and their names all sounded alike to me—used voice mail to gossip about their love lives, to gripe about the partners and to plan their next party. And the other calls I'd listened to were even less interesting. In a switch that would have surprised my fellow lawyers, only the staff used voice mail for conducting business. The only surprise at the end of my first day of my new assignment had been that Helen had programmed her phone so that her messages could not be accessed remotely. It was just like her to hide this feature of the phone system from the lawyers. And the only unexpected message I heard had been recorded on my very own phone:

"Amy. It's Ted Cunningham. I stopped by your office earlier but you hadn't come in yet. I've just had a call from the General Counsel of Declan United. The head of the company is coming to London and wants a personal briefing on our progress on the restructuring. Come to my office as soon as you hear this."

CHAPTER 11

"Ted!" I fumbled with the phone and said guiltily, "You're here. I was just coming around to see you. Just checking the rest of my voice mail messages."

"Is that blasted system still not working? I give up. I don't even check mine anymore."

Oh, but I did for you, I thought, but said instead, "The light's not working but I did get your message. What's happening with Declan?" I searched for a legal pad to cover the papers from Blake's box I'd been reviewing and my notes from the voice mail sessions and was poised with pen and paper ready for Ted's instructions when Kimberly walked in.

"Amy, did you finish your ghoulish task with that box? I came by yesterday but you'd already gone. Oh, Ted, I didn't see you there." That she had missed any of Ted Cunningham's 6'5" frame on my dollhouse size sofa was typical of Kimberly. I'd have less trouble believing that I wasn't the only one listening in on other people's voice mail. "Am I interrupting something?"

"Kimberly. Hello." Ted seemed to take in the dynamics of the situation quickly, and in true ladies' man fashion, soothed both of our egos. "I'm happy you stopped in. I really want to pick your brain about tax credits in France. Why don't you give Louise your schedule of free dates and we can have lunch next week."

While Kimberly and Ted engaged in what passed for politically correct flirting—"picking one's brain" replacing the obvious—I surreptitiously moved the banker's box in question, now empty, under my desk. Following my disappointing meeting with Polly, I'd dumped the remains of the bag of candy into my briefcase where it joined the empty Darlington box until I decided what to do with them next.

"Now, if you'll excuse us, Amy and I were just getting started on some work for Declan. Amy, where was I?"

With Kimberly's mission, to attract as much attention from a partner as possible while at the same time ensuring that my exposure was reduced, a sort of zero-sum game for lawyers, complete, she left without waiting for an answer about the box.

"As I mentioned, Roger Strong, General Counsel for Declan United, called yesterday. The head of the company, Declan Graham, wants a briefing—and I'm hoping that the emphasis is on brief—on DW3's progress in the company restructuring. We have today to get you up to speed and tomorrow afternoon, Friday, to prepare in-house and with the tax advisors. The weekend—I'm sorry, I hope you don't have any plans—can be used to complete our package for our presentation to Mr. Graham on Monday.

"I want you to handle the accountants—Rothman's outfit—and Granlees, the specialist tax counsel, get them in line to meet with us on Friday and to clear their schedule for Monday, push them to prepare an outline of their activities—I'll handle the details on our side. The tax guys in New York have completed a first draft of a backup memo and they were to fax it to me overnight. I'll want you to take a look at that, too."

I was busy taking notes on my legal pad and trying to appear as if I knew exactly what he was talking about. I'd already seen the fax from New York this morning when I'd made my first stop at the fax machine, but I couldn't exactly tell Ted that.

It had been months since I'd looked at the Declan United file and I hadn't paid much attention to the fax but I'd learned from Daniel Blake that it was fatal to appear to be anything less than omniscient. The file that Cunningham had in his hands had expanded as much as I had in that time. As he briefed me on the outline of the restructuring, Ted laid various documents on the floor and organized them like a game of solitaire.

While he stepped out to take a call, I scanned the file marked "Declan Tax Plan" and found the contact details for the accountants. When he returned, I was amused to see him, in a very un-DW3 fashion, sit on the floor with the files around him like Lego blocks. He looked over at me and grinned. His reputation was certainly deserved. Unlike Mr. Blake, Cunningham oozed charm and not venom.

Even though he had just ruined my plans—I had intended to spend the next couple of days looking for Mr. Blake's last temporary secretary—I found myself grinning back. Ted could almost be forgiven his tendency to expect others to do most of the work while he basked in all of the glory. His distaste for getting his hands dirty—"I hate to drive but I love to be driven" was his motto—was well known but from my vantage point I was happy to be along for the ride.

"Chinese sound good to you? Louise will call in an order if you'll tell me what you want."

On hold with the accountants, I nodded my agreement to fried noodles with chicken and string beans. Frustrated, I left a message and tried the tax advisers. While Louise, Ted's secretary, ferried papers from my office, the fax machine and his files, I outlined our plan—the merger (or was it de-merger?) and relocation of Declan's headquarters—and the expected huge tax benefits—to my junior counterpart and what we would need for the meeting based on Ted's briefing. From time to time during my conversation, Ted would come in and provide the thumbs up or silently mouth some additional comments and encouragement. "Great work. Just the right mix of authority and obsequiousness," he crowed.

The smell of ginger and scallions greeted my return from the ladies' room—our dinner had arrived. Louise had already handed out napkins, chopsticks and various containers. She had also cleared a place on my conference table where Ted and I could eat. For the next hour, Ted and I drafted a working outline of briefing points—the more pithy to be distributed to Mr. Graham, a more substantive version for in-house purposes. With our feet up on my settee, we ate and talked, occasionally breaking from the meal to make notes about the meeting. I basked in the camaraderie. Mr. Blake and I had never had such a relaxed and friendly work relationship; the possibility of the thunderclap of his temper had always left me dreading rather than relishing any calm since it was inevitable that a storm would follow.

"Ted, I never did thank you for speaking up for me with Mr. Blake about this file although I guess I would have liked to have told him myself."

"Please, call me Teddy. Oh right, I guess I'd forgotten."

"Well, it certainly made an impression on him."

"How so?"

I was about to relate to Ted my last conversation with Mr. Blake—censored to delete the resignation part—as a jumping off point for questions about his whereabouts that Friday afternoon—as much as I was enjoying his company, Ted was still a suspect—when Helen burst in. Even at the relatively late hour, she was on full-scale military alert, but she visibly cooled down when she saw Ted on his way out to check on the status of Louise's typing.

"There you are. Doesn't anyone check their messages? I've left dozens of messages asking you to call me."

"As you can see, I've been very busy."

Helen ignored the files, the take-away containers, and the mountains of paper Ted and I had generated over the last few hours as minor inconveniences. "Where are Blake's timesheets? You've had plenty of time to prepare them."

"If I recall correctly, I was handed that task precisely three days ago. You've had access to his time for . . . what has it been? . . . over five months now."

"Well, they need to be submitted before I can close the books for the fiscal year. And I'm still waiting for the list. Blake's invitation list for the party. And I don't like being kept waiting." She stomped out of my office.

"Has the dragon lady gone?" Ted appeared at my door a few minutes later.

"Yes. Timesheets, invitation lists. She's really making me crazy, particularly about this party. I almost regret even taking the solicitor's exam. At least you have Louise to do your dirty work."

"What, still no secretary? I'll talk to her. Helen owes me a few favors."

"Right," I said glumly.

"No, I'm serious."

"Don't bother. It will only make matters worse." On the few occasions that Blake had intervened on my behalf with Helen, it had only antagonized her.

"No really. It's inexcusable. You need your own secretary. Besides, I'd be happy to talk to her about something other than that party she's planning. She's spending far too much time and the firm's money on this social affair. We're American lawyers practicing American law and no exam or paper exercise is going to change that perception."

"Is that why you didn't take the exam? You aren't becoming one of the partners in the new English firm either."

"One Bar exam in a lifetime is enough. Going through it a second time with Walter Hughes would be excruciating. But that's not why I've opted out. I don't need the validation. I'm already English."

"You mean if you stay here long enough they'll give you a passport?" I had assumed that he just didn't have the inclination to sit for an exam after all these years.

"Yes. And a telegram from the Queen on your hundredth birthday."

I laughed. "Now that's something to look forward to."

"Seriously, I have dual citizenship, my mother was British. I already have a British passport. I'm not like these English wannabes."

"You went to school here, too, didn't you?"

"Yes, for a few years. My parents divorced and my mother remarried an Englishman and stayed here. But I went to college in the States. A long time ago." He flashed a smile that could only be described as boyish. "Shall we continue?"

"Sure."

We finished the last of our food and retreated to different offices to digest our less than appetizing dessert—the New York office tax memo. I was tired, my feet hurt, and I was already beginning to feel hungry again.

I could get used to this.

When Teddy stopped by my office an hour later to give me his final comments and instructions to incorporate them in the now not so brief briefing paper, he thanked me profusely for all my help at such short notice. He left me with three small words—"Amy, go home"—that Mr. Blake had never uttered to me. They were insincere and illogical—I couldn't possibly go home when he did and finish this work in time for the accountants and the tax advisers tomorrow— but nonetheless endearing. Was being tortured with Mr. Blake's cruelty really all that different from being killed by Teddy's kindness? Either way, I was the one going to end up dead. But with Teddy, his trademark smile, and his way with women, there was a chance I'd die happy. And, if he was true to his word, maybe even with my own secretary.

CHAPTER 12

The grandfather clock chimed five times and there was a tangible feeling of relief in the room, as if we had, as a group, unbuttoned our collective top button on our slightly too tight trousers. We, the lawyers, accountants, tax advisors and assorted minions from the Declan United Group, all knew that Mr. Graham had an evening flight from Heathrow. Transit time from Mayfair, Friday night traffic, minimal check-in for First Class. Working backward with the determination and diligence we rarely applied to our work, we had run the numbers. Mr. Graham would be saying his good-byes, at the latest, at 5:15, if we were unlucky, 5:30. A meeting always went better when one knew when it would end.

And it certainly had not started out well. Ted and I had spent the morning with the accounting firm representatives. They had been well prepared but Ted had wanted the meeting to bear the distinctive DW3 stamp so we had insisted that their presentation notes for Mr. Graham be modified. Louise had been putting the finishing touches on the latest draft of the briefing outline when, in a panic-inducing change of plans, Mr. Graham and his companions had arrived unannounced at DW3's offices, intent that the presentation take place at lunchtime on Friday and not Monday morning whether we were ready or not.

So, while Declan management relaxed over the English idea of sandwiches—colorful and startling combinations—tuna and sweet corn and bacon with avocado—that children might have concocted had they been allowed to finger paint with food; the English idea of potato chips—individual bags of crisps in a smorgasbord of flavors—ready-salted, prawn curry, and beef and onion—that were reassuringly marked "suitable for vegetarians"; and the English idea of dessert—something sticky and sweet, a variation of the usual day old bread, I had stalled for time.

And Ted had charmed and disarmed them. Without notes, he had expounded upon a tax structure that still mystified the tax specialists. His elaborate description of our efforts to date had been remarkable, since I had discovered during my late night with the files that there wasn't actually any progress to report.

That had been four hours ago. The principal tax advisor from Granlees had just finished his speech about tax gains when the clock had struck indicating that school was out for the day. Ted took this as a signal to sum up the discussions.

"Here's how we see the next few weeks. As promised, Stuart Rothman and his team will move ahead on reviewing the benefits of a branch office rather than an actual subsidiary in France—once that's finished, we'll have considered all the potential European sites; the team from Granlees will be outlining the tax consequences of the structure we've agreed upon this afternoon; and finally, I'll be preparing, with some help from Amy, a new organizational chart and the corporate resolutions, finalizing the formations, convening board meetings, and so on, through local counsel as necessary, all the steps that are required to effect the new structure. Agreed?"

No one objected.

"And we will, of course, keep you informed as progress is made. Does that sound suitable to you?"

"Yes. I'm pleased with the progress made to date. This has been very informative." Mr. Graham turned to his assistant, Roger Strong, who now donned the cloak and demeanor of Mr. Graham.

"Yes, we'll be expecting progress reports from both the lawyers and the tax advisers and a final report sometime before the end of our financial year. Let's see if we can fix a date." Strong reviewed his calendar on his open laptop, while we, the ones for whom this particular deadline would be wrenching, kept poker faces and made notations on our legal pads that would hopefully never be read by our clients. He snapped his laptop shut after giving us a date that would guarantee more than a few ruined weekends and, with that motion, the meeting was finished. We all stood as Mr. Strong and Mr. Graham made their way to the door. I found myself smiling numbly while I thought about the mounds of work that lay ahead.

The other men shook my hand and I waited for Ted to show them on their way. When Ted returned, he recounted, for my purposes, the specific tasks he wanted me to undertake or supervise with a timetable that even Mussolini would have had trouble meeting. He gathered his papers and I followed him to Louise's desk where, to my bewilderment, she handed him an overnight bag and airline tickets.

"Are you going somewhere?" When Ted didn't answer, I turned to Louise and asked, "Is he going somewhere?"

"The airport."

"I can see that. Was there a sudden change of plans, after Declan showed up?" I asked Louise as she started clearing her own desk.

"Oh, no. Ted spends every weekend in his family's

place, up in Scotland. I hear it's beautiful." Louise, like most of the other women in the office, was more than a little in love with Ted Cunningham.

"Sorry about those canceled weekend plans, Amy," my foot. Teddy had never intended to let a little matter like work interfere with *his* weekend. Ted was as bad as Blake. Only better looking.

"Have a nice weekend, Louise. Oh, Amy, you're still here." Ted turned in the hallway on his way to reception. He absentmindedly patted his pockets before he pulled out his passport. "Thanks for your help today."

I was still musing on his parting words—"I couldn't have done it without you"—and my pathetic response—"My pleasure." Annoyed for having fallen for his charm, I decided that his motto was fitting after all.

But annoyance disappeared as soon as I returned to my own office. My desk had been cleared. My in-tray no longer resembled a toppling landmark, and what appeared to be the day's mail lay opened and sorted in a separate tray. Before I could wonder whether someone had discovered my plan to look into Mr. Blake's death and this was his or her way of letting me know I was being watched, a young woman, petite with fair hair and even fairer skin, knocked on my door and came in.

"Oh, good, you're done with your meeting. I hope you don't mind, I've tidied up a bit. And I've left some things for you on your desk that someone named Helen insisted that I leave with these instructions. I wrote it down. 'Amy is to stuff these and have the labels ready to go by Monday.' If it can wait, I can help you next week, I've already got plans to go away this weekend, but I suppose I could cancel if you want—and a Kimberly stopped by, no message, and before I forget, someone named Seals called for Susan Jones, but I told them wrong number, and a man, short, talked very fast, looked out the window a lot, does he have a problem? I didn't catch his name, I'm sorry, I'll do better next time, wants you to call him. A woman named Miss Lawrence called—extremely nice, and this was extraordinary, she recognized my accent as Mancurian. I take it she's a linguist. Most Americans never can tell the difference. Her message was brief. 'Send candy.' Said you would know what that meant. I asked if there should be a card, as well, or flowers perhaps, but she'd hung up. Oh, and your husband called from Paris. He's stuck in a meeting there tonight and he might have to stay all weekend. He'll call you at home tonight. There." She visibly relaxed. "Any questions?"

"Just the one." I looked around the room. "Who are you?"

"Didn't Louise, Mr. Cunningham's secretary, tell you? I'm your new secretary. I started this afternoon while you were in your meeting. I'm sorry. Where are my manners? You must be Mrs. Brown."

"It's Ms. But, please, call me Amy."

"Amy, then." She stuck out a tiny hand and introduced herself. "I'm Nicola. Nicola Barnes. But everyone calls me Nikki."

"Private joke, or can any one join in?"

"I'm sorry. I just can't stop laughing. About my secretary. Her name, I mean." Ted Cunningham had not only been true to his word but he also had a sense of humor. A young man who looked vaguely familiar entered my office. "I'm sorry, you had to have been there." Seeing he still looked bewildered, I asked, "Can I help you with something? Reception is just down the hall."

"I know where reception is. I work here."

"Oh, gosh, I am sorry. Amy Brown." I extended my hand. He seemed about the right age for one of the six-monthers. I took a calculated guess, and asked "Jonathan, right?" I'd seen him before with David Knight and Kimberly Sullivan.

"Joshua, Joshua Hall," he corrected me. "But you can call me Josh. Late evening, huh?"

"Well, yes—now that I look at the time. I've been tied up in a meeting all day—haven't even had a chance to check my mail. Just now returning my telephone calls."

"With your condition you really should be on your way home." He pointed to my stomach and then said, "My sister's just about your age and. . . ."

I wondered how this kid could possibly have a sister my age—maybe he meant his mother and was just being polite.

"She's expecting too. About seven months right?"

"A little bit farther along."

"She tells me that she starts to feel really rotten just about this time of day so I figured that you must be about worn out."

"No kidding." I suppose it couldn't hurt to be nice. He was cute in that pedigreed, prep school kind of way. I gave him a wan smile.

"So I was wondering since you seem to be the only one around tonight . . ."

"Really, I hadn't realized everyone had gone."

"Well—I just saw David leave—some family obligation. Kimberly Sullivan just left too."

I raised my eyebrows but did not draw a response in kind. The kid was really wet behind the ears.

"So anyhow, my dinner companion has just canceled and I was wondering if perhaps you'd like to join me—un-less, that is, you have plans with your husband. I just figured since you were here so late that maybe he was out of town. You do have a husband, don't you? I mean I don't want to assume anything these days. I mean, I would be the last one to assume anything."

I smiled at his fumbling attempt to be politically correct.

"Well, I am on my own this evening. My husband's in Paris. Not a bad place to be, but a real bummer for me." I hadn't even thought about dinner. Dinner with Joshua Hall, a six-monther fresh from New York without a reason to dislike Daniel Blake, would be an interesting diversion from murder and the Declan United restructuring. Now, if I were only a few years younger, single, a little less pregnant. I left those thoughts to myself and admitted, "I am hungry. But I still have a few more things to take care of here. I need to make a few calls to the U.S."

"I've already got a reservation, or booking as they say, for two at Koko's. I have things to keep me busy for the next half hour. Would that give you time? I have a car. I can drive there."

"Great." I looked at my watch. It was the afternoon in New York. "Look, let me make these calls, pack up some work to take home and I'll meet you in reception in about an hour."

"That sounds great."

Forty-five minutes later, I started organizing my papers from the briefing with Declan United and the stack of invitations Helen had forced upon Nikki in my absence. I mentally weighed which of the two I was most likely to actually work on at home tomorrow. I chucked my choice into the banker's box.

After unceremoniously tossing the plastic evidence bag in the trash—I may have piqued Polly's curiosity about the culpability of the candy company but I wasn't sure how she'd feel if she thought I was interfering with a police investigation—I threw the chocolates back into their original packaging. I'd arrange to get them to her over the weekend. Before I stacked my briefcase, bulging with the Darlington chocolates and the rest of Blake's "Personal Effects" onto the banker box, and rushed to meet my dinner date, I made one last call to the New York office where I invoked the name of Teddy Cunningham to demand refinements to the Declan tax memo by Monday morning. I'd already learned one lesson from my new boss. Real power was ruining someone else's weekend.

CHAPTER 13

"Here—all that looks heavy. Let me carry that for you. What is this?"

"A pillow. For my back." I'd grabbed it at the last minute. "A present from my husband. The pregnancy equivalent of a toaster." He looked at it and me quizzically. "Don't ask."

"Here, let me get that door for you."

"Thanks." Maybe it would be wise to remember this guy's name after all. We had made our way downstairs to the basement car park when I asked, "What made you decide to get a car?"

"My family's been coming to London for years. We own a place out in Oxfordshire. And when I lucked out on this transfer, er assignment, my dad agreed to let me take the family car. It's usually just left sitting in the barn at the place in the country."

"Isn't parking a hassle?" The firm only had two reserved spaces.

"No, it's not too bad. I live in Earl's Court," Josh mentioned a neighborhood three subway stops west of mine, "and I always seem to be able to find a parking space. Plus not too many people at the office have cars. I can usually park in the building. That is if H.M.S. hasn't driven her Bentley in."

We laughed. Helen's car was commensurate with her girth. After a tedious discussion of traffic in central London, we pulled into a parking space at the dicey end of an area of the city known as Ladbroke Grove close to a restaurant that I'd read about as being very trendy but had avoided because of the neighborhood. Grateful for a new topic of conversation, I said, "My, we have good taste."

"Oh—this place. Well, I've been here a couple of times with people from the office."

I hadn't gone out to dinner for business in ages. I thought back to the last meal at which Mr. Blake and I had entertained some out-of-town clients. The wine steward, who offended Mr. Blake by dribbling some red wine onto the tablecloth, would not have mourned at the news of his demise.

A cool but professional maitre d'hôtel ushered us to a corner table. I regretted that I was there with an office mate and not Steven but resolved to enjoy the company and the food. This was certainly better than eating at home, alone with my usual pasta. We ordered our food and made a toast, me with water, Josh with a glass of wine.

"Cheers, a belated welcome to the London office of Winter, Worthington & Walker."

"Thanks. And congratulations on the baby."

"Thank you. How are you enjoying your rotation so far?"

"You mean the six month quarantine?"

I blushed and choked on my water. "Word travels fast to New York, I see."

"We hear all the gossip—and the less than flattering names. Although, I have to admit, nothing prepared me for H.M.S.!"

"She is something else. I'm sorry about the attitude. Toward the six-monthers. It's just that you all come over so bright eyed and bushy tailed."

"And well paid."

"That too. And it's difficult to get too excited when we know you'll just be leaving."

"About the time we learn where the men's room is."

"So you have heard all the jokes."

"Except that I hope to be the exception."

"Meaning?"

Our waiter interrupted us with our main courses and we immediately dug in and chatted mindlessly about the various projects we were working on.

"What were you saying before about extending?" I managed to speak around a mouthful of vegetable terrine. Dinner was a big improvement over lunch.

"Oh right—I'm hoping to stay on after my six months are up."

"Really?"

"Yes. This has turned out to be such a great experience. It wasn't like that at first. Even though I've been coming to England for many years with my family, the transition from a New York business environment to one in London was more difficult than I expected."

"Just because we speak the same language doesn't mean we always communicate."

"Right. When I first arrived, I couldn't imagine why H.M.S. made such a big deal about calling the New York office. But then I discovered that she meant the *Home Office,* the U.K. department that issues our work permits. Not the *home* office."

"That's funny. That still happens to me. Lucy once asked me if I would be going home early to cook my turkey, you know, for the Fourth of July."

We traded other stories of cultural misunderstandings, enjoying the meal and the conversation and then Josh recounted his initiation to the London office. "And then when I first came, I couldn't get anyone to help me unload my boxes, let alone send a fax. Everyone on staff seemed to be tied up filling out application forms, copying diplomas and Bar certificates for Her Majesty. You would think that her career is resting on this party."

"She certainly seems to think so."

"What's the big deal? I mean, I understand about the anniversary and everything, but was it such a big deal just to waive into the English jurisdiction?"

"The establishment of the English firm was pretty much just an administrative matter once Gideon was hired. We needed an English solicitor to form the partnership. But it wasn't that easy to become an English lawyer, believe me. I had to sit for exams. And sitting for law exams ten or fifteen years after taking your last exam is not fun."

"But what's so important about being an English law firm or being an English qualified lawyer, for that matter?"

"You mean besides being liable for malpractice in two countries? I don't know. You'd have to ask someone else at the firm for the company line. They'd probably tell you that it was to serve the clients, or that it made financial sense, something like that. But I have my own theory."

"Which is?"

"Don't take any of this personally. There are two categories of expatriate lawyers in London. The first group, and I guess I fall into this category, is here, through opportunity or personal circumstances, to do the job. We take our jobs or our careers seriously and see that the only route to credibility is to become locally qualified. The second group, and probably the majority of our lawyers falls into this group, is here because of some mystical belief that England is their true homeland; that the American Revolution was a minor quirk of history that inconveniently prevented them from realizing their true English heritage. Anglophiles. More English than the English. You can hear it in their accents—pitched somewhere between Boston Brahmin and Masterpiece Theater. They embrace all things English. Why else would our offices be in Mayfair, the most picturesque part of London, when all the real players are in the City? And what better way to prove that you belong than to become an English lawyer? Or solicitor, I should say."

"And you're thinking that I'm one of those?"

"There is the farm out in Oxfordshire. . . ."

"Who else falls into your categories?"

"Well, Kimberly's motives are more political than patriotic. If anything, she's a Francophile. The only interest she's ever expressed in London is that it's only an hour from Paris." DW3's very own Diana Vreeland. "Kimberly probably sees becoming a solicitor as another way to secure her partnership. Walter Hughes and David Knight will both become partners in the U.K. firm and both took the exams. I place both of them squarely in the Anglophile camp."

"And Ted?"

"It's funny. He's the only American at the firm with a British passport, but he's certainly not an Anglophile. He didn't take the test with the rest of us because he—his words not mine—'didn't need the validation.' "

"I guess your theory does have some merit."

"Maybe. What changed your mind about the London office?"

"Working with David Knight and Kimberly Sullivan."

"Kimberly I can understand. Every other man in the office would like a chance to 'work' with Kimberly. But David

Knight doesn't strike me as Mr. Wonderful. How is he to work for?"

"Oh, he's been great. He's really great."

I raised my eyebrows and shivered.

"No, seriously, that formal thing. Cold, professional—that's just his way."

"And what about his thing with Kimberly?"

"I've heard about that. I haven't seen anything in their behavior to support that, I mean they are nothing but business-like around me. Even when we're traveling. I think it's just one of those office myths. Besides, you're a great one to talk. We six-monthers weren't just warned about H.M.S. We all got an earful about Dan Blake too. Even if only half of it was true, how could you stand working for the guy?"

"I know, I know." I had heard this lament before, and particularly since his death. Those who had been content to stay silent about Mr. Blake as long as he kept bringing in the money now suddenly felt the freedom to voice their disrespect. I tried to conjure up the words. Steven and I had had this very conversation. "He was mean. I worked for him. And now he's dead. Is there anything else to say?"

"Look. If it's difficult to talk about. . . ."

"No, it's okay."

"There must have been something positive about the experience. Was the work interesting? What about the clients?"

I described our work and the clients in as glowing terms as I could muster, leaving out the bits about catering to Mr. Blake's boorish behavior.

"And you did all his billing?"

"For Mr. Blake's clients, yes, that's right."

"Isn't that normally done by secretaries or lower fee earners?"

I laughed. "You mean, aren't I too expensive to be crunching numbers?" I ran through my usual litany of billing woes. "It's no piece of cake. No pun intended." I pointed to Josh's plate as he finished his last bite of chocolate cake. I explained that I'd also been given the thankless task by Helen of sorting through his timesheets for the period before his death.

"That's gruesome."

"I said I'd been given the task, I didn't say I was going to do it."

"I see. What's become of Blake's clients?"

"Good question. David and Ted have already inherited some. Kimberly, as heir apparent, is taking over a few." I thought back to my conversation with David and the disposition of the files. "How long did you say you've been here now?"

"Just over five months."

"So you were here when Daniel Blake died?" My meal suddenly turned from a friendly dinner to supper with a suspect. "I didn't realize you've been here that long. Were you here when . . ." But I didn't have a chance to complete my question. A waiter came by just then to replenish my water and to pour the last of Josh's wine and then Josh stood and said, "I've just realized. I've left my mobile phone in the car." He felt in the pockets of his suit jacket. "Will you excuse me for a minute while I run out to the car and get it? I had been expecting a call about my plans for the weekend."

"No, go ahead."

He got up and hurried through the tables out to the front. I took the opportunity to finish my dessert but dismissed thoughts of coffee afterwards when I saw Josh's ashen face minutes later.

"What's wrong?"

116

"Someone's broken into the car. It must have been just before I came out because the alarm was still going off. The front window was smashed."

"Did they take anything?"

"Do you have your purse and your briefcase? I couldn't find them in the car."

"Yes, they're here."

"Good, then they didn't get them. But that box you were carrying. It's gone. I'm really sorry. Were there important papers in it? Oh God, what about client confidentiality? I'm so sorry, I should have gone out sooner." Apologetic and panicking, Josh struggled to talk. This guy would never get ahead at DW3.

I didn't know whether to laugh or cry. Facing H.M.S. when I had to tell her that the party invitations she'd forced on my new secretary were gone would not be pleasant. But fear of H.M.S. was not what brought on the tears. Someone would be very frustrated when he discovered that the box he'd stolen didn't contain, as the label proclaimed, "Daniel Blake—Personal Effects."

CHAPTER 14

"Amy, honey, I'm really sorry."

"I don't like the sound of this."

On the Saturday morning following dinner with Josh, I was eating breakfast and listening to apologies. I had had a less than restful night's sleep. Josh had been a real prince, and with my briefcase and pillow in hand—the culprit who'd broken into the car was apparently more romantic than Steven—Josh had walked me to my front door. He'd only retrieved his sense of humor when I warned him of my sixty-eight drunken steps. Until then, he hadn't stopped apologizing from the time we left the restaurant in a black cab. He'd called a tow truck from his mobile phone that he'd discovered he'd had all along and, once satisfied I was fine, left to return to Ladbroke Grove. When I'd found a message on the answering machine from Steven that he was still "stuck" in Paris, a contradiction in terms, and that it now sounded like he would be there for the weekend, I had been tempted to tell him about my amateur attempts to pin Blake's death on someone at DW3. Tempted, but not convinced. Honesty does not always work best over the telephone and the current conversation was proof.

"They've scheduled meetings for early Monday morning and it just doesn't make sense to fly home today just to turn around and fly back on Sunday night, does it?"

118

"So you're there all weekend." The shrillness in my voice turned even me off.

"I said that I'm sorry. I can come back if you want me to. Do you?" This was stated in such a way that my assent was not an option.

"No, no, you're right. It's silly to fly home and turn around and fly back. I'll be fine here. Please call me tonight though, okay?"

"Of course. Will you be at home all day?"

"I'm just going to do some food shopping and run some errands, maybe run into the office for a little while."

"That Declan thing?"

"Right."

"Ted Cunningham doesn't know how lucky he is to have you working for him. But don't stay too long. You need your rest."

"I know."

"Okay. Take care of yourself. I love you. I'll call you tonight."

"I love you, too. Bye."

What I hadn't told Steven, in the interest of marital harmony, was that I had planned on spending Saturday exercising the remote function on the DW3 voice mail system while stuffing invitations in the comfort of our apartment. Multi-tasking, I think it's called. The theft of the invitations, the first sign that I might be right about Daniel Blake's death, called for a change in plans.

By the time Steven had called, I'd already reviewed the mishmash of papers—the Declan file, the evaluation form, the new client form, an annual report, and old phone messages—that had constituted Blake's personal effects, for an hour and was no closer to answering the question "Why steal them?" several hours later. To my mind, there were few things worth stealing—the chocolates, which no one knew I had and that Polly would soon have, and the yellow sticker, which the police had. Packing away my briefcase, I set aside the files of the dead man. It was time to concentrate on dead files.

DW3 hadn't been the first law firm to save money by separating the fee earners from the hired help—the posh, public spaces belonged to the lawyers, and the service staff and their machinery got tickets to the cheap seats, in DW3's case, a rabbit warren of rooms in the basement of the building, home of "Dead Files." Accessible by elevator and stairs, the basement featured a main hallway that led to a fire escape labeled in bold letters—EMERGENCY EXIT ONLY—NO ENTRY—to the right and, to the left, further down the corridor, two doors that were entrances to the library and the back office, the main work area for staff. Both of those rooms were restricted to those of us from DW3 who knew the imbecilic "1-2-3-4" code. The other door on the right led to the underground parking lot where tenants, like Josh and Helen, parked.

Dead Files were located in a storage room in the back office. Its official name, the archive room, implied a neatly organized historical repository of files. In actual practice, the room was an overstuffed jumble of boxes, files, and loose papers and documents, jammed in rather haphazardly onto huge shelves intended for a room double the size of the present site. The shelves were moveable stacks with huge steering wheels on the sides that allowed greater use of space. Unfortunately, the shelves were intended for use in rooms with perfectly level floors, and the archive floor had been laid using the "which corner does spilled water run to" method. When the weight of files on the shelves wasn't perfectly distributed, which was most of the time, the shelves would roll.

Clutching my only companion, the pregnancy pillow, I poked my head around the obvious corners and turned on the light switch located outside the archive room door. For a person with a fertile imagination like mine, the basement fed all kinds of paranoia. But I was unlikely to be disturbed. The first floor security guard had waved me in without requiring me to sign in, his respect for pregnant women even greater than that usually reserved for anyone carrying a briefcase, and I'd come straight downstairs. The other lawyers—I was certain from the mess that David Knight had never been there—wouldn't venture to the archive room on a weekend.

I rolled the wheel on the second of five shelves and started scanning it for boxes marked "Daniel B. Blake," intent on finding some clues. I moved forward when I heard the shelf lurch in my direction. Shaken a bit, I pushed myself against it and straightened it into submission so that it would not reel inwards again. I thought about picking up one of the heavier boxes and using it to prop the stacks apart—as a doorstop of sorts—but I knew I couldn't lift one without hurting myself. A hernia was not something I needed.

The bottom shelf of the stack had files labeled with Blake's name. I sat awkwardly on the floor to read them, pillow propped behind my back, when I heard someone in the hallway just as the light in the archive room went out. Unlike the entrance to my apartment building, the light for the archive room was not on a timer so a person had to have turned off the lights. I shouted out "Hello?" as a greeting as much as a question. "I'm in here!"

"What are you doing?"

"Tony?" I thought I recognized the voice of our office clerk.

My "What are you doing in on Saturday?" mixed with his "What are you doing down here?" Before we continued our conversation any longer in the dark, I finally shouted, "Can you turn the light back on please?"

"Sure." With a click, the place filled with artificial light and Tony appeared in the doorway, clad in black Lycra shorts and helmet, with a bicycle resting against the wall behind him. His attire provided an explanation for at least one of us.

"Sorry. I left my bike here last night. I cycle in and back most days but last night . . ."

"Late night at the pub?"

"Something like that. What about you? I thought working on Saturdays would have ended with. . . ." He caught himself before he finished with the obvious.

"Mr. Blake? No."

Probably eager to change the subject, Tony said, "You need to be careful down here. The shelves sometimes roll downhill." He pointed to the back of the room. "I'll leave a heavy box between these shelves to keep them apart."

"This is where I was when the lights went out."

Tony lifted, effortlessly, a file box and I pointed to the space between the third and fourth shelves. I moved my pillow closer to the files and sat back down. A few minutes later, he shouted goodbye from the hall and I called out thanks.

More than a few files later, I closed my eyes to rest, disappointed that the files seemed to hold no leads. Nothing suspicious, no unreasonable expenses, no inordinate number of billable hours. More than a few minutes later, I stirred from a sound sleep on the floor between the shelves.

Narcolepsy was a part of pregnancy I hadn't expected. I roused myself, marked my stopping point with a yellow post-it note and left to find the staff toilet. Settling back in my place at eye level, I resumed my search through the old files—when the light went out again.

Thinking that another lawyer or staff member or even less likely a security guard was being overzealous about the electricity bill, I called out in singsong fashion, "Hello—it's Amy—I'm still here." When no one replied, I called out, more anxiously, "Tony?" The absence of windows made it pitch black in the archive room and I blinked to get accustomed to the dark before I made a move to the door. But the stack before me was being subtly but forcefully pushed back to the back wall—or "downhill" as Tony had put it. I remembered stepping over the heavy box Tony had placed at the opening of the shelves nearest the corridor on my way out to the toilet but I could not remember stepping over it on the way back in. The stack was getting claustrophobically closer. I quickly took hold of one of the file boxes and tried using it as a wedge as Tony had done before me but the only one I could lift was equally insufficient to keep the shelf from moving forward. The files were starting to get uncomfortably close.

"Wait, wait, I'm in here, don't move the shelves! Stop, stop!"

I used my arms and my feet to try to keep the distance between the shelves greater. Sardonically, I wondered if this giant exertion was anything like giving birth. The pushing was not immediate but slow and steady. I realized not a moment too soon that if I didn't find something to keep the stacks apart I was going to be squeezed among the dead files of DW3. The metal shelves were already much closer than my full arm's length. Fearing that a quick run for it without some resistance to whatever or whomever was closing in on the other side would be dangerous, I kept one arm and a leg in front of me while I tried to inch closer to the open corridor. It was now no longer clear if someone or something was in fact pushing or if, once started, the weight and the downward path of the shelves now had a mind and force of its own.

Thinking fast, I fitted the only thing in the room that came close to supporting me in the ever-narrowing space between the shelves. It provided me the seconds and space I needed to slip out before I was squished like a cartoon character.

I fell to the floor, unleashed from the vise of the now nearly closed shelves. I scrambled to the doorway using my hands before me to find my way in the dark as the orthopedic anatomically correct back support I had previously scorned for being too practical took the full force of three loaded industrial shelves.

I was grateful that my thoughtful but unromantic husband had not bought me an Hermès scarf after all.

CHAPTER 15

"Walter!"

I had raced down the basement corridor gasping for breath after my near escape from the shelves. I'd punched the button for the elevator but when it hadn't immediately appeared, I'd fled up the stairs where I'd run into Walter Hughes in the stairwell on his way down.

"Amy. The elevators are broken."

"Walter, I'm so happy to see you. Did you see anyone just now, coming up from here?" Not waiting for an answer, I panted out of breath, "The shelves. In the archive room. They were, someone was, I mean, the lights went out, and then they started moving."

He looked over my shoulder to the stairs below me and said, "I'm sorry to hear that." Walter wasn't particularly socially adept. Being polite took time away from thinking big thoughts and his failure to establish eye contact was all part of the package. Regardless of the question or subject matter, Walter's comment was bound to be along the lines of "That's great" or the alternative standard reply, the one I'd just heard. If I'd thought running into a hysterical pregnant woman was likely to generate more interest than whatever weighty topic was occupying him at the moment, I was wrong. David Knight had warmed up when confronted with death at the office. Believing there was hope for Hughes, I tried again. "The shelves, Walter, were pushing into me. I could have been . . ."

Walter jingled keys in his pocket, a sign I took for growing impatience.

"Am I blocking your way to the garage?"

Walter didn't respond.

"Never mind then." I stood aside to let him continue down the stairs and then I emerged at street level. Once there, I looked for the security guard. The radio blared but his desk was empty. Debating whether to flee to my office or my empty apartment, I was relieved when Gideon walked in.

"Good morning, Amy." His tone changed immediately when I didn't answer. "You look awful. Are you all right? It's not the baby, is it? You look like you could use a cup of tea."

Daniel Blake had been supplanted as the center of my life at DW3. Another dead man—Earl Grey—had taken his place.

"Feeling better? Your color's back. Here, have a biscuit. The sugar will do you good."

"Thanks, Gideon." I took a cookie from the plate he pushed towards me. "Look, my hands have stopped shaking." I held out my hands over the table at the Market Coffee shop where we'd walked while Gideon had pieced together the scene moments before in the archive room. "And the baby's kicking." I felt a jab in my side where a shelf could have been.

"As my Nan would say, 'you'll soon be right as rain.' "

It was the first time he'd mentioned his relatives to me. Gideon probably had a family somewhere but, unlike his American colleagues, he hadn't shared the intimate details with me. At least not to his knowledge.

"Do you have time for another cup? I'm feeling better but Steven's away and I don't think I'm quite ready to be alone."

"Of course. I was only stopping by to clear up my desk. What about you? What were you doing down in the basement?"

"I was, um, looking through some files."

"Until those unfortunate shelves started rolling? You must complain to Helen."

"Helen? I don't think so. She wouldn't do anything just because I complained. Besides, I don't think the lights went off by themselves." I'd been vague on the details about the shelves with Gideon and had emphasized the darkness and my clumsiness.

"Amy. You can't possibly think someone turned them off on purpose, do you?"

"No, no, of course not. I don't know. Maybe. Maybe I do."

"What and just walk away? Do we really work at a firm with people like that?"

I looked at him for a moment. Gideon had traded the civilized world of Jenkins Cole, a prominent London firm, for the promise of higher wages and possible partnership at an American firm but I saw someone who had gotten less, or depending upon the point of view, more than he had bargained for. Since I'd been back, there had been a slightly unpleasant smell about Gideon. And I didn't think it was just bad hygiene, public school background notwithstanding. The high associated with his recruitment ("We love you! You're great! Come work for us!") had been replaced with reality ("Find that document! Cancel those dinner plans! Bill those hours!") and reality stunk. Nothing

I was about to say would clear the air.

"I'm not suggesting that someone would actually turn off the lights and deliberately send the shelves rolling." It was exactly what I was thinking but I couldn't tell Gideon that. "But if making sure that no one was in the archive room meant taking a few extra minutes. . . ."

"Amy. . . ."

"Can you honestly deny that any single one of your colleagues wouldn't stab you in the back to get ahead?"

"That's a great leap in logic from merely not pausing when turning out lights."

"I know, just answer the question."

"Present company excluded?" Gideon laughed, seemingly unsure if I was serious or not.

"Present company excluded."

"I don't know. I'd like to believe that we are all gentlemen. And gentle women. See, I have learned something since joining an American firm."

"Apparently not enough. Did I ever tell you about the time I was sued for malpractice?"

"You're joking. Malpractice?"

"It was about the time I got pregnant."

"This year?"

"No, I lost the baby. I had a miscarriage just after Steven and I first got married. This was at another firm, just before we moved to Hong Kong."

Gideon shifted his bulky frame in the spindly café chair like he had sandpaper in his trousers. He tipped his teacup and emptied it like a shot glass. Too polite for his own good, he mumbled, "No, I don't believe you've shared that with me," while he waved to catch the waiter's attention. Gideon's contract with DW3 hadn't mentioned the American practice of using the office as a confessional and one's office colleague as priest.

"We'd been trying for a baby. . . ."

"Well, look at the time . . ."

"But that's not the point, I was talking about the malpractice case."

"Right then." Gideon eyed the bill and put some money on the table.

"It's not what you think. I was just part of a larger picture. The big fish was another partner and the firm. Some client got annoyed when we lost a big lawsuit and then submitted a huge legal bill. The client decided to get even by complaining to the Bar and filed a malpractice suit—it was later dismissed and the complaint withdrawn."

"How dreadful."

"Frankly, I was so preoccupied with the pregnancy and then the miscarriage that I never really let it bother me. I knew it would go away. But that's not why I'm telling the story. I found out, later, that the firm had attempted to settle with the client, but only with regard to its big rainmaking partner."

"Money does seem to be rather important."

"But it wasn't the money. The malpractice suit was like a slow death for this partner. Being a lawyer was his entire identity. More important than anything. Enough to leave me on my own to suffer the consequences. That was an eye opener."

Gideon stirred. He lifted an empty teacup and set it right back down. "I think they're watching me."

"What?"

"Not watching me, per se. But keeping an eye on me."

"Now who's being paranoid?"

"Someone was in my office. Going through my things."

"So you do mean per se."

"I don't know. This is my first experience in an American firm. Would the firm do that? Go into my office?"

"How do you know?"

"This morning. Before I ran into you. The files on my desk, my phone. They'd been moved. I thought maybe the cleaning people . . ."

I didn't have to tell him that the cleaning people didn't come in on Saturdays.

". . . I'd left a box of files on my chair. I could swear it had been moved."

"By the same person who turned the lights out on me?"

"You're right, we're both being silly."

I laughed and sat up in my chair and smiled at him reassuringly. "Gideon, we are both being paranoid. I shouldn't be filling your head with my war stories. I feel one hundred percent better and I don't know about you, but I don't intend to spend the rest of this beautiful Saturday afternoon talking about the office. That's our problem, you know, we both spend too much time in the office." We stood up and parted at the door.

As far as I knew, Gideon had no real reason to be paranoid. His box of files was unlikely to have been mistaken for a box with Blake's "Personal Effects." Mistaking his office for another lawyer's office, now that was a more likely explanation. That gave me little comfort. His office was right next to mine.

But maybe I was wrong. About the paranoia. I'd had time to think after my escape from the archive shelves. Maybe it had all been an unfortunate accident. I had certainly been persuasive with Steven when he'd asked about my day in his nightly call from Paris. And after spending a lonely evening listening to DW3 voice mail, I was still no closer to solving Mr. Blake's murder, but I had decided that all my colleagues, and not just Gideon, were paranoid.

"Welcome to the Winter, Worthington & Walker voice mail system. The party you are calling is not available. Please leave a message after the tone or press the star key for more options."

"This is a message for David Knight. You'll be receiving written confirmation of the wire transfer but I wanted to confirm the fax number you've given me. Please call me, Mr. Hausmann, at extension 213."

David's paranoia was justifiable. Having client correspondence sent to his home fax in light of the holes in DW3 technology made sense. I hadn't known that David had a fax machine at home. If Mr. Hausmann had as much trouble as I did—I tried the number several times but it was constantly engaged—he would never get through.

"David. It's Kimberly. I hear that Amy was in the meeting with Cunningham and Declan management. I thought that client was . . . I mean why wasn't I given that assignment? And I still haven't heard about Blake's office. Is there something about the partnership decision you're not telling me? Look, forget I asked. It's not fair to ask you these questions. I'll see you in Paris."

Kimberly's partnership paranoia seemed to be struggling with her natural confidence. I would bet on the confidence winning. Ted should watch his back.

"This is a message for Gideon Chapman from Liz

Headley. I'm calling from Accounting in New York. I've been going over your timesheets and before I go to the Lawyers Committee I thought that maybe you and I could have a little chat. My extension in the New York office is 3309."

No lawyer wanted his name mentioned in the same breath as the Lawyers Committee. Just because Gideon was paranoid, didn't mean someone wasn't actually out to get him.

"This is a message for Walter Hughes. It's Adam from Adam & Eve Publications. It's about those documents you ordered. Call me at the office."

I hung up on the receptionist for an escort agency who answered the number in the phone book for Adam & Eve Publications before she could regale me with the roster for "Delicious Dates." Why was I not surprised to find that I had not been calling a religious bookstore? Maybe it had to do with the Penthouse magazine I'd found in Walter's pigeonhole my first day of snooping. Paranoia was too good for Walter Hughes.

"Josh. David Knight here. I'm ready to give you comments on the memo. And we need to talk about your request for a transfer. I'll be away all week but will be calling in."

Junior associates, like Josh, needed little, if any, encouragement to feel paranoid. A voice mail from the managing partner would be sufficient.

"Ted Cunningham? This is Roger Strong from Declan.

Wanted to talk to you about the meeting on Friday. Please call me when you can to discuss personnel issues."

I was the only "personnel" involved in Declan. My mind raced back to the meeting. Had I said the wrong thing? Had I been too inattentive? Did Strong prefer male attorneys? Now who was being paranoid?

Chapter 16

Puffy ankles, hemorrhoids, tender breasts, itchy dry skin. I had been too preoccupied—nothing like a little detective work to take one's mind off the perils of pregnancy—to notice that at some point in the last week the sum of my parts had become a greater burden than my whole. This was difficult since the swollen whole had started to resemble a beach ball on stilts. With a weak bladder. Maternity leave and an end to my volunteer murder investigation could not come a moment too soon.

After light streaming in my bedroom window had awakened me at 11:00 a.m. on Sunday, I had wriggled out of my nightgown while I ate breakfast and, with a piece of toast in one hand, I had thrown on an old shirt of Steven's and struggled into my only pair of leggings that still fit, with the other. Not exactly dressing for success but then my clothes had never been the real obstacle to my career advancement.

I contemplated my body parts as I struggled up the stairs to DW3's first floor offices an hour later. The sight of open elevator shafts reminded me of my conversation with Walter yesterday and I wondered whether the only men at work were the ones on the sign. I made a pit stop to the kitchen at my end of the floor to deposit some leftovers. I'd come to the office equipped with plenty of food since I now struggled not with nausea but with a non-negotiable hunger. Satisfied from my session with voice mail the night before that nothing worthwhile had been recorded, I made my way to the fax machine to read the weekend's accumulation of incoming faxes.

The place felt empty. The disruption of elevator services that I had just ignored was a good reason to expect it to stay that way. Busy lawyers could hardly be expected to walk up one flight of stairs.

I stood at the fax machine and read, uninterrupted except for the annoyance of an incessantly ringing phone, that Kimberly, David and Josh would be having a very busy Monday morning if they were going to meet a U.S. client's deadline, and that Walter Hughes would soon be manipulating shipping invoices to fend off a federal government investigation. Based on this forty-eight-hour period of correspondence, the only crime DW3 lawyers could be charged with was murder by boredom. It was a shame that Hughes hadn't given his fax number to Adam & Eve Publications.

The annoying ringing started up again just as I was finishing with my reading. I looked around for its source, worried that a ringing phone might mean that someone was in the building or was expected. I stepped out into the hall and put my ear to Helen's locked door, but the sound did not seem to be coming from within her office. I strolled past Hughes' office and the rooms that housed his extended office family and jumped when one of those phones rang shrilly. The other phone, now ringing intermittently, must have been placed on mute and it grew fainter as I got further from the office I had just vacated. I returned there and waited silently for the ringing to start again.

A few extremely quiet minutes later I was rewarded with the renewed sound of ringing. I picked up the phone on the incoming fax machine but only got its screeching mating call. I spun around at the fax machine dedicated to outgoing faxes. It had always been strictly off limits for any incoming faxes by edict of H.M.S. It emitted a soft whir. Happy to have identified the source of the ringing phone, I found myself in a quandary whether to answer or let the machine perform its unauthorized function.

"Hello?" Answering didn't mean that I had to identify myself.

"Who is this?" An extremely unpleasant male voice, heavy on the English accent, boomed into my ear. The mute button unfortunately did not extend to the receiver and I held it away from me.

"What number are you trying to reach?"

"I have been trying to send a fax to this number for the last hour but no one answers. My girl doesn't work on Sundays and I'm not familiar with these bloody machines. I say, has it come through? Whose girl are you?"

I rankled at the suggestion that I was anyone's girl. I bit back a response—a variation on the backside of the offending male and to whom did it belong—to this pompous, chauvinistic pig. "To whom are you sending a fax?"

"Mrs. Smith. Sorry, Helen Matthews-Smith. She insisted that I get in touch with her over the weekend even though it's not our usual practice. She assured me that she would be waiting to hear from me."

I should have known. It was typical of H.M.S. to declare the machine off limits and then use it as her own personal fax machine. "And what was it you were sending?"

"Menus, of course. Wine selections. Centerpieces. I must have her comments on whether the cold poached salmon will be passed by waiters or sliced and served by our man at the buffet table. I told her that these details could

136

not wait until the last minute."

"I'll look." Normally, after outgoing faxes had been transmitted, they were routed back to the lawyers through interoffice mail. I was relying upon that system to keep informed but I hadn't expected any incoming correspondence from this machine. Today there were several pages in the fax tray, including a two-page fax from Lord—the English aristocracy had really fallen on bad times—Terrance Piggott-Carruthers Catering. "Yes, it's here."

"Thank heavens. And could you be a dear girl and make sure that Mrs. Matthews-Smith gets that fax as soon as possible?"

"Of course." I waited for the click of the receiver before inserting the two pages into another indispensable piece of office equipment and hitting the "on" button. Madam H.M.S. would be having her salmon shredded today.

Piggott-Carruthers had not been the only one to whom Helen had given the outgoing fax number. The tray included a request from the florists for an advance payment. And interspersed between a hand drawn diagram from the caterers of the layout of the buffet—one wouldn't want to leave such an important item to chance—and a bill from a wine shop for champagne, was a ten-page fax from the Geneva branch of Securex Bank. I wasn't a banking lawyer but I had lived overseas long enough to recognize standing instructions for a wire transfer. I flipped through the fax—it looked like about a year's worth of monthly transfers from an account in Geneva to one in the Cayman Islands. The account numbers were partially redacted and the legend on the top of each page mentioned that the originals with full information were being sent by post. But the amounts, several thousand dollars, were not what caught my eye. The instructions were faxed to the attention of Daniel Blake.

Before I could read the fax to determine why the very dead Daniel Blake would be getting faxes, I heard someone coming. Escape into the hallway would have meant a possible face-to-face confrontation with Helen who was clearly expected. The fax room offered little room for hiding. I crouched on hands and knees behind the file cabinets and hoped that for once the machines would not run out of paper. Trying hard to remember the instructions from the baby books I'd been reading, I concentrated on breathing.

My unknown companion in the room left within minutes. I sat up, now exhausted from sitting so still, and then with even more difficulty, stood up and walked back over to the fax machine, figuring that Helen would have gone back to her office to rave at Piggott-Carruthers for failing to send her the latest menu. As much as I would have enjoyed listening in on that conversation, I knew that I only had a matter of minutes to look at the banking documents I had just seen before she came back to look for the missing menu.

She would be looking for the layout and the bills as well for they still sat in the tray but the wire transfers were gone.

I left the room as soon as I could. Whoever had been here, and it was certainly not Helen, should have signed in. If I got to the main reception desk without running into anyone, I could check. The lights were still off in the hallway leading to reception. I headed for the stairs but froze when I heard the booming voice of Helen berating the guard at reception for not stopping her to check her pass. He must have been wondering what he had done in a past life to deserve such wrath.

Any minute, H.M.S. would be coming up the stairs. I considered my choices. I didn't think I could make it back to my office without running into either her or whoever had taken the Swiss bank fax. The maintenance men had been and gone. They had blocked off the passage to the ladies' room with their equipment but had not fixed the elevator. I could take the steps down, hoping to avoid the scene in reception, but that route meant the basement. After yesterday, I was intent on avoiding that area at all costs. I could take the stairs up, but I knew that access was blocked once I got past the second floor. The workers had left a sign directing women to the toilet on that floor. H.M.S. would, sooner rather than later, make her way up there. I knew I couldn't lift the equipment that barred my way. Which left me with only one option for hiding. The men's room.

I flicked on the light switch and immediately regretted not taking my chances with H.M.S. I rarely went into Steven's bathroom. He, the pack rat, and I, the minimalist, were happy not to share sinks. And I had only ever been in one other public men's toilet and it had been memorable for all the wrong reasons. I'd been returning with some girlfriends from Spring Break. We'd already covered endless miles of interstate through North Carolina when a sudden thunderstorm had made driving nearly impossible. We had pulled into the first gas station we could find. It had hams and fireworks and chewing tobacco but no ladies' room. Not deterred, we ran through puddles and pounding rain to the men's room where we battled for space with an army of cockroaches and a year's supply of half-empty bottles of beer. Or we convinced ourselves that it was beer. Hitching the dripping hems of our sundresses to our waists, we had straddled cracked toilet bowls and peed in rhythm to the downpour. We had laughed about it all the way back to Ohio.

The smell of stale beer from that men's room in North Carolina would have been an improvement to the odor emanating from the DW3 facilities. A trail of dark wet grime snaked its way up the mirrors like a primordial ivy above the sinks. Cigarette butts floated in the urinals. I didn't get close enough to see if they were Helen's brand. I entered the first stall but immediately exited when my sneaker slid on the floor. Rolls of unopened toilet paper lay stacked at the doorway, as if the cleaners had been afraid to enter for fear of disturbing the beast within. If this was what lay on the other side of the Glass Ceiling, Kimberly was welcome to break through. No wonder Daniel Blake had been such a grouch. He had probably been permanently constipated. He would not have wanted to linger here.

I walked to the stall furthest from the door and lamented not having turned off the lights. But mostly I lamented being pregnant. The proximity of the toilet, however disgusting, was like a red flag to my bull of a bladder. I considered dropping my leggings and maternity underpants, miles of white cotton fabric large enough to double as a parachute and designed to dispel any notion of ever having a passionate love life again, and relieving myself. But the slam of the door and the sound of a zipper being unzipped stopped me. I held my ears for what seemed like an eternity while I peered through the space between the stall door and frame in order to catch a glimpse of the person. I couldn't and didn't want to see his face. The snippet of conversation I'd heard—he'd taken a call on his mobile phone while finishing his business—wasn't enough to identify a voice. But I caught enough of a glimpse of his new waxed jacket and Harrods bag to know it was David Knight. He had walked out the door past the sinks without stopping. The clean desk theory apparently didn't extend to clean hands.

CHAPTER 17

I wasn't eager to accuse the multi-tasking David Knight of anything—fraud, embezzlement, murder, bad hygiene— solely on the basis of his appearance in the men's room just after the fax for Mr. Blake had gone missing. I didn't know for sure that he'd been the person to take it from the outgoing fax machine. Pretending to have just arrived, I strolled through the reception area and looked around casually to see whether anyone else had surfaced and headed back to my office. My affected nonchalance was disturbed when Walter Hughes came walking out of it. After a week of reading his mail and listening to his messages, I now had a different view of Walter and his big thoughts. Walter's mind was certainly elsewhere—in the gutter. And he was probably looking over my shoulder in order to keep from looking at other parts of my anatomy.

"Amy."

"Walter."

"I've left a file on your desk for you to read and to see me about tomorrow morning. I meant to speak to you yesterday about it but you seemed otherwise disposed." He directed his comments to an area up and to the left. "Shipping invoices. Government investigation. Fraud? Authenticity? Yes, look for fraud. Interview the clerk whose signature appears as the clerk of record. I've drafted a plan of action, it's there with the file. Statute of limitations needs to be considered but that's a non-issue in these types of cases. Compliance with export-import controls, yes, that's our best strategy." He stopped rocking on the balls of his feet to indicate he'd finished his analysis. "That should cover it." He turned and walked away.

"Nice to see you, too, Walter." Finding a dirty mind lurking behind the curtain did not endear Walter Hughes to me. I made a note to myself to research Securex Bank, the bank named on the fax to Daniel Blake. I moved the pile of shipping invoices from my desk where Walter had placed them and pulled the Declan file toward me. Faxes read, mail scanned, voice mails accessed, tomorrow's research organized, I was ready to do some real work when the phone rang. Expecting Steven, I was surprised to hear a woman's voice.

"Amy?

"Polly?"

"Good, I'm glad I got you. I didn't want to leave another message. Did you understand?"

"About the candy?"

"Yes."

"I got it. Thanks, Polly. I'm glad you changed your mind. Are you at your office? I could stop by today. I've got it right here."

"No, that's why I'm calling. I'm at a conference all weekend up in Birmingham. On chocolate, sponsored by the Federation of Cocoa Growers. Isn't that great?"

"Great." I couldn't imagine a worse way to spend a weekend than with an assembly of Pollys comparing notes on cocoa. The rolling shelves seemed less forbidding with every passing hour.

"Thought I'd network, make a few new contacts in the

business. It was just a stroke of luck that brought me here. I was reading the *Cocoa Trade Journal*, in preparation for working for you, and I saw that this conference was already scheduled and I thought 'why not?' I'll miss my weekly lecture at the British Museum—Musical Instruments in Art, we're up to the harpsichord. I can always rearrange my session with my Urdu tutor, and my Bible as Serious Fiction Book Club won't be pleased by my absence, but I promised to practice on the train."

"The harpsichord?"

"No, the Urdu. I'm brushing up."

"Right." Did I say every passing hour? I meant minutes. "So when would be a good time to drop off the candy?"

"I'll be back tomorrow morning. Why don't you stop on your way home?"

"Fine. I'll see you then."

"Oh, and Amy, about changing my mind." Polly then hemmed and hawed and made lots of noises about highly unusual circumstances. She described again her two, but really infinite number of hypotheticals. She outlined her ideas for investigating Darlington: telephone inquiries, shopping for random samples of candy from various Darlington outlets, sending the candy to the lab for analysis. When I pressed for her point, she abandoned her earlier pretence of taking on the case for the intellectual challenge. Appearances aside, Polly was more like a Winter, Worthington lawyer than I had first appreciated. In the end, she'd changed her mind and agreed to look into Darlington for the obvious reason. The money.

My money. I was going through the motions of earning it when Steven called.

"You should go home."

143

"I'm on my way as we speak."

"We're all off to dinner. I'm likely to be back very late so don't worry if you don't hear from me."

"Okay. I'm tired too. I'm just going to go home and get into bed."

"So this is goodnight?"

"Right. Goodnight. I'll see you tomorrow night."

Lugging my briefcase, I signed out and was barely out the door when I remembered my leftovers in the refrigerator upstairs. I juggled whether to leave them or run back upstairs and take them home for tonight's dinner. With my current out-of-control appetite, I'd probably eat them in the cab. The cleaning staff zealously cleaned out the fridge every Monday morning—it was the only task they attacked with regularity—and the thought of a meal going down the drain made me turn around.

"I left something, I'll be right back." The guard barely looked up from his mini TV and the Sunday evening football match as I waddled back up the stairs for the second time that day.

I retraced my steps, through reception, past my dark office, Mr. Blake's empty office, and David's palatial office, through the dark hall and into the kitchen. I had flicked off the main light switch when I'd left moments ago and didn't bother to turn it back on. I knew my way to the kitchen in the dark. I bent down to the level of the under shelf refrigerator and the room was illuminated for an instant by the tiny light inside. I stood up, pasta bowl in hand, but must have risen too quickly as the room swam in front of my eyes. I grabbed the wall to steady myself. I must be hungrier than I thought. I would be home in ten minutes so I resisted the temptation to have dinner there and then, but in my staggering I must have hit the kitchen door because I felt a rush of air as the door closed shut. The door was incongruously and probably illegally propped open with, appropriate for a fire door, a fire extinguisher, but today it wasn't there. I tugged at the door. It steadfastly refused to open. I had no idea whether it was intended to keep any potential fire out but it was doing very well at keeping me in.

I looked at my watch. I hadn't seen another lawyer since my encounter with Walter. The football game in which the guard had been engrossed wouldn't be over for another hour. I'd start pounding about then. But two hours later I was exhausted from pounding and shouting. This must have been the same guard who'd been on duty the night Mr. Blake had died because I had made enough racket to raise the dead but apparently not the sleeping.

Unlike the offices on the street side of the building, the kitchen had windows that actually opened, in this case, onto a small portico that ran the length of the exterior of the back side of the building. The maintenance men used this terrace—just wider than a ledge—for access to the HVAC system. At the end of the ledge was a door marked "Fire exit—No access without permission" which led back into the building at a right angle to the kitchen door.

Frustrated by my lack of progress in getting the guard or, for that matter, anyone's attention, I figured that if I could ease myself through the kitchen window and out onto the ledge, then I could come back into the building through the fire exit door. The window was about three feet high and three feet wide, easy enough for me to crawl through if I stood on a box of kitchen towels. I considered the merits of leaving the warmth of the kitchen but it held no other attractions for me—I had already eaten the pasta that had got me into this mess. Unless I could make a meal out of artificial sweetener and an expired container of milk, I was left with someone's leftover take-away that had long since lost its distinctive international character—Indian? Chinese? Turkish? It had the universal smell of garbage.

I stepped onto the box and climbed up through the window. Miscalculating the distance onto the ledge, I landed hard on my right ankle. The trip back if I needed to make it would not be an easy one. This was not a comforting thought when, after having inched my way across the ledge to the door, I discovered that it, like the fire door in the kitchen, was locked from the other side.

At the end of my first semester of law school, a precocious fellow classmate asked one of our professors what one lesson he, the professor, would want us, his students, to take with us from his class on our journey into our second semester and the mysteries of corporate law. As our torts professor, he had spent the better part of three months regaling us with stories that were heavy on gore and light on law. We had expected something practical, like, "Learn how to read X-rays, the future is in asbestos." So we were surprised by his one word response—"humility." Don't be too sure of yourself. Don't be afraid to admit to mistakes. Don't allow the law degree to inflate the ego. It was a lesson that I was to learn again and again for I had made a legal career out of being humbled by Daniel Blake. I doubted, however, that heeding the call of nature down a drainpipe was the humbling experience that my professor had had in mind at the time. Even the vile men's room would have been less degrading.

But my night on the ledge—as I had expected getting back into the office through the kitchen window had been much more difficult than getting out, and I had the scraped palms to prove it—had been an extremely educational experience. I learned that the truism that the cleaners came in bright and early Monday morning was a myth, that sound proofed windows kept out all kinds of undesirable as well as desirable noises, that the guards must have had a better night's sleep than I did, and that being first in the office had certain advantages in addition to impressing the senior partner—like providing a great means to steal a cigarette in a smoke free office. Helen was not happy to discover that she was not alone when she lit her first cigarette of the day.

"What are you doing out here?"

"I might ask you the same question but then again it is rather obvious." I pointed to the cigarette in her hand. She immediately dropped it to the floor and stamped on it where it joined a small pile of tell tale butts. "Look. I'm in no mood to chat. I thought I heard something early this morning and I stepped out here just to have a look around."

"And you didn't have a key so you locked yourself out-side." She twirled her own key chain.

"Right." I didn't want to admit my stupidity to H.M.S. I had some dignity.

She eyeballed my obvious dishevelment and my weekend attire. Even my most unattractive maternity outfit was more becoming than my Sunday night through Monday morning wear.

"And you expect me to believe that you were planning on wearing that to the office today?" She looked at me with a sneer.

"There's no putting anything past you, now, is there?"

"Let's just say that I won't ask any more questions and then I won't be forced to tell the managing partner that our expecting Ms. Brown was last seen wandering on the out-side ledge in an outfit that she clearly slept in."

What I did not need was Helen butting into my business,

sleuthing or otherwise. She had already made my life miserable enough. I asked, eager to negotiate, "So what's the deal?"

"How about I didn't see you and you didn't see me? This will just be our little secret." She smiled and pulled out another cigarette that she lit to taunt me. H.M.S. clearly believed that she outranked the Surgeon General and could ignore his health warnings.

The thought of my entering into any kind of a mutual conspiracy or agreement with Helen appalled me but I didn't want to draw attention to myself as detective. Or this new role. Office idiot. And how willing would Her Majesty have been to trade silence for secrets if she'd known that all of her precious invitations had been stolen?

"Fine." Why did I feel like I was making a pact with the devil?

"I love this time of day." She crossed her arms across her massive chest. "No ringing phones, no screaming lawyers." She took a deep breath and, if there had been any justice in the world, would have then fallen into a coughing fit brought on by too many fags on too many similar beautiful mornings. But she didn't. "Can you believe he's really gone?"

"I take it you mean Mr. Blake?"

"*Your* Mr. Blake. I always knew him as Daniel. Do you know how I first met him? We were both in the New York office. I mean, I was working as a secretary then for one of the senior partners and he was on home leave from one of the Asian offices. He had dropped in to see Larry Worthington, and I could hear their conversation, dropping all these foreign names—Macao, Shanghai, Bangkok. Daniel was still married then but there was talk of a separation. He was, I don't know, maybe in his fifties, and I was very young. I'd never been out of New York. It all seemed so exotic and thrilling to me. I think I decided then and there that somehow I was going to live overseas. That I was going to have an exciting life, too." She inhaled sharply and then dropped the butt.

And marry Daniel Blake, I thought.

"And some dreams do come true." And with a vehemence she usually reserved for lawyers, she ground her shoe into the smoldering, discarded cigarette. With her back to me, she surveyed the courtyard for a moment and then said, "It's still early. The cleaning people haven't even arrived yet. If you scoot, you can make it out of here without having to explain your appearance."

Had I been too busy in my search to consider that Daniel Blake had been deceived about the chocolates not because he'd been despised, but because he'd been loved? I looked at my companion on the ledge from this new perspective but all I saw was the same old Helen, who, as if reading my mind, huffed and then turned around and unlocked the door.

I stepped past her into the stuffy air of the office corridor and quickly turned back into the kitchen to retrieve my briefcase which, unlike me, had spent the evening in relative luxury. The heat from the appliances, although a welcome change from the outdoors, did little to warm me. I was chilled by the sight of the opened door, the fire extinguisher back in its usual place as door prop.

CHAPTER 18

I burst into my apartment and basked for a moment in its familiar smells as though I'd been gone for months and not merely overnight. Even the dark and drafty hallway seemed welcoming for a change. I shed my attire and stuffed every last piece of it in the laundry basket. Grabbing a robe from the bedroom closet, I walked down the hall to check the answering machine for frantic calls from my concerned husband wondering where I'd been.

"Amy, it's Steven. I'm calling at around 10:00 p.m. on Sunday evening your time. You must already be asleep. Just called to tell you that my flight leaves at 2:00 p.m. I'll probably go straight into the office and call when I get in. Love you."

So much for hysterical husbands.

A shower worked out the kinks in my muscles. My back, neck and arms ached from my attempts to use my jacket as a pillow on the concrete. I had eventually chosen warmth over comfort and had ended up wearing my jacket and using my arms as a headrest.

Donned in a clean, comfortable nightgown, I placed a carton of fresh squeezed orange juice, a bottle of mineral water, a banana and some cheese and crackers on a tray in the kitchen and carried them back to the bedroom. I downed the bottled water in just a couple of gulps and rested my head on a pillow and thought about last night.

For years Steven had been begging me to go camping, to sleep under the stars, and to learn to appreciate the great outdoors. My one night out in central London had not changed my mind. I'd seen no stars, no wildlife (for which I was thankful) and nothing that would have endeared me to spending any amount of time away from the luxury and bathroom of a five star hotel.

But I had seen the fire extinguisher propping open the kitchen door. Maybe women's brains did shrink when they became pregnant, and in my tiny mind I had just imagined that it hadn't been there the night before. I'd listened, in vain, for movement in the kitchen during my all night vigil. Helen would have mentioned the closed door and the missing extinguisher, even if only to embarrass me. Someone had waited for me to go into the kitchen and closed the door by removing the fire extinguisher. And that could only mean one thing: someone had wanted me out of commission. Maybe not out on a ledge, but at least locked in the kitchen. That same someone must have replaced the fire extinguisher shortly after I'd made my move onto the ledge. Before my head grew heavy with too much thinking, I drew the cord on the telephone at the side of the bed toward me and lifted the receiver to call the office. Lucy would be there but no one would be expecting me yet.

"Good morning, Winter, Worthington & Walker. How can I help you?"

"Lucy. It's Amy. I'm not feeling too great. I'm going to get a little more rest and be in late. Has Nikki arrived?"

"Your new secretary? Some people are coming up in the world!"

I laughed. "You've met her then?

"Yes, she seems like a lovely girl. Not that Helen agrees."

I'd forgotten that Helen hadn't been the one instrumental in hiring Nikki.

"I haven't seen her, but let me just check."

"Lucy, before you do. Have there been any calls to Helen, or to David Knight, from that detective who investigated Blake's death?"

"You mean that divine D.C. Lawson?"

I hadn't remembered anything particularly divine about him. "Yes, him. Has he called?"

Lucy rustled some papers as if looking for message slips. "You mean today? No one's called for either of them today."

"No, not necessarily today."

"Can't say that I remember, and I would do. He was, er, sorry, another call, I won't be but a second."

I ate the rest of the cheese while I waited for Lucy to come back.

"Amy, are you still there? Now, what were we talking about?"

"Nikki." I didn't want the idea planted in Lucy's head that Lawson had a reason to call.

"Right, you were checking on Nikki. Right. It's been crazy here this morning. Hold while I ring her."

"Nicola Barnes."

"Nikki, hi, it's Amy."

"Oh, good morning, Amy. Where are you? Are you at your desk? I didn't see you when I came in."

"No, no, I'm at home. I'm a little tired from the weekend. I'll be in, but later. You can direct any callers to my voice mail and I'll check them later. Could you tell

Ted's secretary, Louise, you've met her, that if Ted needs to speak to me about anything urgently, he can call me at home but if it can wait, I'll be in eventually. And that short, weird guy, that's Walter Hughes, if he drops by or calls, give him the same message."

"Got it."

"Now, put me through to Helen Matthews-Smith. She's the office manager who you might have met . . ."

"How could I forget?"

". . . on Friday. Her extension is . . ."

"I've got it right here."

"Great, thanks Nikki." I might as well face the music about the missing invitations while I had a few ounces of energy left this morning.

"Welcome to the Winter, Worthington & Walker voice mail system. The party you are calling—Helen Matthews-Smith—is not available. Please leave a message after the tone or press the star key for more options."

Probably still enjoying her morning routine. I rushed to speak as soon as I heard the tone.

"Helen. It's Amy. I'm calling at 8:30 a.m. on Monday morning. I've just told Lucy I'll be in late today. In any event, I wanted you to know as soon as possible. Some of my things were stolen from Joshua Hall's car on Friday evening and, um, the anniversary party invitations were in there. So, um, I'll need more invitations. Hope this won't cause too much inconvenience. Thanks. Bye."

I amazed even myself at my cowardice in delivering the message by voice mail when I had just seen her in person minutes ago. She would have a fit. I was too tired to care about her reaction. All that mattered to me was my bed. I closed my eyes, hoping for dreams of babies and not nightmares of misplaced fire extinguishers.

"Good morning. It is still morning, isn't it?"

"Hi, Lucy. Has anyone been looking for me?"

"Only Helen. You've been warned. If there's anyone else, you'll have to check with Nikki."

"Thanks. Any word about when and whether they're going to fix the elevators?"

"You'll have to check with Her Majesty I'm afraid."

"I've already talked to her about it. The elevators," Kimberly said as she pulled angrily on a small suitcase and a litigation bag on wheels. "I had to carry these up the stairs." Pausing in front of Lucy's desk, she moaned, "Is my driver here?"

Lucy said, "No, but . . ."

"Then it looks like I'm going to have to carry them down, too. If anyone calls, we can be reached at the Paris office." She stopped short of saying "civilization."

"Who's 'we?' " I asked Lucy as Kimberly departed.

"Who do you think? David Knight. It's their sixty-seventh trip together this year. Not that I'm counting or anything. He must have gone straight to the airport."

"Amy?" Nikki came around the corner into reception as Lucy and I giggled over Kimberly's dramatics.

"Nikki, hi. I was just on my way . . ."

"Your husband's on the line. I've got him on hold in your office."

"I'm coming. Talk to you later, Lucy." I barely said hello to Gideon and Josh Hall who both inquired about my health.

"Steven?"

"Hi, sleepy head."

"Hi, yourself."

"Who answered the phone, another one of those temps?"

"No, this one seems to be mine for as long as I want her." I'd forgotten to mention her to Steven over the weekend.

"That's progress. I'm just about to leave for the airport, hoping to catch an earlier flight. Your secretary said you were coming in late."

"I had a busy day yesterday," and I launched into a sanitized version of the previous evening. We laughed over my scatterbrained al fresco adventures. I omitted the more dangerous details—like the climb onto the box of kitchen towels and the fact that I had actually spent all night on the terrace. He was still getting over the idea that my pillow, through absolutely no fault of my own, was now as flat as a pancake.

"Amy, you have got to be more careful! Oh, before I forget, you do remember that we're having dinner with my cousin tonight, don't you?"

"Right." I had forgotten but in keeping with the tenor of the conversation, I didn't tell Steven. I mentally checked the contents of our freezer and said, "Pasta. Let's have pasta."

"Sure, I'll cook."

"And will you promise to come home on time?"

"I promise. I'll even try to be early."

"If that happens, I'll be so surprised, I'll cook."

"Sounds like a plan. I've got to go now, love you."

"Me too." I was thinking of his promise, mentally weighing the odds that he'd get there before our guests said goodbye. Oh, the lies we tell ourselves. Nothing compared to the lies we tell our spouses.

Having visited the voice mail systems of my colleagues over the weekend, I turned my attention back to my own. The red light was still not working and my "old" but really "new" messages informed me that H.M.S. had returned volley for volley, as if our quiet moment on the terrace had never happened. She lambasted me as only she could—her tone and words delivering more of a punch than a torpedo. I held the phone at arm's length but could still hear her recorded bellow.

"How could you be so careless? You have spoiled any remaining chance of this event going forward on time."

The "event" again. Helen's big day. Why didn't she spare us all the trouble and just elope?

"Your negligence will cost the firm money in more printing and mailing costs. I delayed long enough on Blake's account. Now you're doing your best to screw things up. Don't you know this is important to the partners?"

She shouted out my failings like roll call. I pressed the button for the next message and closed my eyes when Helen's voice screamed from my phone again. She'd switched topics but only a little. I gathered that, despite my best passive-aggressive plan, the invitation list that Helen had implored me to search for in Mr. Blake's papers and that I had trusted to the interoffice mail had eventually found its way to her although even that had not satisfied her.

"This list you've sent me can't possibly have been the people Blake intended to invite."

According to the all-knowing Helen, Mr. Blake certainly would have invited more people. And her complaints about whom he had intended to invite, like the tape in my machine, seemed endless:

"Judge Tustin's dead."

She didn't appreciate the irony in a dead man inviting a dead man.

"Lawrence Worthington's retired and partners, retired or not, aren't getting invitations."

I had thought that he was dead but I was wrong. The firm name would have to be changed to Two Dead WASPs and a Worthington.

"This Sir Gordon, he's not even in the social directory. And I can't read the other names. I'll need a new list and right away. Perhaps you can get your new secretary to help."

My changed circumstances were the real reason for her wrath. She ended with veiled threats to run to the partners with tales of my misbehavior. My finger poised on the delete button, she ended with a painful postscript.

"And don't think for a moment that I've forgotten about those timesheets."

I hung up, dialed her extension, and left my own message.

"Helen. Amy. I got your messages. I resent your insin-

uation that I broke into Josh's car, that I deliberately sent you the wrong invitation list and that I am purposely avoiding preparing Blake's timesheets. I am in my office if you would like to discuss this in person or with David Knight. You might want to bring your cigarettes."

CHAPTER 19

"Are you all right? I heard voices, well, shouting really, and I didn't know if it was okay to come in."

"Nikki, I'm sorry. I was just, never mind, what is it?"

"These were just delivered." She held up a parchment card like the ones I'd seen last week and asked, "And I was wondering what you wanted me to do with them. Helen, the office manager?"

"Yes."

"She left a note with them." She started reading, " 'The deadline for mailing is today but if you are too tired from last night'—that part's underlined—'then I'm happy to discuss postponing with David Knight and . . .' "

"You can stop. I get the idea." I'd let Helen win this one. "Okay, there's a list of my invitees on the machine at your desk, or at least there should be. Could you just run off the labels, and stuff and label the envelopes?"

"No problem. There's also something here about a Mr. Blake. Is it Blake? His invitations. I take it he was your old boss?"

"Yes. Mr. Blake." I fought back an unexpected flow of tears. "He's dead." I wiped my face with a tissue from my desk. "I'm sorry." The invitations, the shelves, the kitchen, lying to Steven, the battle with Helen, the possibility that my imagination, like my appetite, was no longer in my control. The last few days had taken an emotional toll that I couldn't blame on hormones or even chocolate. At least not directly. "I had a difficult weekend. And then Helen . . . I don't know what's gotten into me. A baby, I guess." We both laughed to break the tension. "I, I, I'm fine. I'm fine, really." I sniffled a bit and said, "Go on."

With a worried face, she spoke softly and said, "I thought maybe we could send invitations to the names in his address book, if he had one, or I don't know, his Christmas card list but I've already looked through the documents on my computer and there aren't any records in his name."

I was beginning to really like this woman. One step ahead, even of Helen. I thought for a moment. "They must have removed his diskettes and other documents from his secretary's computer when he died."

"I asked Louise and the clerk, Tony, right? And they weren't sure but thought maybe . . ." She paused.

"Yes?"

"They thought that all that stuff had been put in his office, Mr. Blake's, I mean. I'm happy to have a look around if you don't want . . ."

"No. It's okay. I can handle it." I had resisted the pull of Mr. Blake's office since my return even though I knew sooner or later I had to at least look at what I considered to be a crime scene. "I'll have a look around. Why don't you get started on my labels and, as soon as I find Mr. Blake's, you can do those." I looked at my watch and saw that it was lunchtime—every day now measured in increments of meals and not billable hours. "The day's still young. We've still got all afternoon."

"Right. This shouldn't take long. Is there anything else?"

I looked at the Declan files and Walter's shipping invoices. I was in little danger of getting any real work done today. "Well, there is a little something. I'd do it myself but . . . I hope you don't mind."

"Of course not."

"It's a bit of a puzzle, really. I'm trying to locate one of our former secretaries—I shared her with him. Mr. Blake, I mean."

"Right."

"Yes. Well, um, the last secretary we had working for us, well, to tell you the truth I just can't remember her name but I remember the agency—Morrison's—and well, I need to speak to her about some work she was doing for Mr. Blake before he, um, passed away." The agency would be suspicious of my American accent. "I could go directly to Helen but . . ."

"I'm sure I can find out without having to go that route. Leave it with me." She smiled.

Quick learner, diplomatic, takes initiative. This temp was a keeper.

"Good. Now, I'll go get those addresses."

Nikki lingered at the doorway for a moment. "Pardon me for being forward but I can tell just from the way you work, how you spoke about him just now, the two of you, you and Mr. Blake, I mean, must have made a great team."

"I suppose you could say that."

"You must miss him a great deal. It must be very hard. Losing a boss like that."

I nodded. And in the biggest lie in a day fraught with falsehoods, I told the biggest one of all.

"He was the best."

One conversation around the water cooler and Nikki would be disabused of the notion that Daniel Blake had been a great guy, I thought as I followed her the short distance to Mr. Blake's office. Blake's desk, only slightly smaller than the oak tree that had been felled to build it, and his well worn leather chairs had been removed, replaced with dainty furniture—the generic pattern screamed rental—that seemed dwarfed in the space. Personal items of Blake's—diplomas, Bar admission certificates, pictures and photographs—had been taken down, leaving noticeable patches. The walls would definitely have to be repainted. David Knight had mentioned in passing that the office would remain empty until London had another partner. I'd be surprised if Kimberly hadn't already sent the dimensions to her favorite interior decorator.

I felt detached from memories of the former occupant and pulled one of the rental chairs up to a stack of boxes marked with Blake's initials and a standard DW3 routing form that directed the boxes to the archive room. Flinching at the memory of my experience with the shelves and at the category selected from the menu of options, "Dead Files," I removed the lid of the first box and found draft application forms for the English law exams. I relished the thought of Helen searching for them and left them in their place. After rifling through boxes of old client files, I finally found the diskettes I'd come for in a box with expense reports and other documents. I put the diskette marked "Address list DBB" in my pocket and sifted through the documents to see if there was anything else that should be resuscitated.

A memo half way down the stack of papers caught my attention. Marked "First draft" and typed on plain paper, it still bore editing marks, and I recognized the format as an internal Winter, Worthington & Walker memorandum addressed to members of the firm management committee from David Knight. Joshua Hall, or "JH," however, had actually drafted the version I held in my hands and his hand-written questions and David's perfectly penned responses provided a lively counterpoint to the typed text. I wondered how the document had landed in files destined for the archives and not the shredder. But the answer became apparent as soon as I read the subject matter, "Summary of Events Relating to the Death of Daniel Benedict Blake: Legal and Practical Consequences." Dead partner, dead files, easy mistake.

Not that the subject matter was surprising. Typical of an organization that valued proper punctuation over people, the event hadn't taken place at DW3 until it had been memorialized in memo form. Certain that the door was closed behind me, I read with curiosity:

Daniel Benedict Blake joined Winter, Worthington & Walker after graduating from Harvard Law School. He trained as an associate in the corporate and banking sections of the international department and after a six-year apprenticeship was named partner in the New York office. Shortly thereafter, he made the first of several transfers to the firm's foreign offices before his last assignment in the London office.

Josh Hall took the prize for rewriting the past. In three short sentences, he'd managed to describe the most colorful character in DW3's history in the grayest of terms. The truth was much more interesting. Daniel Blake had cut his teeth on the Asian practice of DW3-New York, with short but memorable stints in most of the firm's Asian offices. He'd made the most of the go-go years—the heady '70s and early '80s when American lawyers in Hong Kong could waltz into negotiations in Beijing and waltz out with bills paid and reputations intact.

But he'd been sent to Hong Kong for a permanent posting when his temper was no longer tolerated Stateside. He was a moneymaker so there'd never been a question about his success. It was just that his meanness, according to the senior partnership, was better tolerated from a distance. A very long distance and multiple time zones away. Hong Kong, with its colonial atmosphere of white man at top and local Chinese native at bottom, suited him, and the partnership, perfectly.

He was already beyond the firm's retirement age when our paths had first crossed. I was an expatriate housewife in Hong Kong with a law degree from a mediocre law school, no Asian experience, and no real prospect of a job, the typical dilemma of what we expatriates refer to as the "trailing spouse," but I had something that made me invaluable to DW3. An infinite amount of patience for cranky old men and an ability to read just about anyone's handwriting. Despite the firm's reluctance to hire me—a non-Ivy Leaguer might have diluted the DW3 gene pool—I eventually became indispensable, the one Mr. Blake turned to when he needed someone to find a file or a phone number. Someone to rage to after hours. Someone to fire.

In the years leading up to the 1997 hand-over, Hong Kong-trained local Chinese lawyers began taking on more responsibility. In response to a not so subtle shift in the dynamics of an historically colonial relationship, DW3 had moved Daniel Blake to London as a reward for a job well done, the last step before Blake's retirement. There would be, the powers-that-be thought, an easing of old man Blake, by then, into his late seventies, quietly into that good night. Of course, there were those among the partnership who would have preferred that he had stayed in Hong Kong, figuring that sooner or later he'd antagonize the Chinese who, they secretly hoped, would take care of a problem none of them had had the guts or ruthlessness to address. They had had visions of Daniel Blake in a dunce cap forced to confess and labor in a re-education camp.

But Mr. Blake hadn't used his move to London as an excuse to slow down. To his credit and ultimately the firm's benefit, he had brought in business from his rich Hong Kong cronies searching for a safe and vaguely familiar harbor for their fortunes away from the new landlords of Hong Kong, the Chinese Communists.

But none of that would find its way into this memo. I skipped the rest of the bland discussion chronicling the highlights and achievements of Daniel Blake's career and focused on the next section.

MEDICAL DETAILS An autopsy established the cause of death as anaphylactic shock after ingestion of nuts, specifically, nut oil found in chocolate candy consumed by our late partner. An emergency vial of adrenaline was found just out of his reach under his desk.

This conformed to my memory of a clenched fist reaching toward something.

A coroner, sitting at——(DK—I'll supply details. JH), concluded that the severe and fatal reaction to nuts was insufficiently rare—a five percent fatality rate among reactions is "normal"—to render it an "unnatural cause."

There was little that was "normal" about Daniel Blake, particularly when it came to his allergy. How many times had I heard him scream "No nuts!" to harried waiters? He had learned the phrase in at least five languages. When we had traveled to more remote parts of Asia together, he had insisted that I hand the waiter a card printed with the warning in the local dialect. I had helped him carry small vials of adrenaline for self-injection, the only feasible remedy short of a speedy trip to a hospital. In the safety of civilized London, where language differences were few and his own eating habits predictable, such precautions had seemed to be unnecessary.

I had witnessed an attack just once, in France. We had gone through the "no nuts" ritual with the headwaiter. Coupled with Mr. Blake's usual rudeness, the "no nuts" routine had put us in the head waiter's extreme disfavor but I seriously doubted that what came later had been anyone's fault. We had finished three courses and were just starting on dessert when I heard an unpleasant choking sound emanating from Mr. Blake.

He had clutched his throat and gasped for breath. I whipped out the travel first aid kit from my briefcase and he managed to self-inject a life-saving dose of adrenaline. The manager, apologizing in languages even our French host couldn't understand, had called an ambulance and Mr. Blake had been whisked away. It was the last time he'd gone to France. Later, in his hospital room, where the nurses had already threatened to strike in response to his orders, his doctor had warned that his type of allergy would only get worse with every subsequent exposure. The next time could be fatal. And it had been.

A copy of the draft coroner's report is attached.

I couldn't find a report but tried to make sense of Josh's descriptions of IgE production and mast cells and antigens

166

and allergens. Even skimming the next three pages of scientific and medical details, my head swam. I found myself agreeing with David's note to Josh.

(JH—Can't we just say he was allergic to nuts? DK)

The cold legal prose couldn't disguise the fact that Mr. Blake had died a painful but relatively fast death. My eyes watered as I continued reading.

Even if Blake had been successful at injecting this remedy, it was unlikely to have saved him, according to medical opinion. A fatal reaction was practically guaranteed by the combination of nut oil found in the chocolate candy and his heart medicine, which exacerbated the effect of the natural toxin.

He had never stood a chance.

CHAPTER 20

The police investigation answered most of the questions left open by the post-mortem and reinforced the decision not to call an inquest. **(Josh—Shouldn't we have names here? DK)** Blake had eaten chocolates from a container manufactured and sold under the name of "Darlington." The container did not bear a price tag and a receipt was not found among the items left on his desk. Police described it as an "impossible task" to track the route of the candy to the deceased's desk. According to conversations with the investigating officers, Darlington confirmed that the uneaten candies were not a standard assortment. The label did not shed any clues on origin beyond "Made in England." The bar code on the bottom of the box identified the box, but not its handpicked contents, as one that had come from a distribution center in Slough that supplied all of the greater London area. Darlington had sold over a thousand pieces of chocolate that day from its outlets in central London alone. The company does not maintain daily records of sales of its product from the counters of the luxury department stores.

Police questioned staff at the Mayfair outlet, the closest Darlington store to the London office, but no one recalled seeing a man of Daniel Blake's physical description.

No wonder. The police had asked the wrong question. There was nothing remarkable about Blake's appearance: "short, balding, elderly, with a voice practically void of an accent" would not have triggered a recollection. But the screaming, the rudeness, the demanding tone, no sales clerk was likely to forget that customer.

Blake's secretary, a temporary discussed in more detail below, thought that she recalled seeing him opening the box early that day. Another interviewee had recalled seeing the box of candy on his desk that Friday afternoon.

I assumed Josh meant me. I'd told D.C. Lawson, who'd come by the hospital frequently at first, always keeping what he probably considered to be a safe distance from any potential projectile vomiting, the same story I'd told him in my office—that I'd seen the box that afternoon. I was under doctors' orders not to be bothered and Lawson had been kind and gentle, and usually limited our meetings to discussions of the timing of my departure on Friday and arrival on Saturday—and I had been consistent with those answers.

Investigating officers confirmed that Blake's day had been "fairly routine." No one could remember precisely, but practically everyone had been in or near his office that day.

It would have been impolitic to acknowledge that everyone usually avoided Daniel Blake like the plague.

According to records maintained by Lucy De Veres, London office receptionist, and confirmed in our own interviews with building security, there had been no clients in the office that day. The last person to have seen him alive had been his secretary who had left the office at approximately 5:45 p.m. The secretary (**Josh—NAMES PLEASE! DK**) *had not known of his allergy—because of the unusual arrangements made by the firm for temporary secretarial services for the late partner and his associate, Amy Brown. During the past few years, fourteen agencies had each sent a total of three girls, making this particular woman temporary number forty-two.* (**JH—Do you think it's necessary to tell NY this? Let's discuss. DK**) *Her appointment had ended that day.*

No one interviewed remembered seeing Mr. Blake again until the discovery on Saturday morning by Ms. Brown. (**DK—Under the circumstances I haven't talked to her. Do you think there's any chance she'll sue if she loses the baby? JH Josh—Don't be ridiculous. This is *Amy* we're talking about here. DK**)

No wonder he'd wanted to take me to dinner.

With the exception of his elderly housekeeper, Mei Leow, Mr. Blake lived alone. Mrs. Leow had been out of town and consequently no one became concerned when he did not return home that night. The security guard attributed his failure to discover the body during his night rounds to two reasons (1) Mr. Blake always left his lights on; and (2) the scent of certain fruit in the guard's native country bore a striking similarity to day-old garbage and, even less appetizing, a loosened sphincter. (**Josh—Delete! NY will not appreciate. DK**)

I agreed.

A description of the building security, which should have followed, was notable for its absence but it was clear that the memo wasn't an exercise in truth telling but in covering the London managing partner's ass. What Josh should have written and what everyone, except New York knew, was that security was laughable. Anyone coming in the front door after hours had to show a security card and sign in at a register kept at the guard's desk. But the management company followed a policy of hiring recent immigrants. Although this policy fed our liberal consciences, it did little to improve our safety. Easily cowed by symbols of authority, the timid guards hesitated before questioning anyone in a suit with a briefcase.

Even if, by some stretch of the imagination, a security guard had barred entry through the front door, easy and impermissible entry was still possible from the basement through the parking garage. The elevators and the stairs that led to the upper floors also went to the basement. Because the elevators and the stairs were both located behind the guard's desk, access to the parking garage meant easy access to the rest of the building. Guards purportedly patrolled each floor on the hour but it wasn't something to set a watch by. In short, the security system, much touted by the management company, was as effective as the building's "no smoking" policy. All the guards smoked. When they weren't sleeping. And all that David Knight had done to protect DW3 personnel and client files during his reign as managing partner, was to fit the main entrance and the doors to the basement with a key pad with the elementary "1-2-3-4" code.

No evidence suggested that the candy had been forced upon Mr. Blake and the police pointed to the more gruesome

*details of the post-mortem on the deceased's stomach con-
tents as a probable explanation of why he had failed to exercise his purported caution. His stomach was empty except
for some chocolate candy ingested earlier in the day. There
was no physical evidence that someone had stuffed the mor-
sels in his mouth. There was no record of anyone entering
the office after hours. It seems reasonable to conclude that
he'd eaten the candy because he had been hungry.*

*A police search, perfunctory as it became increasingly
clear that death was due to natural causes, and our own,
more thorough, internal investigation, revealed that
nothing unusual had occurred in the days leading up to or
immediately following his death. No funds had been withdrawn from client accounts. No business deals had been
affected. No suspicious deliveries had been made. Nothing
was missing. Our search covered bank accounts, files, and
personal belongings.*

Under the heading, "Legal Consequences," Josh had included the report's first, unintentional light relief:

*LEGAL CONSEQUENCES Blake's death did not
trigger the Health and Safety at Work rules. Death after
indulging in chocolates after hours is not the kind of "accident" that the legislation was intended to cover (e.g., fac-
tory floor type incidents).*

I could just hear the partners in New York breathing a
collective sigh of relief that their London office would not
be condemned as an unsafe workplace. The discussion that
followed was far from funny.

PRODUCT LIABILTY Because of recent publicity in

the U.K. press regarding the dangers associated with allergies to various ingredients, including nuts, Darlington posts signs in each of its stores warning of the possible presence of those ingredients in its candy. Such warnings were not mandatory at the time of the incident.

I would have to tell Polly.

The Darlington container was labeled in compliance with the relevant food labeling laws. A box of handpicked assorted chocolates does not have to be labeled with exact contents, an exception to otherwise rigid rules.

I read through the summary of the labeling rules quickly—they were slightly less laborious when delivered in person, with gusto, by Polly—and slowed for the analysis that followed.

*An argument that the candy was "defective," a legal hurdle for initiating a product liability action, would be difficult to win. (**DK—Could we sue the drug company? JH**) Some of Darlington's candy contain nuts and are intended to have nuts. In addition to having signs at the point of sale, Darlington prints the warning—"May contain nuts"—inside the lid of all its boxes and containers. Darlington and its lawyers could easily argue that, in his hunger, frailty, or impatience, Mr. Blake had ignored or merely not taken the time to read the warning.*

Even I, who had protested that Mr. Blake would have been more careful, had to agree that, at the best of times, when hungry, he had had the patience of a two-year-old.

173

Darlington is understandably loathe, however, to have its name associated with a death—bad for business for a law firm but devastating for a candy company—and has offered some form of payment in exchange for a release and an agreement by James Blake, son of the deceased, and the firm, not to disclose the name of the candy company in public statements about Blake's death. **(Josh— Did we ever sign anything? Check w/ Kimberly or Walter—DK)**

James Blake has apparently agreed to payment of an undisclosed sum. There is, however, no likelihood of any great financial windfall for the family or the partnership. The "going rate" in England for the life of an elderly man, especially one whose death was, it could be argued, in no small part attributable to his own failure to read the label, is probably in the range of £——. **(DK—How much should I put here? JH)** *A different result might be achieved if an action was filed in the United States.*

James had been lucky to have been paid funeral expenses. He'd taken the news of his father's death as I had expected, calmly and without emotion, when I'd called him later the next day after I'd been assured by my doctor that the baby was going to be fine and that all I needed was plenty of rest. James had decided against a Stateside funeral. That would have implied some degree of sentiment that he didn't feel. I recalled a conversation that Mr. Blake and I had had years ago after one of James' visits.

"Do you think he'll ever forgive me for leaving his mother while she was pregnant?"

I had probably offered some inanity while thinking to myself that no, James will probably never forgive you. The awkward silence after I told him of his father's death was confirmation that forgiveness was not part of the familial relationship.

He'd stopped by the hospital after the funeral. He'd told me that a few of the lawyers from the New York and Hong Kong offices had been there. A few clients. Mei, his father's housekeeper. He'd been impressed with the good showing from the London office—most of the lawyers, their wives, Helen, Louise, Lucy and Tony. I hadn't contested that staff attendance had probably been less a show of respect than an enthusiasm for the open bar afterwards.

I turned back to the report and the final section.

Practical Consequences *The death of a fee-earning partner in a worldwide partnership has several practical consequences with respect to the continuing financial viability of the firm, in general, and the London office, in particular. Plans for the celebration of the London office anniversary, inter alia, have been postponed, but not as some suggested, cancelled, as a sign of respect.*

A cancellation, I knew, would have been over Helen's dead body.

Perhaps convinced of his own immortality, Mr. Blake had died without leaving a will. This was in clear contravention of firm policy.

I grinned. What had they expected? Daniel Blake hadn't acted contrary just to annoy the partnership, he had lived to contradict. He would disagree with my opinions regardless of how meaningless. If I had recommended a restaurant, he would eat there and then regale me with how bad the food, the service, and the atmosphere were. If I had recommended a book, he would read it and deliver an opposite viewpoint.

Aside from being profitable, he had been everything that the firm had not wanted him to be. Greedy. At Christmas time, clients would send gifts—a case of wine, a basket of fruit or a box of chocolates, like the one that proved to be his downfall. Unlike the other lawyers in the office, Mr. Blake had made sure that the boxes were delivered to him personally, opened by him personally and ingested in their entirety by him personally. Egotistical. He would take 100% of the credit for any project, whether team or joint or solo effort. And he'd been petty. Imperious. Secretaries would type exactly from his handwriting, warts and all, and he would correct his hand-written originals to prove to some imaginary arbiter that the mistakes were the typists' and not his. He would snap his fingers or, more frequently, clap his hands to get the attention of waiters. Maitre d's all over the world cringed when he walked in. All ego without a trace of humility. By the time I had started working with him, his bad habits had run out of check for so long from a combination of colonialism and financial success that there had been no hope of changing him. And by dying at the office without a will, he had confounded firm policy to the end.

*We understand that under the relevant laws of intestacy his only descendant is his son, James. Blake left a considerable estate, with assets in the range of ——. James is currently in negotiations with the Internal Revenue Service and the Inland Revenue. (**DK—What number goes here? Should we expand on other financial arrangements? Should I mention offshore accounts? JH Josh—No, leave it to me. I've already been in touch with Hausmann. DK**).*

In line with his son's request, Blake's personal belongings (office furniture, artwork) have been transported to his former home, 1739 Hampstead Row. In an arrangement not unusual among U.S. law firms with foreign offices, the house was, at the time of Blake's death and continues to be, leased by the firm through a managing agent, Williams Estates. Allen Williams has agreed to an extension of the lease under the same terms of the previous tenancy until alternative arrangements can be made for the live-in housekeeper and the disposition of Blake's personal property. Discussions concerning the re-negotiation of rental terms or alternatively, a possible purchase, are ongoing, through Williams, pending finalization of advice from U.K. and U.S. tax counsel. We await the return of items taken from firm premises by the police in the course of their investigation. David Knight has undertaken to reassign client files.

I was already intimately familiar with those plans but I sat back at the revelation in the next paragraph.

Although past the firm's retirement age, Blake was still responsible for over —— active client files, representing —% of the London office billings. He had announced his retirement to the managing partner of the London office, to take effect at the end of the fiscal year to coincide with the naming of new partners and his death merely accelerates those plans. **(DK—Should I mention Kimberly here? JH Josh— No, I'll discuss numbers w/ Ted and Walter—DK.)**

The typed text ended abruptly and David's final comments covered the rest of the page:

Josh—A good first effort. Simplify the science

177

part, and make sure the next draft covers insur-
ance policies, contractual obligations, a strong
conclusion and recommendations for the fu-
ture—NY loves that sort of thing. Also the memo
should reflect conversations with the people I've
listed below. You may think of others. Check
with Teddy and Walter on the next . . .

I stopped midsentence only when Nikki tapped me on the shoulder and said, "I've found her."

"What?" I looked up for a moment but held out my hand to silence her. "Just one second. I want to finish this." I pulled out the computer record of Blake's files. "Here's the diskette." I ran through the rest of David's comments, and the attached list of names. "I'm sorry, what is it?"

"I've found the temp."

I looked back at the names David had written, and said, "So have I."

Nikki, too excited by her success in finding the temporary secretary to wait a moment longer, said the same name that appeared at the top of David's list, *"Susannah Jones."*

CHAPTER 21

"Susannah Jones?"

"Yes, I'm Susannah Jones." Nikki's urgency had more to do with the fact that she had Susannah Jones on my telephone than, as I had mistakenly believed, her eagerness to share her discovery. I'd carried Josh Hall's draft memo—well written but wrong—with me as I rushed to my desk to chat with the woman who'd last seen Mr. Blake alive. We were barely past hello and I could already tell that it wasn't going to be a friendly conversation.

"I'm calling from Winter, Worthington & Walker."

"Yeah, that's what the girl said. What's this about?"

"I don't know if you remember me, we worked together, my name's Amy Brown."

There was a pause before she replied. "Yeah. I remember you."

Blake had chewed up and spit out so many secretaries, I would never have remembered her. I had kept a civil but discreet distance from the young women—and like the six-monthers, their gender never changed—who occupied the desk outside his office. I had learned early on not to take sides. Taking sides was never an option when the outcome was a foregone conclusion. He would scream. The secretaries would leave. There were variations on the theme. He would scream, they would cry and then leave, or sometimes scream back and leave. In all cases, Mr. Blake would emerge triumphant. He never seemed to understand that his was a Pyrrhic victory. Screaming never got the work done.

Had she been the gap-toothed, posh-accented, public school graduate, or the leggy model who had been temping between assignments? I tried but just couldn't conjure up a face to fit the name, but as we talked more her voice came back to me, a London accent affected by British pop stars hoping to establish street credibility. On Susannah, it had been the real thing. When I explained that I wasn't calling to offer her a job, her next words, "Look, I don't know what you think" came out something like "Lookit. I don know wha you fink you're after. The coppers know everyfink."

"I'm sure you told them everything but I just wanted to ask you a few questions about that day that maybe hadn't occurred to them. I promise it won't take long. Please?"

Another pause. "So what is it that you are so hot to know?"

"I'm sorry, I don't mean to upset you." I didn't remember her being so unpleasant. And it was hard to believe that she could be upset about Mr. Blake. "I just wanted to talk to you about that last week. The last week you worked for me. And for Mr. Blake. Do you remember much about what he spent his time on? Did anything unusual happen that day or even that week? Did he seem agitated about anything?"

"Agitated?" A smile came through the phone. "Who would notice? He was agitated all the time."

"You're right. But did anything or anyone seem to upset him more than usual?"

"You and him seemed to go at it pretty good. Him and H.M.S. went at it."

Nothing unusual there. "Anyone else?"

Her agitation returned. "I just don't remember. I told the police all of this."

"What about the candy? Any idea how he might have got it? You checked his mail. Did it come in the mail? Did anyone take it into him?"

"Why are you asking all these questions? I told the police everything. I don't remember anything else."

"It's just . . ." I wasn't sure what I should tell her. I didn't want to feed her some line about vegetable fat in chocolates or cross-contamination. Polly's research didn't even make that much sense to me. "I have my reasons, but I think that or have reason to believe . . ." I heard myself sounding like a pompous lawyer. "I knew Mr. Blake really well and I know he wouldn't have eaten that candy unless he knew or had been told that it didn't have nuts in it and . . ."

"Look, someone's asking for me. I've got to go."

"It will only take a minute."

"This should all be in his timesheets."

"Yes, but you hadn't done his time for that month. They left me to do his timesheets after he died."

"Sounds like something that woman, Helen, what was it everybody called her, H.M.S., would do."

"No kidding. Look, I just have a couple more questions."

"He was always writing something down in that little black book. His diary." She paused and said as if surprised, "I'd forgotten that. I told him I needed it to start his timesheets. He couldn't find it. Said something about asking you and then he snorted. I thought he was about to blow his top again so I just went back to my desk."

His diary. Blake misplaced it with the same frequency he

changed secretaries. I'd wasted plenty of billable hours trying to track it down, and had seethed when it turned up in its usual resting place, his top desk drawer. And, too intent on defying Helen, I hadn't realized that I couldn't do his timesheets, and I didn't have a prayer of solving his murder, without it.

I had just started explaining to Susannah that I'd found a note on the candy when I'd heard the buzz of the dial tone. Scanning Josh's memo for the name of the managing agent for 1739 Hampstead Row, I rang the number for Williams Estates.

"Allen Williams, please."

"Allen Williams speaking. How can I help you?"

I explained, with as few details as possible, that I had been house hunting in Hampstead and had liked the looks of 1739 Hampstead Row. Mr. Williams reluctantly confirmed that a prestigious U.S. law firm held the lease to the property but was in the process of negotiating for an extension.

"Is it possible to just get a bit of a look around, in case they don't extend?"

"Well, I could make a few telephone calls to my contact to see if we could make some arrangements, but that could take a few days. It's a bit awkward, the current tenant, well it's really all rather frightful, but . . . when did you say you were going back?"

"Tomorrow, I'm afraid."

"Mind you, I can't within the terms of my agreement with the owner and the tenant give you access but I suppose if you were to . . ."

"Is the house empty or is someone living there?"

"The house is vacant for now, but the old Chinese

woman who worked for the former tenant still goes in everyday. Or so it seems. Every time I've been there she's been cleaning although it is mystifying how an empty house could possibly be dirty."

I hinted that my employer might be willing to pay a premium over the current rent for what I, one of its most valued employees, had decided was my dream house. After some hesitation, he said, "There could be no harm in your admiring the house and striking up a conversation with the Chinese maid, get a look-see that way. No harm, no foul, isn't that what you Americans say? Maybe even offer her a job, she seems to come with the house." He laughed at his own joke. "If that doesn't work, then come back to me. I'm sure we can work something out."

By the end of our conversation, I'd decided to take my chances on the maid but Williams had practically agreed to give me my own key and a personal tour. It had only taken the magic words, Seattle, software, and stock options. Whoever said only Americans thought the world ran on dollars and cents never met a London real estate agent.

The taxi driver was silent. I was happy to avoid the usual exchange, prompted by my American accent. After a half dozen years of the same routine, I had considered having a placard printed with the standard responses: Ohio; five years; yes, except for the weather; and no, I have never been to Disney World but I understand it's very nice.

Lost in my thoughts about the memo and the idea that Blake had been planning to retire without telling me, I hadn't noticed the trees and expansive green lawns that signaled that I had arrived in my destination in North London. I knew from experience that it would be difficult to flag a cab down in this neighborhood and was even hard pressed without a compass to find my way back to Chelsea. As one of those expatriates for whom London ended at Oxford Street to the North and the King's Road, or if I was feeling adventurous, the Embankment, to the South, Hampstead was another country. I asked the cab driver to wait at the end of the horseshoe drive.

I had been to the house on Hampstead Row only once or twice before. I didn't like, or maybe I was just incapable of, thinking of Daniel Blake as having a life outside the office. As far as I was concerned, he put himself, along with his week of identical dark blue suits, on a cedar hanger in a closet for the night until the office beckoned the next morning, like some vampire who'd gotten his days and nights mixed up. But even despicable old men like Mr. Blake, for whom the office had been his life, had a private persona that differed from his office one. On the rare occasions that I had had to call him at home, he'd answered in such a meek, sweet voice that I had hung up convinced that I'd reached the wrong number. Little wonder Steven had trouble believing my horror stories.

I rang the doorbell and, peering through glass panes on either side of the door, I could see the entranceway, complete with Persian carpet, antique Chinese urns and rosewood table, but no inhabitants. I banged the knocker for good measure and waited another ten minutes but still received no answer. I had guests arriving for dinner and, as much as I wanted to, I couldn't afford to linger. My feet made crunching noises as I trudged down the driveway back to the taxi.

Just as I told the cab driver to take me to St. James and Polly's office where I still needed to drop off the candy, I heard the sound of a door opening behind me and turned around to see Mei, Mr. Blake's elderly Chinese housekeeper, who I'd first met in Hong Kong at a time when home entertainment was de rigueur. She had silently served hors d'oeuvres and drinks at the dinner parties Mr. Blake had hosted at home over the years. Mr. Blake's ire had been directed at her for the usual capital offenses, spilled wine or cold soup, but unlike our series of temps, Mei had taken his insults in stride and stayed. She had probably hurled Cantonese invectives at him when she retreated with the rest of the staff into the kitchen.

She was wearing her usual uniform: black pants, white blouse, gray cardigan, yellow rubber gloves, house slippers and blank expression. I had thought she would have retired now, and that, as D.C. Lawson had said, she had moved to Chinatown, but, as greedy Mr. Williams had predicted, I had interrupted her from cleaning. Some habits had not died with Daniel Blake.

"Mei, hello."

"Miss Brown. Hello. I only just heard the door."

"I . . . I'm sorry to disturb you." I mumbled something about sympathy, which she silently acknowledged with a nod of her head. "I came by to check on some office matters. Some mail that had not been delivered to the office and that I thought perhaps had made its way here." I didn't want to draw attention to the fact that I had only come to look for his diary. I mentioned a file that I knew Mr. Blake had never worked on.

"There's been no mail for several weeks now. I don't know anything about Mr. Blake's business matters. I've been staying at my cousin's son's place since Mr. Blake died and," she hesitated for a moment and then said, "I just came in to do some cleaning."

"For the new tenants?"

She gazed past my shoulder. "Yes, for the new tenant."

I wondered whether it would be David or Kimberly. Or David and Kimberly.

"Would you like to look through his things? They've been sorted, some are packed and labeled for shipment to James along with the furniture but perhaps some business items have gotten mixed up. It's taken a bit longer to get things together than he expected."

"Well, I might as well look while I'm here." Trying not to appear too eager, I followed her back up the drive after motioning to the black cab that I would just be a few more minutes. This ride was going to cost me a fortune.

The house had the aroma of furniture polish and fresh cut flowers. I looked around for reminders of its previous occupant but the scent made me feel like I had entered the lobby of an expensive hotel, rich and luxurious but impersonal and entirely too clean. Mr. Blake's presence seemed to have been vacuumed, dusted and polished right out of the woodwork.

Mei, ahead of me, straightened pictures and rugs as we walked through the house. How difficult it must be to have had responsibility for such beautiful things, the cleaning, the tending, but not to possess them. An apartment down in Chinatown would be as tough a move for her as a ticket back to Hong Kong.

She led me to a door on the right of the hallway and I knew finally that we were in Mr. Blake's office even before she flicked on the switch that lit two Chinese porcelain lamps and I saw the familiar furniture. It was going to take a lot more than bees' wax and linseed oil to remove the familiar mixture of after shave, perspiration, pencil shavings and old age that made for the most personal of perfumes. The room reeked of Daniel Blake.

"You miss him."

186

"Yes," I answered as I found myself, like Mei before me, drawn to the desk placed before the bay window. I caressed the gleaming wood grain as if by touching this inanimate surface I could conjure back the old man in the flesh.

"These are going to James. He's coming to London at the end of the month to make some decisions about the other furniture, what to sell, what he'll keep. Do you want to go through these?"

"Yes, yes. Thank you." I'd almost forgotten why I was there. Mei left, and I pretended to sift through papers and boxes of tax returns and bank statements until I knew she was out of earshot. I went back to the desk and pulled drawers out gingerly looking for Mr. Blake's diary. It would have been easy to spot. Not for him an orderly Filofax or Rolodex, Blake's diary resembled a young girl's scrapbook. In addition to scribbles that passed for appointments, each page usually had clipped to it a ragtag collection of taxi receipts, credit card slips, cocktail napkins bearing telephone numbers, and business cards, reminders of what he had been doing and who he had been doing it with on a particular day.

But the top desk drawer, in fact all of the drawers, had been emptied.

I took one last deep breath from the memory well and made my departure.

"Thanks so much. I'll be going now." I called out to Mei. She had traded the rubber gloves for a giant apron miles too big for her tiny waist. She wiped her hands as she approached me.

"Did you find it, the file?"

"No." I considered whether to ask her about Blake's retirement or to confide in her about what I believed was Mr. Blake's death or, more precisely, murder.

"Was this what you were looking for?" Mei reached into one of the deep square pockets of her apron and pulled out Mr. Blake's diary. "I was saving it to hand to James."

Trying not to betray my excitement, I took it from her. "Yes, actually this is one of the things I was looking for."

"Then you should have just asked for it. Such indirection, I believe, is not what Mr. Blake would have taught you."

"You're right, I'm sorry."

"That's all right. You were always his favorite you know."

I was startled by her comment. Before today, we had never exchanged more than formal pleasantries.

"Thank you." Embarrassed, I changed the subject. "It's a really beautiful house."

"Yes. Beautiful."

"Will you stay on, I mean, as housekeeper?"

"No. I don't think so." She looked at me and not at the house.

I looked at my watch. "I've got to go. Thanks again."

"I wish you all the best with the baby. Please take good care."

I found myself wanting to hug her goodbye. To clasp her sparrow-like frame to my chest as if I could clasp a memory of Mr. Blake to me. She shrank back as if I had actually spoken my intention. The image of me embracing her goodbye was suddenly as absurd and distasteful as touching Mr. Blake, something I had avoided doing in the years we'd known each other. The mental picture of physical contact with him was enough to hasten my departure.

That, and being late for my own dinner party.

CHAPTER 22

Very late. Later than Steven, who up until my arrival had been the gold standard for late in our house and I hadn't even taken the time to stop at Polly's office.

"Where have you been?" Steven shouted from the kitchen with his back to me as I entered the apartment.

I couldn't answer the truth, Hampstead, without an explanation and since I could already hear our guests chatting in the living room, I avoided the question and asked instead, "Am I late?"

"I've been calling the office non-stop for the last hour. Lucy said she hadn't seen you since this afternoon." He turned the tap to stop the running water, wiped his hands on a towel and hugged me. "I was worried. Where were you?"

"So I am late."

"Amy."

"I was at the doctor, silly, no reason to get alarmed. I was late for my appointment which meant I missed my turn so then I had to wait, and then I wanted to discuss . . ."

"I get the picture. Is everything okay?"

"Healthy as an ox." I backed out of his embrace and patted my stomach.

"Why don't you change? I can manage here."

Happy to avoid any pointed questions that I'd be unable

to answer truthfully, I set my briefcase on the counter and left the kitchen. I could hear Steven offering drinks to another arrival and pointing someone in the direction of the living room while I washed my face and put on something more comfortable. I wiped my face on a towel and caught a glimpse of myself in the mirror. I was still experiencing sleep deficit from the night before but I didn't look that tired. The plumpness and glow from my pregnancy belied the melancholy I'd experienced in the cab flipping through the pages of Blake's diary. I hadn't been able to decipher much from his scattered notations but it had not looked like the schedule of a man about to retire.

All four of our guests were sitting in the living room, a tableau of wine glasses and earnest conversation, when I entered.

"Hello." I gave Steven a sign that he could go back into the kitchen and that I would take over the hospitality role. "I'm sorry I was so late. Doctor's appointment. Does everyone have something to drink?" I turned to the only stranger in the room and said, "Hello, I'm Amy Brown, Steven's wife. You must be Peter. I understand you've just joined Steven's office. Have you met everyone?"

"Yes, Steven introduced us." The Sandlers, another American expatriate couple with whom we'd been friends since the beginning of our time in London, both smiled.

"And Scott, we met several years ago at your other cousin's wedding—it's wonderful to see you again." I kissed Scott's cheek and then addressed the group. "I hope everyone's hungry. Steven's making tortellini."

They all made noises of hunger and pleasure, content to have someone else cook. Playing the usual parlor game for expatriates, the Sandlers had already learned that Peter had graduated from Yale, their alma mater, and had dated Karen's younger sister's roommate. Scott Goldman, Steven's backpacking cousin, was looking at some family photographs, happy for free food and booze. His ears perked up when he realized that Karen and I knew each other from the same law school he would be entering in a year. We chatted a few more minutes, degrees of separation established, and then I excused myself to help Steven with dinner.

The first course was already on the table and, from the aroma wafting from the stove, it was clear that Steven had made considerable progress on the rest of the meal. The table had been set and candles were lit. I resolved to be late more often.

"Amy, could you pass the cheese, please?"

"Sure, Scott, please help yourself to more. Can you just pass this down?" I handed a bowl to Peter at my left.

"Any ideas for names for the baby?" Karen asked.

"We can't agree on boy's names but, if it's a girl, we were thinking of Sophie. Aren't we, Steven?"

"Sophie Goldman. That sounds a little like a Communist organizer from the '30s doesn't it?" Peter turned to Steven and asked.

"Who said this baby was going to have Goldman as a last name? Brown is a perfectly reasonable last name. My family likes it."

"I agree."

"Thank you, Karen."

"Of course it's going to have Goldman as a last name. Goldman is a great last name."

"You're not in the least prejudiced, Scott. Your last name is Goldman, isn't it?"

"But he's right, of course the baby will be named Goldman."

191

I looked at my husband and said, "We'll see. Would anyone like more wine?"

"So, Amy, what's happening at Wither & Walking?"

"It's Winter, Worthington & Walker." Karen corrected her husband.

"Whatever. All those law firms sound alike to me. Does that woman, the really . . ."

"Beautiful?" I asked. Jim was an incorrigible flirt.

"I was going to say something else, but if you insist, beautiful and . . ."

"You were going to say beautiful," Karen interrupted.

"Beautiful and smart, how's that, woman still there? What was her name, Kim?"

"You mean Kimberly Sullivan?" No man ever got my firm's name right but they all managed to remember Kimberly's. "Yes, she's still here. How do you know Kimberly?"

"She goes to my gym. I've seen her there, run into her at the juice machine."

"A likely story. Just ignore my Neanderthal husband. What's it like working there, now that your old boss is gone? What was his name?"

"Mr. Blake." Our friends had occasionally heard dramatized versions of Blake's tantrums.

Steven turned to Peter and Scott and explained, "Amy's boss died recently, at the office."

"That's terrible. Had he been sick?" Scott asked.

"Well, he was pretty old," I said.

"Amy found him, didn't you, Amy?" Karen looked at me for confirmation.

I nodded.

"Oh my god, you're kidding," Scott gasped.

"It was quite a shock." Steven took my hand.

"But I'm over it now. Back at the office. Life goes on."

"But that must have been awful for you."

"What happened Amy? How did he die? If you don't mind talking about it."

"No, it's okay. I don't mind," I said and I realized that I meant it. I'd been consumed with thoughts of Blake's death recently and it felt good to talk about it. "Anaphylactic shock. He was allergic to nuts and he ate some candy with nuts." I filled in some background on my job at Winter, Worthington for Scott and Peter up to the day I'd discovered Blake's body. When I'd finished, Scott spoke, "Uncle Mort has that allergy, did you know that, Steven? He has to be really careful. I guess no matter how hard you try to avoid them, accidents will happen."

Jokingly, Steven said, "But this may not have been an accident. Amy thinks someone killed him."

"Steven!"

"Well, you said so yourself, he wouldn't have eaten that candy if . . ."

"Amy, you're kidding. You never told me that!" Karen grabbed my arm across the table.

"What do you think someone did, use a hypodermic needle and inject nuts into . . . I'm sorry, I know this isn't supposed to be funny, I'm really sorry, I shouldn't say this . . ."

"Say what?"

"Just say it, Jim." Karen rolled her eyes.

". . . Inject nuts into his Fanny . . . Farmer?"

Everyone around the table, except me, groaned and Steven said, "Jim, you are awful."

"Were they British? I could see how it could be murder if they were British." Karen was a dear friend but she did have a tendency to engage in the verbal equivalent of the

Boston Tea Party—dumping on the British—at every social occasion. A vegetarian who turned into a carnivore the minute she left British airspace, Karen was convinced the local tap water would kill her. Death by British candy was consistent with her idea of a British conspiracy to reclaim the Empire with bad food.

"But why would anyone want to kill an old man?" Scott, the youngest among us, asked.

"Was he old?" Peter asked.

"Really old, wasn't he, Amy?" Jim, who'd finally stopped laughing, looked at me.

"Have you thought about motive, Amy?" Karen, at least, seemed to take the matter seriously.

"I really don't think. . . ."

"You said he was a lawyer, didn't you?" Jim, the only non-lawyer in the room asked.

"Yes."

"Well, wasn't that reason enough?"

CHAPTER 23

"Not another lawyer joke, enough, enough. Let's change the subject," Steven said as he downed the rest of his wine.

While everyone laughed at the macabre possibilities in a box of candy I rose and asked, "Can you excuse us? Steven, can you help me carry this into the kitchen?" As soon as we were out of earshot, I turned to him and said, "Steven, I really don't think we should be talking about this in front of other people."

"But of course the baby's going to have my last name."

"Not the baby, stupid. Blake. The note."

"I'm sorry. You're upset, aren't you? I wouldn't have mentioned it if I thought you would be. You seemed fine a moment ago. And it's not as if it's a secret. You told the police. I was just making conversation."

"I know. Sensational conversation." A burst of laughter resounded from the dining table. "But, well, can we just drop it?"

"Of course."

"Good." I slammed a pot on the counter.

"You're still upset. What is it? Is there something you're not telling me, Amy?"

"Not now, Steven. We have guests."

"They can wait. You did take the police the note, didn't

you? And the resignation letter?"

I nodded.

"We agreed that that would be the end of it."

"I know, but, it's not just the note that makes me think he was murdered, there's more to it than that."

"Any more Parmesan?" Jim Sandler appeared at the door.

"Oh, Jim, sure." I handed him a block of the pungent cheese and a grater. "Do you mind doing it yourself at the table?"

"No, sure. About that comment in there earlier, I . . ."

"Don't worry about it. I'm fine. Go. Grate cheese." I smiled momentarily and then turned to Steven. "Where was I?"

"I think you were going to tell me . . ."

"All these things have been happening and I think they've been happening for a reason."

"Amy, what are you talking about?"

"First, there was the break-in. Joshua's car. All that was stolen was the box of invitations. I mean of all things to steal, why that box unless . . . ?"

"Was there anything else to steal?"

"Josh's mobile phone. The car."

"Maybe the guy had a box fetish."

"Steven, I'm serious. That box was labeled Daniel Blake's 'Personal Effects.' That was the only reason to steal it. And there's more. There was a fax. An incoming fax on the outgoing fax machine."

"What's so weird about that? Maybe the incoming machine was broken. If I got suspicious every time a piece of office equipment inexplicably broke down, I'd drive myself crazy. I have days when it feels like the whole office is turning against me. Like some weird Stephen King movie, you know the one where the car turns on its owners. Or that movie where the television sucks people into some other dimension. But I don't go around thinking that the office has been haunted, like you do, by the ghost of Daniel Blake past." Steven was trying his best to add levity to the situation.

"The fax machine wasn't broken."

"So blame it on the fax operator. Good old human error. Amy, what's this really all about? You lost a box of invitations. You told me yourself that the worst part about having that box stolen was having to tell that witch of an office manager. I really think that you're overreacting. Maybe going back to work wasn't such a good idea after all."

"It was for him. The fax. It was for Daniel Blake. But he's dead. And what about the shelves?"

"You've always told me those were an accident waiting to happen."

"And then there was the fire extinguisher."

"What fire extinguisher?"

Dead silence from my side as I transferred the last of the vegetables from the roasting pan to a serving dish and Steven poured the remains of the sauce into a bowl.

"Amy. What fire extinguisher? What aren't you telling me?"

"Well, you know how I told you that I must have hit the door in the kitchen and that it closed when I got up too fast?"

"Yes."

"The door is usually propped open with a fire extinguisher. It's just that I didn't see it—the fire extinguisher—after I hit the door but when I came in the next morning . . ."

I guess it was the words "next morning" that struck him.

"What do you mean 'the next morning?' "

My belated confession to the full story of being locked out of the office was delayed by Jim's reappearance at the doorway to ask if we needed any more help. I smiled gratefully and handed him the platter of vegetables and asked that he set it on the table but not before looking at Steven and saying, "We can talk about this later."

The meal was an unqualified success from our guests' point of view. They missed out, however, on the urgent whispers delivered with clenched teeth that Steven and I exchanged in the kitchen between courses. With each dirty serving dish I returned to the kitchen, Steven dug further into my machinations, extracting from me the unabridged version of my overnight stay on the ledge, while I tried to change the subject by delving deeper into why he was so sure that the baby was going to be a Goldman. Steven was getting somewhat redder by the moment but the Chianti masked the truth behind his glower. We reverted to charm and idle chatter with our guests. We talked of the usual frustrations with London, the Tube, the weather, but in the kitchen turned on each other. By the time we'd started making coffee for dessert, I'd provided full details on every questionable event in the office, including what I thought really happened to the pregnancy pillow, which prompted a change in battle positions. Questions like "What does my mother have to do with the baby's last name?" were answered with "I never liked that pillow anyway."

"Why?"

"It was an appliance."

"It was not an appliance. Appliances have motors. It was not an appliance."

"A precursor to an appliance, then. It felt like an appliance. Let's just forget about it."

"You brought it up."

"No. You brought it up. 'Amy thinks someone killed him,' " I said mockingly. "Well, it's true. I do." We'd come full circle. "Steven, forget about the ledge and the pillow and the shelves for the moment."

"I'm sorry that I brought up the subject at dinner. But I'm glad I did. At least now I'm hearing what's really been going on while I've been out of town. I don't care about the pillow. All I care about is you. You could have injured yourself and the baby."

"But I didn't. I'm fine. Just listen for a minute. I don't think any of these things would have happened if that note hadn't been planted deliberately. I think Daniel Blake was killed and that someone knows that I know that."

"Amy. Now you are really talking nonsense. Even the police. . . ."

"They're doing nothing. In his own indecipherable way, Blake wrote everything down in his diary. I think someone wants that diary and has been looking for it in the box, in my office, in Gideon's office, in the archives. It all makes sense. David Knight says Blake was going to retire, but he had his calendar made out through the end of the year. It's all there. Look, I'll show you. Where's my briefcase?" I looked around the kitchen but didn't see it.

"I put it at the end of the hall," Steven said over his shoulder as he placed cups and saucers on a serving tray. "Amy, we can't just ignore our guests. I'm going to serve this coffee and dessert and then we're going to sit down and discuss this."

"I'll be right back." I walked past the dining table to retrieve my briefcase. Eager to show Steven that I had evidence, somewhere in the diary, I emptied the contents of my briefcase on the counter. Turning the pages of the diary to the months after Blake's death, I accidentally tipped open the Darlington box. I dropped my hands and let the diary close as I hesitated, staring at the scattered chocolates. Hadn't there been more than half a box returned in the evidence bag? The pieces on the counter didn't amount to much. My fingers tapped, counting each piece, as I tried to remember just how many there had been. I had eaten two. Blake had eaten at least the one, I thought grimly. I read the Darlington label, looking for a number to counter the fear that some were missing, but all it had was a measure in kilograms. I couldn't convert metric measures without a cookbook and even then I always got it wrong. Was my brain really shrinking with pregnancy, as recent so-called experts claimed? The part that allowed me to visualize a box of candy seemed to have deteriorated first. And when I heard Karen Sandler call out from the dining room, I stopped counting. And breathing.

"Amy, where are you? Come join us for coffee and chocolates."

I bit back a wave of nausea, and closed my eyes, wishing that I'd stayed in Hampstead. Would our guests laugh if they knew they might be munching on a murder weapon while sipping from their tiny cups of espresso? I was only an amateur at this sleuthing business but even I knew that biting into evidence was a major no-no. "This is gross. Gross, gross, gross," I whispered to myself and then shouted back, "I'm coming." In my husband's last misguided attempt to play host, he'd served a 1985 Chateau Margaux in paper cups at a Fourth of July party after the beer had run out. It was just like him to have seen the Darlington box in my briefcase and to have assumed that I had bought it to serve as dessert. I vowed never to express breast milk. He'd be sure to serve it as coffee creamer.

"Are you coming out or are you going to stay in the kitchen the rest of the evening?" Steven spoke loudly for our guests to hear and jerked his head in their direction. "What are you doing?" he whispered.

"Steven. They're eating the chocolates," I whispered back.

"I know. I'm sorry."

"But . . ."

"I know. Look, I said I was sorry. Come on, they don't seem to mind."

"I'm not worried about them minding, but . . ."

He grabbed my arm and led me into the living room with our guests. "Here she is. Amy's annoyed. It wasn't enough that I cooked dinner. I've failed my domestic duties because I didn't fix dessert, too."

"Amy, who needs a big dessert? This is just right." Jim licked the tips of his fingers. I mentally weighed my choices in a social dilemma that I doubted Martha Stewart had ever faced. Should I rudely snatch pieces from astonished guests or play the greedy host and pretend to grab them all for myself?

"Don't give him grief, Amy. At least he *bought* dessert. That's more than Jim ever does."

Steven handed me a plate and said, "For you. Your favorite. Champagne truffles. Hand dipped. I bought them in Paris." He smiled the smile that made me fall in love with him and said quietly, "A little better than an appliance, don't you think? I hope you don't mind sharing," and then to our guests said, "You didn't think I was working the whole weekend did you?"

I exhaled and reached for a piece of candy.

CHAPTER 24

"Are you sure you want to give these to me?"

After a fitful night's sleep during which I had worried about the possible disappearance of some of the candy and mentally retraced every moment my briefcase had been unattended over the last few days, I'd arrived at Polly's office just as she had been unlocking the door. I'd been invited in for a cup of coffee but it was turning out to be an adult education course on the brew. I'd seen an espresso machine in her office on my first visit but had assumed it was in the same category as the vacuum cleaner: part of the household armory. She lectured on beans, roasting methods, proper storage, water temperature and muttered to herself about Italians while she twisted knobs and turned levers. I was about to agree with her final pronouncement, "This machine is a product liability suit waiting to happen but it makes a great cup of coffee," when she'd questioned whether I wanted to hand the candy over to her.

"Yes, I'm sure." I laid the box on the desk. Even if I hadn't imagined the reduction in the number of chocolates, I still thought the truth about Blake's death could be found in them. Or in his diary. Or the candy and the diary. Who was I fooling? I didn't know who or what or whether Darlington's connivance would lead me to the truth. But giving the candy to Polly meant the candy would be safer than it had been with me.

She moved the box aside and then frowned when I handed her my copy of Josh Hall's memo. "What's this?"

"I thought you'd find it useful. It fills in some of the gaps in my information."

"Amy, I'm not sure about this."

"It was in the trash."

"Don't you have a bin and shred policy at your firm?"

"Let's just say it fell through the cracks."

"Amy."

I wanted to scream, Polly, can't you stop being pedantic for one minute? Instead I pleaded, "You're my lawyer, I'm giving it to you to hold on for me."

Polly didn't stir.

"I'll take one hundred percent responsibility. Please just read it."

Polly took a few minutes to read the memo while I sipped my coffee. A few minutes later she said, "All right. I've read it. And I'll keep it. But against my better judgment. Now, since you're here, let me tell you about my research and the conference." She pulled out a note pad from a giant plastic folder with the word "MENSA" plastered all over it. "I've made a few calls. I spoke to my usual contacts in enforcement and the press about Darlington. They were all generally complimentary about the company. By the way, the name is misleading. The company isn't actually in Darlington but in some industrial estate outside of Manchester."

"Okay."

"Darlington used to be a family-run business and it still has a great reputation, good labor-management relations. It's known as a contributor to the local community.

Nothing that helpful either way there. Then I did a quick computer search, looking for lawsuits, complaints, health scares, that kind of thing . . ."

"Any reported cases of fatal allergic reactions to Darlington chocolates?"

"No. Not from this research. But I didn't expect to find any. And this," she pointed to the memo and said, "confirms my reasoning. James Blake agreed not to disclose the name of the company in connection with his father's death."

"Yes. That's right."

"I'm sure Darlington would have made any other family experiencing a similar loss sign a similar agreement."

"You're right. What about other problems?"

"My research turned up zilch. But I did meet some Darlington people at the cocoa conference." She tossed me a business card the color of dark chocolate with white embossed lettering and the capital "D" I'd come to recognize. The name on the card read, "Philip Fletcher, Director, Public Relations."

"Smell it."

"What?"

"Go ahead, smell it."

I held the card to my nose and breathed in a mixture of Nestlé's Qwik and printer's ink.

"Scented business cards." Polly smiled as she spoke. "They need some fine-tuning but these guys take their business very seriously. They were making them up at one of the trade booths. Neat, huh?"

"Yeah, neat." Not that I'd take someone very seriously who'd hand out perfumed business cards. The comics responsible for lawyer jokes would have a field day.

"I had a very interesting conversation with this man, Mr.

Fletcher. A nice guy, not too bright, typical P.R., loved the sound of his own voice. I saw his name on the list of attendees and once I saw the Darlington group, I followed him until I could get close enough to read his nametag in the hospitality lounge. Don't worry, I wasn't conspicuous."

Polly, the social outcast, limping, toting a MENSA bag, and stalking her prey into a bar. And I had thought pregnancy would pose a surveillance problem.

"I told him I was a lawyer specializing in food matters and that I was considering writing an article about the industry—using his company as a model—lots of free publicity—he ate this up. Of course, once he runs the idea by company management and his legal department, he'll change his mind. I explained to him that before I went any further into my research, I wanted to get some information from the company, an insider's view, if you will, of the company and its overseas operations, if any.

"He said he'd send me the company's annual report. I didn't tell him this, but I'd already downloaded that and other information from one of the on-line services. Those showed the Manchester plant and a U.S. plant, but I wanted to get a better feel of the operations from a living person. Mr. Fletcher, after several chocolate Russians—I'm a Scotch drinker myself, can't understand how anyone can confuse dessert with a good stiff drink. . . ."

"Polly?"

". . . He was happy to oblige. The company has only one overseas concern, a manufacturing operation on the East Coast of the U.S.—Paramus, New Jersey. The New Jersey plant supplies all of the U.S. outlets and it's fully operational. No new information there.

"I wanted to draw him out on the vegetable fat derogation, so I asked him whether any of the candy manufactured in the U.K. was ever sold in the American markets or vice versa—there's no way chocolate with vegetable fat would sell in the U.S. market—and he said certainly not. He said it didn't make sense to manufacture a delicate consumer luxury product and then ship it overseas when the U.S. operations could furnish all the company's American needs."

"I wrote all this down later," and she referred to her notes. "He said, and I quote—'Our handmade truffles would never survive the trip unless, of course,'—he got a huge laugh from this—'they flew there.' Then his public relations ego and the alcohol took over.

"He told me how he, or Darlington, that is, had just landed a contract with a major carrier to be its official candy. According to Mr. Fletcher, first-class passengers will be eating Darlington candy with their champagne and caviar, soon, if not already. The company already has a long-standing relationship with Royal Crest Hotels. He went on about how Darlington's New Jersey operations also supply Royal Crest—you know, the U.S. hotel chain with the crown logo."

I had a vague recollection of a commercial with a man with a heavy Brooklyn accent and a crown on his head pretending to be a part of the royal family.

"That little box of chocolates that the maid puts on your pillow at night is none other than Darlington's and, if Fletcher has his way, Darlington's will be on every pillow on every bed."

"Right."

"Fletcher explained that this new venture and the Royal Crest relationship were all part of his plan to modernize Darlington's reputation—to be, and again I quote, 'the chocolate of your dreams.' You should have heard him. Dreaming in bed was definitely not what he had in mind for anyone lucky enough to eat Darlington chocolates. Unless it was a wet dream. Talk about believing your own ad campaign. Advertisers have a lot to answer for. . . ."

I didn't want to hear how advertisers were as stupid as consumers. Did this woman not like anyone? "Polly. What about the theory that Darlington's warning about the nuts is just a sham, the—what did you call it—'lip service' scenario?"

"Well, I'm still working on that. I didn't want to come right out and say the 'n' word."

"Nuts?"

"Right, and by the time Fletcher was finished going on about his P.R. coup, he was incoherent. We exchanged business cards and I promised to call him later this week to follow-up on my research. I'll call him after I've made some other inquiries. And it'll be a few days before we get the lab results."

"Okay. Thanks Polly." I wasn't sure how any of what she'd just described was going to help me find Blake's killer but it was more progress than I'd made on the seamier side of the case. "For all you've done so far, and the coffee . . ."

"Want another cup?"

"No, I should be going." But I felt heavy and glued to my chair, not eager to leave her office for the possible dangers that might await me in my own.

"You look like you could use it. Although studies about caffeine in pregnant woman suggest . . ."

"I know." I didn't want a mini course on caffeine again. "I don't think one more cup will hurt me." She handed me another steaming cup. "This is delicious."

We sat in silence for a moment and then Polly said, "I've heard all the stories about Daniel Blake. He sounded like an ogre."

"I know."

"I've got to ask. Why are you doing this, going to all this trouble? You could lose your job for giving this memo to me. Why?"

Steven had asked the very same question last night. Our guests had departed soon after I'd stopped stifling my persistent yawns. Happy that the missing chocolates had not turned out to be dessert, I turned my mind back to remembering just how many pieces should have been in the Darlington box. The theft from Josh's car, the rolling archive shelves, the fax to Blake, even my night on the ledge. Were they all flights of my imagination, as Steven suggested? Or had they been attempts, not to retrieve Blake's diary, but to get at the candy? I had just about convinced myself that I was a victim of my hormones and that Steven had dropped the questions, thankful not to repeat the litany of events that made me believe that someone had killed Blake, when Steven had set aside his nighttime reading. Conscientious consumer, the exception to Polly's rules, he'd taken to reading every book ever published on babies and I didn't have the heart to tell him that they weren't likely to come with international warranties. He'd taken my hand and said with concern in his voice, "Amy. What's really going on here? Why are you torturing yourself with all these thoughts of murder?"

"Because there has been a murder, that's what I've been trying to tell you."

"I know, I know. But let me tell you what I think is really going on. Why you're so convinced that he was killed. I think you're letting pregnancy . . ."

"Not that again."

"No, let me finish, pregnancy and well, grief, get in the way of rational thought. You don't want to admit it, but I know you. Deep in your heart, you cared for that old man. If he hadn't died, you'd still be working for him, and complaining."

"But I'd resigned."

"Only after working for him, not just once, but twice. If you didn't feel something for him, then tell me, why did you stay?"

I had looked away from Steven. Why had I stayed? The only useful purpose I had served at DW3 had been to keep Mr. Blake in line and out of everyone else's hair. That was no reason to stay. I could have said that I saw a glimmer of charm or good intentions behind his maliciousness but that would have been lying.

There had been reasons for staying that even I had hated to admit to myself, let alone to Steven. A small part of me had admired and envied Daniel Blake. Although his behavior could be a disgrace, it had achieved results. He was rewarded for being bad. His success was proof that all those years of being told to "Act nice," "Be polite," "Be a good girl," "Say thank you," lessons that I still followed, might have been good training for a mother from a '50s sitcom— June Cleaver came to mind—but the Eddie Haskells were now taking over the world.

But there had been other more complicated reasons for staying that had only surfaced with his heart attack a few years ago. Not eager to admit to Steven that he was right, I had grown fond of the old guy. He had insinuated himself into my life. Like the bad weather in London. Everyone complained about dull and rainy skies, but the entire population didn't pack its bags and move to sunny Ibiza. And, to be fair, some of his most annoying habits had become almost tolerable as he got older. Over the last couple of years, he had been transformed into a grumpy old man. Curmudgeon had started to replace cruel.

And buried there in the recesses of my brain was the real unspeakable reason I had stayed. He had needed me and I had needed to feel needed. We had developed a kind of symbiotic relationship. He had played his part of cranky senior partner and I had responded as expected—cajoling him one minute, praising him the next. Our roles had worked so well that, at times, I had wondered who was writing the script. Back in America, there would have been some kind of support group for our pattern of behavior.

"I stayed for the obvious reasons," I had said instead. "The money. The opportunity to learn at the feet of a legal master," I had said sarcastically, "You know me. Inertia."

"Keep telling yourself that, Amy. But this is your husband you're talking to, not some Winter, Worthington attorney."

When I hadn't responded, Steven had said, "You only have a few more weeks until maternity leave. Promise me that you'll forget all of this nonsense about murder and concentrate on our baby. Can you promise me that?"

"Sure." Not for the first time had I told my husband what he wanted to hear.

"You've got to be more careful in the office with your condition. No more visits to the archives. No more overnight stays on ledges. And no more dinner dates in dodgy areas with young single men from the office. Promise?"

I had promised.

"And even if, by some stretch of the imagination, someone did intend to harm Daniel Blake, you'll let the police do their jobs. They're the experts, right?"

I had nodded and closed my eyes hoping for sleep.

"Amy?"

"I'm sorry. I drifted. I seem to be doing a lot of that lately. You asked 'why.' There are a lot of reasons. I guess one of them is guilt."

"Guilt?"

"Yes. I feel guilty. Don't you ever feel guilty?"

"Guilty? Guilty of what?"

"Guilty about anything, or everything. You know how there are some people who admit to crimes they haven't committed? It seems crazy, but I understand. I'd do the same thing. Confess, I mean. If the police arrested me, then I have to be guilty of something." I looked at her but her face was blank. "I'm not making much sense, am I?"

"Not really."

"Let me give you an example. When I walk through the green line, the 'nothing to declare' line in the customs area at Heathrow Airport, it's like an invitation. To declare. I go through the line and 'guilt' screams from every pore. It's not enough that my conscience works overtime—my whole body gets in on the act. My eyes shift, my palms sweat, my pulse throbs. . . ."

"Uh-huh."

". . . and I become this heaving, breathing neon sign of guilt."

Polly stared at me, dumbfounded.

"I guess there are the Daniel Blakes of the world. He could commit the worst transgression and walk away without feeling even the slightest remorse. And then there are the normal people. Normal guilt. And then there's me. The smallest oversight causes the greatest feelings of guilt. 'Guilt' is my middle name."

"But what do you have to feel guilty about?"

"I'm not . . ."

Polly, a quick study on emotions as well as electrical appliances, interrupted. "I get it. You're feeling guilty because you thought badly of him while he was alive and now you're compensating for it by overreacting to his death. Classic Freudian or was it Jungian, no, it'll come to me . . ."

I nodded, pretending to agree. Polly could believe whatever she wanted. Clients didn't have to explain their motives to their lawyer—all they had to do was pay the bills. I may have been willing, like Steven suggested, to admit to mourning a loss that no one else shared. All my years of working together with Blake should have meant something. But, as I tried in vain to explain to Polly and had avoided telling Steven, grief wasn't the only reason I was hiring her or spying on my colleagues. D.C. Lawson had attributed Mr. Blake's death to bad luck. Because of my uncontrollable hunger that afternoon in his office, I'd eaten two pieces of candy that I distinctly remembered did not have nuts and, without knowing it, had increased the odds against him. I had then removed the only shred of evidence that pointed to murder. Unless I wanted to feel guilty for the rest of my life, I had to find who or what was responsible for Blake's death. I needed to find someone else to shoulder the blame.

CHAPTER 25

A week had passed since I'd struggled with the question "Why" over coffee with Polly. A week, seven days, fifty-six non-billable hours of reading other people's mail, prying in their empty offices, comparing the entries in Blake's diary with his client files—I only had two more months to go— waiting for Polly to come up with something on Darlington, avoiding unpleasant encounters with office equipment and Helen, gaining more weight, pumping Lucy for office gossip, and listening in on voice mail while juggling the demands of Teddy's and Walter's clients.

"I'm calling for David Knight. Mr. Knight, it's Francois from Le Printemps. I'm just calling to confirm your reservation for dinner for two on the 15th at 9:00. Your usual table. That's Wednesday. We look forward to seeing you. À bientot."

"Theodore. It's Helen. The caterers will need access to the kitchen and the garden pavilion for the party by 4:00 on Thursday. Have I thanked you enough for agreeing to have the party at your place?"

"Walter. Chewy. Let's make sure we talk before this goes any further. I'm tied up with appointments all week.

We can talk at this bash on Thursday. If not, it will have to wait until the next session. Give my best to Barbara and the children."

"This is a message for Kimberly Sullivan. Allen Williams here from Williams Estates. I recognize the number. It's a pleasure to be working with another lawyer from Winter, Worthington. We don't normally show properties on the weekend but I'm sure in your case we can make an exception. Would next Saturday be convenient for you?"

"This is a message for Gideon Chapman from Liz Headley. Mr. Worthington will be in London the day before and the day after the anniversary party. Can you please keep your calendar free? One of us here will be in touch."

My co-workers were too busy with their social calendars to commit a crime. For them, the operative question wasn't "why" but "when." But, at last, the answer to "who" was emerging.

"Josh. David. I just got off the phone with Hausmann. When's a good time to meet with him? Let my secretary know. And what's the status of the current draft? Let me know. Worthington will be here soon and he'll need an update."

"Polly?"

"Amy? Is that you? I was just getting ready to call you again. Why are you whispering?"

"I'm at the office. I don't want anyone to hear me."

"Well, I can barely hear you. Can't you speak up? Or just close the door?"

"My door is closed. Look, I need that memo I gave you. I don't mean that I need it back, I need you to look at it for me. In the section on Practical Consequences, toward the end, there's a handwritten note about Blake's finances."

"Hold on." I could hear papers rustling and file drawers being pulled open before she finally said, "I've got it. 'Practical Consequences.' God, remind me not to die at your office. Talk about bloodless."

"Can you read it out to me?"

Polly read over the phone, " 'We understand that under the relevant laws of intestacy his only descendant is his son, James. Blake left a considerable estate, with assets, in the range of'—that's left blank."

"Go on."

"Okay." She continued reading, " 'James is currently in negotiations with the Internal Revenue Service and the Inland Revenue.' Then in the margin next to that section, there's a handwritten note. Shall I read it, too?"

"Yes."

" 'DK—What number goes here? Should we expand on other financial arrangements? Should I mention offshore accounts? JH Josh—No, leave it to me. I've already been in touch with Hausmann. DK.' That's all there is."

"Yes, that's it. That's all I need to hear. Thanks Polly."

"But don't you want to hear about the chocolates?"

"Not right now. I'll call you back."

Minutes later, I glanced furtively around the fax room where I'd hid the Sunday someone had taken the fax from Securex bank addressed to the late Daniel Blake. I scribbled a note to myself on a piece of paper. The incoming fax machine swallowed it up while I punched in the telephone number from David Knight's voice mail in his first message from Mr. Hausmann, the same number that I had called unsuccessfully the Saturday I'd nearly been shelved and that I had assumed was Knight's personal machine. I pressed the send button and made a 180-degree turn to wait for the outgoing fax machine to receive it. I had already searched for a number on the inviolate outgoing machine but Helen had been thorough in removing all identifying numbers. David's access to the restricted machine must have been a managing partner's perk. In seconds, the machines were talking to one another and the outgoing machine spat out my handwriting. It had traveled across several miles of phone lines just to make the short distance across the room.

I'd found a connection between Knight and Hausmann and Blake. Back in my office, I was going through Mr. Blake's diary for some connection between the bank, Securex, and Hausmann and Blake. If Blake had been required to remember any account numbers more difficult than the simple sequence required to enter the office, he'd have to have written them down somewhere. The last page of his diary looked like a page from an illegal gambling operation.

"Amy, good, you're here."

"Ted. Hi."

"What's happening with Declan?"

I summarized my calls and the recent exchange of faxes while I mentally wondered how many Hausmanns might work in a Swiss bank.

"Wonderful. Real progress. That's what I like to hear. I knew I could count on you." He looked at his watch. "I have a conference call in about fifteen minutes that I've got to prepare for but, before I forget, how's the new secretary working out?"

"Teddy. I'm sorry. I never thanked you for stepping in and arranging that for me. It's been great, she's super. Nikki . . ."

"Is that her name?"

"Yes, can you believe it? Of all the names . . ."

He shook his head. "Old man Blake would probably be laughing right now."

"I doubt it. Anyhow, she's wonderful. I don't know what strings you had to pull. . . ."

"Louise took care of the logistics. I just had to make a couple of phone calls."

"Well, I am forever in your debt. Helen's not too pleased but . . ."

"About that . . ." Teddy looked at me sheepishly. "Promise you won't get mad?"

"Oh, no, what about Helen?"

"Well, I had to do a little horse trading to placate her. I'm really sorry but to keep the peace . . ." He looked around my office and my eyes followed his. Oak bookcases, an upholstered settee that sat perfectly under the windows, color coordinated silk rugs, and tasteful artwork accumulated from years in Asia. I had one of the grander offices—whether I deserved it based on seniority or servility was unclear. No one else had ever wanted to be as close to Blake as I had been. Was H.M.S. declaring eminent domain now that he was dead? I dreaded the answer to my question and I asked, "Not my office?"

"Oh, no, it's not as bad as all that. I thought you'd figured it out already." He pointed to Blake's diary on my desk and I blushed when I realized I'd left it open on my desk. "I promised her that you'd do the old man's timesheets."

As a young law school graduate, I had naively thought that I had broken the chain of my family's blue collar past. I didn't punch a time clock but I only had to be in a law office one day to understand the importance and value of time. Every minute, every hour of every day was potentially a billable moment that could be translated directly into fees. The parchment, printouts, and prose were just props for what had remained unchanged since before Mary Magdalene. Just like the prostitutes in Shepherd Market, lawyers charged for their time. In their inimitable way of plain speaking, the English had got it right. We weren't lawyers, we were solicitors.

And, like the working girls, "enjoyment" was the last word I'd ever use to describe my relationship with the billing tools of the trade—timesheets, billable hours, or anything having to do with my nemesis—not Helen, but numbers. The reason I'd gone to law school.

Unlike my fellow law school classmates, I didn't faint at the sight of blood. And let's face it, that fear of blood was what brought all of my classmates to their destiny—but for that minor failing, wouldn't we have become the doctors our mothers had wanted us to be? I could easily have seen myself wielding a scalpel and a driving iron. No, my medical career was shelved and my legal career blossomed for an entirely different reason. Numbers. I am innumerate, a problem that kept me out of calculus class and medical school. I can't balance a checkbook or calculate a tip. I over-tip or, worse still, under-tip because I can't do percentages in my head. I nearly failed Tax class in law school since it had involved adding and subtracting (or was it deducting?). I've never completed a tax return. For what other reason had God created accountants?

And there was something else about numbers that made the law the right choice for me. The simple problem of reaching the right answer—the one and only right answer. With numbers, you're either in or out of the game. No gray zone where words can be massaged so that no one can really tell if you know the answer or not. No nuances, no qualifications, just the right answer in black and white. No arguing both sides of an issue. Who had ever heard a mathematical theory include the words, "on the other hand?"

An inability to perform simple division without a calculator and a dislike for being limited to one correct response. Who else but me would be responsible for preparing Daniel Blake's timesheets?

And no one had understood the value of time better than Daniel Blake. Always a conscientious worker, he had toiled his requisite eight hours, and to the detriment of family—he had no friends—usually more. It was just that he had kept most of what passed for billable time entries in his head. He'd take little notes in his diary to remind himself to bill a part of his day to some client. He'd look over the scraps of paper he'd clipped to his calendar and muse over them. He'd drive Tony and Lucy crazy by forcing them to recreate month-old telephone records. He'd have a Nikki plow through client files to reconstruct a day. But eventually he'd come to rely on me to fill in the blanks, sort out his timesheets and finalize his bills.

And Blake's bills were far from ordinary. There may have been a time when billing had involved the briefest descriptions followed by a dollar figure that usually but not always reflected some basis in reality—the number of hours worked multiplied by the attorney's billing rate with the usual rounding off to a nice even number, preferably with lots of zeros at the end. But "brief" descriptions had gone the way of the dodo bird and they'd been replaced with computer-generated descriptions of our activities calculated on a quarter hour basis that ran for pages and pages showing each participating attorney's time and how he spent it. The simple matter of calling a client to discuss a project manifested itself into multiple lines on a computer printout that identified to the learned observer not just by whom and to whom a call had been made but when, where and why. Aside from the possibility of fabrication—which occasionally did happen—there were no longer any secrets about the practice of law—any mystery had been coded, computed and spat out.

And so, using computerized printouts that summarized our time, I would draft, in meticulous detail, narrative descriptions on heavy parchment that were intended to explain or obfuscate, depending upon the point of view, in laymen's terms, the wonders of Blake's advice and counsel. Where once the four little words "For Professional Services Rendered" would have sufficed, a lengthy tale as much fantasy as fact took its place. And I frequently spent so much time and effort crafting these masterpieces to Mr. Blake's specifications that it had become the absurd practice for me to bill his clients for time spent billing his clients.

It was one thing to pore through Blake's diary on a secret mission of my own making. It was another thing entirely to have to decipher his chicken scratches one last time for the pleasure of Helen Matthews-Smith. I had been spared the onerous task of preparing his final bills—they would require a partner with the authority to sign them and the skills of a diplomat to explain why they were being sent post-mortem—but I had not been spared the gloating. I was just filling in the last day, happy to finally be able to return to my search for Mr. Hausmann, when a familiar scent wafted into my office.

"Good. I see Theodore's spoken to you. Will you be done soon?" Helen folded her arms and waited for an answer.

"If I'm not doing this fast enough to suit you, I'm quite happy to let someone else do it." I was finished but I didn't want to give Helen the satisfaction of an immediate answer.

"Maybe you can get your new secretary, Nicola," she spat out the name, "to help you."

"Did someone say my name?"

"Nikki, good, there you are. Just the person I'm looking for. As I was saying to Helen, Nikki, my new secretary, has been a lifesaver. What's up?"

"You had a call. Lucy took a message at reception. Polly Lawrence. Do you need the number?"

"Oh, no, I have it. Thanks."

"Polly Lawrence. Isn't she that crippled American woman?"

Always the sensitive administrator. "I think, Helen, the word's disabled. Yes, she limps. Nikki, can you start typing these? Thanks. You'll have your timesheets soon, Helen. Now will there be anything else? If you don't mind, I've got real work to do."

"Mr. Hausmann, please."

"Otto Hausmann?"

"Yes." Otto would do for now. I waited for an extension to ring but my hopes faded when I heard *"Guten dag"* and not the expected "hello." I crossed my fingers and hoped for a multi-lingual miracle. "Do you speak English?"

"Nein." Otto launched into an incomprehensible conversation and I mumbled, "Thanks very much." I set down the receiver and crossed off Otto and tried the next name and number the local branch of Securex had given me. "Yes, I'll hold."

"Amy." The smell and unfortunately the woman attached to it were back.

"I'm on the phone."

Mimicking Daniel Blake, Helen ignored me and waved the papers she was holding under my nose.

"I'm sorry. Something's wrong with our connection." I spoke to a recording of Vivaldi, but I didn't want Helen to think I'd hang up without a fight. "I'm going to hang up and dial again."

Nikki, obviously distressed, came in behind Helen and said, "Amy, I . . . "

I looked at the papers Helen had finally stopped waving. They were the timesheets I'd just handed Nikki.

With a dramatic flourish Daniel Blake would have admired, Helen brandished the pages at me and announced in some personal triumph, "These will have to be redone. You've missed two hours."

CHAPTER 26

There was an official annual billable floor by which young lawyers at DW3 were compensated—a different number was bantered about from time to time. For most of us, the magic number was eight, eight billable hours a day, 240 days a year. Eight was the number the computer recognized. If an attorney did not account for eight hours of every day—even eight hours of vacation time—then the firm's computer spat out the offender's name like a nasty seed. This then brought you to the attention of the dreaded Lawyers Committee. The consequences were not pretty.

To avoid expurgation from the system on those infrequent days when they could not allocate a full eight hours to paying clients, lawyers turned to the magical 600 numbers—the administrative numbers that allowed for creative timekeeping and a full complement of eight hours. Perhaps they did some professional reading—a quarter hour here or there. Perhaps they chatted a little too long at the coffee machine—rack up a half hour to 600. Lawyers may profess to be bad at numbers, but their timesheets, and the mental gymnastics in which they engaged in the effort to reach eight hours, were proof to the contrary.

DW3 Accounting ran on numbers and not names. It had no respect for the dead and would not have hesitated to bounce Mr. Blake's timesheets back for the days for which

PAMELA EDDY

the threshold eight hours had not been met, had Helen not
discovered my miscalculation in time. Even Her Majesty
had to bow to the power of the computer. And because I'd
somehow failed to account for two hours of Blake's time in
the timesheets I'd just completed, I had to bow to the
power of Her Majesty.

I had already spent the previous days laboriously going
back over Mr. Blake's indecipherable diary trying to divine
who had killed him. I had just reluctantly, but I'd thought
finally, prepared his billable hours as a quid pro quo for my
new secretary. Now I had to account for his unproductive
hours and, Mr. Blake, like most lawyers, hadn't left a clear
record of how he'd wasted his time. And I was caught up
short, so to speak, by two hours, when I got to his last day.

Steaming after witnessing Helen's victory dance, I
flipped to the last page of recorded time. Off the top of my
head, I had already allowed for fifteen minutes for conversations that I remembered that Blake had with Helen that
day. I even added some time for my own conversation with
him. "Firing Brown for the 100th and final time" which had
been the description I imagined came the closest to describing our meeting, became "Disc. w/ AB." As much as I
enjoyed manipulating the old man's time to spite Helen, I
found myself sniffling as I typed out the narrative for the
last two accountable hours of what had turned out to be
Mr. Blake's final day.

It was amazing how something as dispassionate as time
entries could evoke such strong emotions. Blake had written
in his usual scrawl "Conf. w/ RTC." That conversation
with Teddy counted towards Declan United's billable hours
but because I knew the personal direction that meeting had
taken—I'd suffered the consequences—I also included it in
Blake's 600 account. Still fifteen minutes short, I decided

224

to resort to my usual method for balancing the non-billable books—I'd just make something up—but I paused when I looked closer at a notation at the bottom of the diary page for Blake's last day. Obscured by a paper clip, the writing had been smeared and was nearly obliterated. I realized that I must have overlooked it in my earlier search. In the tiniest of Number 2 pencil scratchings, Blake seemed to have scribbled what looked like "Meet w/ DK" but I couldn't be sure. Blake had told Helen that he'd wanted to talk to David. Was Blake's notation a reminder or a record of a real conversation? Trying to recall the events of that afternoon, I reluctantly set aside the diary when the phone rang and didn't attempt to hide the impatience in my voice when I answered.

"Amy Brown."

"You said you'd call me back."

"Polly. I'm sorry."

"I just got off the phone with Darlington and I thought you'd want to know."

"I really can't talk right now."

"Why? Do they tap your phones over there at Winter, Worthington or something? I wouldn't doubt it. Have you read that recent decision on the expectation of privacy in an office? Talk about 1984. Maybe we shouldn't be having this discussion."

"No, no, it's okay."

"Good, then shut your door and speak softly. I'll make this quick."

"It's already shut. What is it?"

"It's just a hunch, really. About Darlington. I didn't find any reported safety citations or other problems. Nothing reported or official, at least, but . . . I did a little further digging."

"Uh-huh." Listening with half an ear, I held Blake's diary up to my desk lamp and looked at the letters more closely. Hadn't David said something about skiing?

"The company, the Manchester plant, that is, the entire operation shuts down for a month in the spring after the Easter holiday. The exact dates change every year."

"How very European of them." I turned the page clockwise to see if the letter "D" could be a "P" instead. Blake's hieroglyphics were always difficult to read but rarely was so much riding on the right interpretation. I heard Polly cough and remembered I was supposed to be on the phone. "What does a holiday have to do with nuts in chocolates?"

"I'm getting to that. The company's been shutting down for a month for years, really ever since production started. Except last year. Last year, they shut down for the week *before* Easter. An unexpected extra week of holiday. But my contact said no one was celebrating. The run-up to Easter after Valentine's Day is, as you can imagine, a very hectic time for candy companies and the last thing a small company needs is an unscheduled shut down just before a major holiday."

"Why would they shut down then?"

"During the usual spring closing, the plant undergoes routine maintenance, machine overhauls, technical improvements, that sort of thing. And here's where the 'lip service' scenario comes into the picture. My contact said, and this is unsubstantiated, that there had been some kind of production problem that led to the earlier holiday."

Polly suddenly had my full attention. "And in this case only a few weeks before a box of Darlington chocolates landed on Mr. Blake's desk. What is the shelf life for a box of chocolates?"

"Well, unless an assortment contains fresh cream, longer

than you'd think." Polly waited for me to digest this information and then added, "I decided to test my theory that Darlington had shut down early to clear up a little nut contamination. You remember the Public Relations man I met?"

"With the chocolate-flavored business card?"

"Scented, not flavored. Flavored implies taste and not just aroma. If it had been flavored then technically, under the rules, the card would have qualified as food. Even in England, paper, albeit not nearly as unappetizing as what passes for food, particularly dessert, in this country, is not, well, 'food.' "

"Okay, okay. I remember him. Mr. Fletcher. Did you ask him about the shutdown?"

"Well, I couldn't exactly ask him directly. At the conference he mentioned his campaign to modernize so I went with that. I told him I'd heard the company had recently been upgrading its facilities and that, just last spring, in fact, had installed separate production lines for its various lines of chocolates."

"And what did he say?"

"He suddenly remembered an appointment. With his lawyer, no doubt. The lab reports on the candy samples I bought over the weekend aren't back yet, so we still can't rule out the vegetable fat problem. There's no way for us to prove when the candy he ate on that night was made without more information. It has been months since Daniel Blake died. You may have the box of leftovers but he ate the real evidence. Who knows what the autopsy looked for besides nuts?"

I held the phone in one hand and the diary in another. Uncertain what to do, I asked, "Polly, what do you think?"

"I think the company is hiding something—production

problems, quality control, cross-contamination, something. But I'm not optimistic that we'll find any cracks in the Darlington system on our own. We'd need access to their facilities, their production records and personnel. This is a job for the police and not a couple of lawyers."

It was discouraging to hear a smarty pants admit defeat. Polly seemed satisfied with my assurances that she was right, that investigating Darlington was daunting, and that as soon as we heard from the lab I would go to the police with our findings and suspicions about the company. She was easier than Steven to convince that I would do as I said. But unlike Polly, I needed more than empty assurances to convince me that Darlington and not David Knight had something to hide.

One of the general rules of contract law is that in order to have a binding agreement, there has to be a meeting of the minds. It's one of the first things they teach you in law school. A mutual understanding between the parties. Farmer Jones could hardly be bound to sell his farm in County A to Farmer Smith if Farmer Smith thought he was buying a farm in County B.

Lawyers were notorious for not applying any of the basic rules they learned in law school to themselves. It wasn't as if they were exactly holding themselves above the law. It's just that when two or more lawyers got together, it was a foregone conclusion that there would not be a meeting of the minds. Each would have left a meeting convinced that he knew what had been discussed and what had been agreed. And each, when questioned later, would have his own version of how the minds had met. That version would just be diametrically opposed to all other versions. How many times had Mr. Blake turned to me after a particularly vitriolic exchange and said, "I thought that went well, didn't you?" Had we been in the same meeting?

But I had been in enough meetings with other lawyers to know that this trait was not unique to Daniel Blake. For a partner with his eye on the bottom line, a two-hour meeting might later be described as a half hour conference attended by him only, for an anxious, ambitious senior associate, an hour long strategic counseling session, for the paralegal for whom overtime kicked in at 5:30, a marathon session, and for the junior associate worried about billable hours, the same meeting took on epic proportions.

This egocentric interpretation of events might have been just a necessary part of practice; after all, litigation was a re- sult, and a lucrative one at that, of this failure to reach agreement. The real problem arose when it came time to bill the clients. Then, reconciling the different versions of the same event during billable hours became an art form. When it came time to describing downtime, the time cov- ered by the 600 numbers, the tendency to see the world with a singular view meant that lawyers rarely if ever drafted the fiction that passed for non-billable hours in identical ways. But there was no money to be made in comparing lawyers' non-billable entries. Glaring discrepancies were re- corded but never reconciled.

A few hours after I'd talked to Polly and dispensed with the notion that Darlington was to blame for Blake's death, I'd enlisted the help of a faceless assistant in New York Ac- counting who didn't know that I wasn't entitled to copies of the administrative printouts for all of the lawyers at the London office. I sat reviewing the descriptions that usually went unread and comparing the non-billable time entries, the 600 charges, for Mr. Blake and the other lawyers with whom he'd spent his last day. For the first time, a meeting of the minds was not the goal. I was instead hoping to find an obvious difference in the descriptions of the same events. Like David Knight's description for that day. Eight hours of vacation time. How had he managed to ski in the Swiss Alps and also meet with Mr. Blake in London?

Chapter 27

"Ms. Brown?"

"Yes. This is Amy Brown."

"It's Susannah Jones. I got the message that you called again. I really wish you'd leave me alone. I'm only returning this call because the agency said it sounded important—lost files or something. I don't know why you're calling me again but I really don't want to talk to you, or to anyone from your firm. The police have been back to me about some note and if I'd seen his diary. I'll tell them what I told you. I don't know anything."

"I'm sorry. Please don't hang up." I was surprised to hear the police had contacted her. Who would they contact next? "I just need a quick word." If the police were looking for the diary, then I really didn't have much time. "That afternoon, can you just tell me again who was in Mr. Blake's office, what he did that day?" I had Mr. Blake's diary and a copy of the timesheets I'd prepared for him, now with the missing two hours, in front of me. I intended to go through every entry if necessary with her.

She inhaled a cigarette loudly in my ear. "I don't have much time. I told the office I'm on a cigarette break and I have to get back in just a few minutes."

"It's important."

"He knew that I was finishing up my assignment and he

made me stay to the bitter end." This was said with a choked laugh. "Let me think. Like I told you before, H.M.S.—she and Mr. Blake were going around and around about something."

I checked off the entry with the discussion with H.M.S. It wasn't in Mr. Blake's diary, but I had heard practically every word and I had added them to his time entries myself.

"And Walter Hughes and one of those clerks who works for him, they were hanging around, although I don't think Blake took the time to talk to them."

I checked the diary and the timesheets. There was no entry for Walter Hughes. Mr. Blake wouldn't have known the names of Walter's assistants, so I made a note on another sheet of paper, "Hughes," with a big question mark.

The voice on the other end of the line lost some of its belligerence and she ticked off the events of Blake's last day almost as if rehearsed. "Mr. Cunningham—he's the tall, handsome one, right?"

"Yes. Ted."

"He came by."

I checked the diary and my timesheet reference to Ted Cunningham.

"And, of course, you were in there."

I remembered too well. That conversation, in sanitized form, had been recorded. "Was there anyone else?"

She paused and drew on her cigarette. "I don't think so. It was a very busy day. I'd wanted to finish up with the active matters since I knew I wasn't coming in on Monday. Plus H.M.S. had left me a pile of things to work on, all related to the lawyers' party. It was unfair to leave a new temp in the dark and I knew H.M.S. would just dump the new person there without any instructions."

"And can you remember what else he did that day?

What about that morning?"

The irritation returned in an instant. "Do you really need to go over this again?"

"I'm sorry. I'm almost done. Forget about that day. What did you do for him on other days?"

"You mean like his morning routine?"

"Yes, like that."

She seemed to relax. "I'd come in. Bring him a cup of coffee, that decaffeinated stuff. Then I'd get settled, have my tea, then I'd check his e-mail—those came through on my computer, since he didn't have one—and voice mails."

Her voice grew almost wistful as she moved from the memory of the morning routine to the day. "He spent most of the morning on the phone. I put through several calls for him. He talked to Mr. Tong a couple of times. A Hong Kong operator connected one of the calls."

I recognized the name of a client from Hong Kong.

"Oh, yeah, I remember, he talked to some American man, Mr. Seals, something about a South American deal, a restaurant or something."

"I think he called for you. He must have wanted to speak to Mr. Blake." I made a note to ask Nikki for Mr. Seals' telephone number if he called again.

"And James Blake called. I didn't know he had a son. Anyhow, Mr. Blake got off the phone real quick when I passed him a note that he was holding on the other line."

"Was there anything else?"

"That's all I remember. Look, I've told you all I know. Now leave me alone. I've got to go or I'm going to lose this job."

The only remaining entry in Mr. Blake's diary and the timesheets that I hadn't checked off—"Meet w/ DK" was still there when the line went dead. If I was going to find out whether David Knight and Mr. Blake had been together that Friday, I was going to have to speak to the dead. Or something close to it.

"Steven? It's Amy."

"I know who it is."

"I need to check my telephone. Can you call me and leave a message on my voice mail?"

"Amy, what are you up to?"

"Can't you just do it? Tony promised to fix it but it's been ages and it's still not working."

"All right. But if this is some funny business . . ."

I hung up before he could finish the sentence. I let the telephone ring a few minutes without answering until the message light lit up. In my best Daniel Blake-like fashion, I yanked the cord from the wall. I then crawled on my hands and knees in a bad imitation of a python that had swallowed a small animal and plugged it back in. As I expected, the flashing red light did not reappear but Steven's voice on the recorded message came through loud and clear.

> "Welcome to the Winter, Worthington & Walker voice mail system. The party you are calling—Daniel Blake—is not available. Please leave a message after the tone or press the star key for more options."

I pressed the star key and Mr. Blake's extension. Just as the temporary secretary replacing Susannah would have done on the Monday morning following Susannah's departure, had Mr. Blake been alive on Monday. Or as the police might have done at his death, had Mr. Blake not unplugged the phone and turned the red flashing message light off. Or as any other occupants might have done, had they not all been dissuaded by Mr. Blake's fate, and Kimberly's claim, from taking over his office.

"Hello, Daniel Blake. You have four old messages."

"Daniel. I know you're there. Do you know how infuriating it is when you don't answer your phone? We need to speak and it's got to be today. If you don't call me back, I'm coming down again."

H.M.S. didn't need to identify herself.

"This is a message for Mr. Blake. I don't know if he checks his own messages. In any event, I'm calling for Walter Hughes. We'd, or actually he'd, like a meeting with you this afternoon if at all possible. Please call when it's convenient. Extension 695."

Susannah had remembered seeing Walter Hughes hovering. I checked off his name and erased the question mark I had written in my notes earlier.

"Mr. Blake. This is Kimberly Sullivan calling. I just got off the phone with New York about the partnership interview process and I understand that I need to speak to all of the partners during the next few months. I am in the office all next week. Could you please have your secretary call mine to set up a mutually convenient time? Thank you."

Kimberly was already sounding partner-like.

"Dan. David Knight. I got your message, at least I

235

think this message is from you, that you wanted to talk.
I'll be in the office on Friday evening. A friend is picking
me up at the airport. Depending on the traffic, I'll be there
no later than seven."

Unlike David Knight's non-billable hours, voice mail
didn't lie.

I hung up the phone and stared at the bald patches on
Blake's wall. Shaken by the voices on the phone, I sat im-
mobile, lamenting that I hadn't prepared Blake's timesheets
when Helen had first asked.

"Amy. What are you doing in here?"

"Josh. Hi. Just thinking."

"This is a great office, isn't it? Are you thinking of
moving? This furniture has got to go, but. . . . Hey, did you
hear? Tony's finally got voice mail working again. The
cleaners have been unplugging the cord when they vacuum.
Our message lights should be flashing and all systems back
to normal in no time."

At any earlier time I would have panicked at Josh's news
that Tony had solved our phone problems but the information didn't faze me. I didn't need to continue listening in on
calls. All I really needed was an opportunity to confront
David Knight and Kimberly. Preferably in a public place.
With plenty of witnesses. Dinner at Le Printemps around
9:00 tonight seemed just right.

CHAPTER 28

"This is the place. You can let me out at the corner." The taxi pulled to the right, several doors down from the number for Le Printemps.

"That'll be five pounds, love."

While I counted out five pound coins with my trembling hands, the cabby chatted. "I hear that place," he motioned behind us, "has good grub. Too rich for my blood."

I smiled. I kept my reply simple. "Mine too." The cabby wouldn't believe that I wasn't going there to eat even though I'd worked up quite an appetite since my conversation with Josh in Blake's former office. I'd spent the rest of the afternoon filling in the blanks to David Knight's day on the Friday he'd claimed to be on vacation.

After some prompting—had she seen Kimberly leave with David Knight that week? how did she know that *Dorthea* and David and not *Kimberly* and David had been in Switzerland together?—Lucy had checked her records to see where David Knight and Kimberly had been the week that Blake had died. Lucy had confirmed that Kimberly hadn't been to Switzerland but she had been to a part of France that was less than an hour's drive from where the Knights had stayed. The *frisson* of excitement created by Lucy's discovery meant that other details of David Knight's travel plans were revealed. Lucy had arranged for a car to pick David up that Saturday morning at the airport but the driver from the car service had noted that there had been only one and not two passengers: since both of the Knights' tickets had been issued to "D. Knight," either one of David or Dorthea could claim to have made the earlier trip, if questioned later. Kimberly had returned on Thursday evening, giving her ample time to meet David at the airport on Friday.

Lucy had also booked the hotel for the Knights but, as I discovered when I phoned from the privacy of my office, its staff was far more discreet than Lucy. Even with my authentic American accent and my not so authentic cough, I had been unable to convince the hotel manager to take my call. His assistant had insisted that Mrs. Knight put her request for copies of her and her husband's itemized tariff for their stay in writing.

But I'd had better luck finding Mr. Hausmann. It had taken me a dozen phone calls but I finally found the right number for him and for the bank account from the back of Blake's diary and I'd convinced Mr. Hausmann to provide the details of the Securex account. As I had suspected, there was an empty balance.

Daniel Blake would have been as susceptible as the next man to the lovely Kimberly, particularly if she had come to his office on Thursday night bearing a box of candy. With Kimberly as accomplice, David Knight could easily have entered DW3's offices after hours undetected. And either of them could have been in the office during the weekend of my ordeal with the shelves and the kitchen. As I'd learned, just because voice mail said David was in Paris, and Kimberly was meeting him there, didn't mean it was true. Who really knew where all those high-flying attorneys went once they left the office?

Opportunity, means, a wife willing to supply an alibi. With a simple box of chocolates and Daniel Blake out of the way, David Knight could have everything: a beautiful, ambitious woman who'd sleep with a partner, or help kill one, in order to make partner, a new house in Hampstead, and spending money. He just hadn't counted on me.

I handed the cabby the fare, took a deep breath for courage, and strode purposefully toward the restaurant. The front door looked to the casual observer like just another private townhouse but a sign nearly hidden behind a manicured boxwood tree bore the name, "Le Printemps." It was just turning nine. David Knight was a stickler for punctuality, just as he was for neatness, and I was not surprised to see him already at his table. But what I did see provided a new slant on the picture I'd painted in my mind, and the confidence I'd felt while safe in the taxi began to wane. For David Knight was not having a secret interlude with Kimberly. She must have been plotting her path to partnership back at the office. He wasn't even having a quiet dinner with Dorthea, his loyal wife. She must have decided to stay in Baden. He was with Joshua Hall. And they were holding hands.

"Madam. Do you have a reservation, madam? The name of your party, please. Madam, madam, are you all right?"

I had expected to be the one in control of this situation, that I would lay the incriminating cards on David's table and leave his conscience—I knew Kimberly didn't have one—and D.C. Lawson to do the rest. I certainly had not expected this.

"Madam?"

I realized that I had been blocking the entrance to the door. A man I assumed to be Francois waited patiently for me to speak to him. For the first time, I played the pregnancy trump card and feigned a moment of weakness that was actually not far from being the truth.

"Oh, I'm so sorry. I just feel a bit faint." I thrust my not inconsiderable tummy in his direction.

"But of course. Can I direct you to a table?"

I was as embarrassed as he was. "No, I don't see my party. Perhaps you could point me in the direction of the ladies' room."

"Just to your right. The waiter here will show you." He grabbed a passing waiter who looked like he should be on the cover of GQ. I had a new appreciation of why David Knight liked this restaurant. On my way to the ladies' room, I glanced over my shoulder to check if perhaps my eyes had been mistaken but even from a distance I caught the look that passed between David and Josh. It was not one that usually moved between senior partner and first year associate. Like fear or hostility.

I splashed cold water on my face in the ladies' room and reassessed my line of attack. I tried to use the pay phone inside to call D.C. Lawson but his direct line was engaged. I had more success with Polly. After correcting my pronunciation and observing that no policeman could ever afford the prices, she agreed to send the police to Le Printemps if she didn't hear back from me in fifteen minutes. For good measure, I grabbed a knife and fork from the nearest unoccupied table. Safety precautions in place, shoulders squared, I breathed in and out like I'd learned in Lamaze class, and walked back to the dining room.

"David, Josh. Good evening."

They jumped back from their near embrace. Their faces turned the color of the starched napkins in their laps.

"Amy. It's not what you think." Josh, the eager one who,

just a few weeks ago, I had considered a real catch, fumbled with his chair and stood to offer it to me.

"I'll take this seat, just for the moment." I grabbed an empty chair from the next table and clumsily moved it so that my back was to the restaurant and I faced them both.

"Is everything all right?" The maitre d' had spotted my intrusion.

"Yes, Francois, Ms. Brown is one of my dear friends. She decided to join us at the last minute. Right, Amy?"

"Yes. If you don't mind. I'll have a sparkling water please."

Francois knew what side his baguette was buttered on. He left us alone.

"Well, well, gentlemen. What have we here? No." I put my hands up as if to ward off traffic. "I'll do the talking. I'll be quick. D.C. Lawson will take care of the rest of the details."

"D.C. Lawson? What does he have to do with this?" Josh again. David Knight still hadn't spoken except to handle the nosy Francois. "Have you been following us?" Josh asked. "She's been following us. I told you she was beginning to suspect something."

Josh had probably smashed the windows to his own car to get to Mr. Blake's diary.

"Be quiet, Josh."

At least one thing hadn't changed in this pairing. It was clear that Josh had not toppled the traditional power structure even though David had flouted the usual conventions.

"Let's hear what Ms. Brown has to say. Maybe she's here to negotiate. That is your purpose, isn't it, Ms. Brown? That husband of yours not making enough money to meet the expenses of the new baby? Nannies and private schools can be very costly I imagine."

241

Even the wagging tongues back at DW3 that claimed David Knight had ice water in his veins would have marveled at how coolly he was taking my discovery.

"Oh, I'm not here for blackmail. I don't care about your romantic liaisons. You can sleep with the Queen for as much as I care. And I'm appalled at the suggestion that you would think I could be bought off. I know about the ski trip to Switzerland—you were there but you left a day early. I imagine in order to spend some more time with the friend who picked you up from the airport. A day earlier than you told the police *and* me. Did you tell Dorthea that it was urgent business? Of course, that's not what you put down in your timesheets. Eight hours of vacation time, wasn't that how it read?"

"You're here because I lied on my timesheets?" David Knight's laughter made the waiters stop in their tracks and the other guests look up from their menus. Caught unaware by the strong show of emotion—this was restaurant as religious experience, where people came to suffer for food, not to enjoy it—everyone turned back to their companions as soon as the reverential hush returned. David lowered his voice and said, "Every lawyer who ever passed the Bar lies on his timesheets. It's part of the game. Or didn't they teach you that in law school? Now, as you can see, we're in the middle of a private dinner."

Ignoring David's request, I turned to Josh as another piece of the distorted picture fell into place. "How convenient that the parents let you have the family car. Especially convenient if the passenger you've picked up from Heathrow wanted to enter the office without using the main entrance or signing in after normal business hours. You could drive in from the airport, park the car and sign in. The guard had no reason to suspect that you were not alone. The night receptionist left at her usual time and the reception area would have been empty.

"At which point you could have the little conversation that Mr. Blake wanted." I turned back to David. "He recorded the time, you know. It's all there in his diary in black and white. I'm not making it up. And your voice mail message is still there, right on Mr. Blake's machine. I didn't know he used voice mail but apparently his secretary checked for his messages every day. And I know about the wire transfers. And the closed account. You really should learn not to leave important documents lying around."

Josh and David glanced at each other at the mention of the wire transfers.

"How convenient that the two of you get to write up the official version of the investigation of Blake's death. There was no investigation, was there? A complete, but eloquent, fabrication. I thought maybe you were just stealing from him but now I see that it must have been blackmail. Did he find out about the two of you? Were you able to cover your tracks with the wire transfers? It's only a matter of time and the right questions before D.C. Lawson figures it out too. And to think that you'd even suggest that I could be bought off. Daniel Blake was a lot of things—greedy, unpleasant, and, I guess in the end, a blackmailer—but there's no amount of money that could buy me off from bringing his murderers to justice."

As I laid my hands on the table, I sensed a change in the atmosphere and a shift in control. I had had my day in court but I was no longer on the winning side.

"Murder? Do you think that I murdered Dan Blake, or that we murdered him?" Now it was time for David to get shrill. The ice had gone from a solid to molten lava quicker than was scientifically possible. He was seething and the people at the next table looked at us and drew their chairs tighter around their table.

Knight lowered his voice. I was forced to move my head closer to the table to hear him.

"I may be guilty of a lot of things. Poor judgment in getting romantically involved with an associate. Duplicity in living the lie that I was happily married. Dishonesty in presenting the face of heterosexuality to the world when I have known in my heart that I am a homosexual. But I have never been party to murder."

"How do you expect me to believe you?"

Josh who had kept quiet and who appeared stunned by my presentation now spoke up. "Because it's true. Do you think we cared more about propriety than human life?"

"You've lied about everything else that happened that day, why should I believe you? What about the trip to Switzerland?"

"You're right. I ended my trip early. I wanted to spend part of the weekend with Josh."

"What about the Swiss bank account and the wire transfers after Mr. Blake's death?"

"Daniel's private account. He had an elaborate arrangement for tax purposes, and he had asked me before his death in anticipation of his retirement to begin making certain changes, shifting money from one offshore account to another. I've been trying to sort it out. I have a power of attorney."

"You were there on Friday night. Mr. Blake wrote it down that you spoke. Yet I know you told the police that you hadn't come back until Saturday morning. It's all down in Mr. Blake's timesheets. Josh must have given him the candy and written the note that afternoon." A memory of bumping into one of the six-monthers as I left the office that night jumped into my head. "And I saw you. I saw Josh that night. And then Blake went back into the office and started eating and . . ."

David interrupted. "If we look at the ascertainable facts, the evidence if you will, that you have presented, you'll see that I, in fact,—and Josh—have left a 'trail' as you kindly describe it, of evidence. That leads you to conclude that we have something to hide. I say the opposite is true. Mr. Blake's non-billable hours describe a conversation that we had. That is true. I did not record the conversation since I had my full complement of eight hours of vacation time. Why gild the lily? You state that I lied to the police about my arrival back in England. That is also true, but as you can see, I had a compelling reason"—at this point he took Josh's hand and raised it to his lips—"that has absolutely nothing to do with murder. I would be willing to go to the police right now and confess that indiscretion. You suggest that I have been raiding Mr. Blake's bank accounts in an effort to mask my own blackmail. All I can say is that there is a perfectly reasonable explanation for my dealings with Blake's financial affairs. Daniel Blake's personal banking practices may not always have passed muster with the IRS or the Inland Revenue. He had his reasons for the wire transfers. Beyond that general description, I'm not willing to discuss it any further with you. It's a confidential matter between attorney and client. I will discuss them with the police but not with you.

"What I am supposed to have done to a box of chocolates to turn it into a murder weapon is simply unfathomable. Had you bothered to read the final draft of the whitewash or the cover-up or whatever your derogatory terms are for the firm memo that Josh and I submitted— how you got your hands on a draft in the first place I don't know but I can guess." Reverting to the partner and associate roles, David tapped Josh's arm and said, "Remind me, Josh, to speak to Helen about our shredding policy." He then resumed, "As I was saying, had you seen the final version, you would have known that, after our further inquiries, we satisfied ourselves that Daniel Blake's eating candy with nuts was just an unfortunate accident. As for how you knew that I would be at this restaurant tonight, I hesitate to accuse you of listening in on private conversations."

He had filleted my argument like the fish the couple at the next table was enjoying. When they weren't trying to eavesdrop on our conversation. More lawyers out for dinner.

"Amy. Secrets are not good, not among partners, not among husbands and wives, not among office colleagues. I'd managed to live a secret life for most of my adult life, but with the love and strength of my new relationship with Josh, I've decided to stop living the secret. You see, I wasn't talking to Daniel about my affair with Josh. Daniel already knew of my sexual orientation. He didn't approve but he wasn't about to damn me for it. You may think that you knew everything about Daniel Blake. But even he had his secrets. We all have secrets and I'm sure you understand that better than most."

Why did I feel that the tables had really turned? That David and Josh were the lions and I was the sole Christian at the table.

"You see, Daniel Blake and I were talking about what you believe to have been your little secret. We talked about many things, plans for the U.K. partnership, Walter's plans, my ski trip. But that wasn't what was weighing on Daniel's mind. No, Mr. Blake and I talked about your resignation. Funny, I don't recall that coming up in any of the interviews with D.C. Lawson or with any of the partners at Winter, Worthington. I certainly didn't see a resignation letter among the documents returned with the files from Mr. Blake's desk. Could it be that our Ms. Brown has something to hide? Accusations of murder have been made on the basis of less."

David raised his hand to get the attention of a waiter. "I think that we will order now. If I'm not mistaken, Ms. Brown won't be joining us for dinner after all. She seems to have lost her appetite."

CHAPTER 29

I came to work the next morning convinced that I would be met at the door by H.M.S. barring my entrance until I turned over my security pass, or, at the very least, by men in white coats wanting to take me away. Temporary insanity was the only plausible explanation for my reckless behavior the previous night. But I walked in without fanfare. Lucy greeted me with the news that all of the partners were at a meeting outside of the office with the visiting partners from New York. The festivities upon which H.M.S. was pinning her next promotion were tonight and the office was quiet.

Resisting with difficulty the urge to listen to my colleagues' voice mail and pilfer through their mail, I confined myself to my own.

> *"Amy. David Knight. I've talked it over with the chairman of the Lawyers Committee in New York and we both agree that it makes sense that you go quietly at the end of this week. The office will be informed that you'll be starting your maternity leave a little earlier than planned. You will be expected to attend the firm event tonight—the program has your name on it and I want to avoid any undue attention to your absence. After last night, however, your continuing at Winter, Worthington, is out of the question. You'll be receiving a formal letter to that ef-*

fect. This is not the kind of message I would normally leave on an accessible line, but I am willing to attribute your little delusional scene to the stresses of pregnancy and bereavement. I do strongly suggest that you seek professional help. "

I could just imagine what David Knight thought of me. And I hadn't even had the opportunity to accuse him or Josh of attempting to hurt me with the library shelves. Or to recount the compositional breakdown of European chocolate. I listlessly crossed off the previous day on my calendar—I could look forward to beginning my maternity leave early under the worst of circumstances—unpaid maternity leave *and* no job to return to—and pushed the button for my other messages.

They were poignant reminders of what I was leaving behind. Gideon had called to see if he could take me to lunch on my last day. His tone indicated that he knew more than he was letting on. He had become intimately familiar with the Lawyers Committee and I assumed that the word was already out in New York that I was leaving. Ted had asked that I bring the latest fax from Declan United with me to the party so that we could go over it together there. Tony had called to see whether my message light was working. As Josh had already explained, Tony had discovered that the cleaning people had been inadvertently unplugging phone cords with the vacuum cleaners. No gremlins, not even a glitch. And H.M.S. had called to remind me that all of my belongings had to be out of the office before I left on maternity leave so that a new lawyer could move in during my absence. The menace in her voice meant that she did not know yet about last night's fiasco. Like the partners, she was out of the office, presumably busy with last minute party details.

At least I hadn't lost my sense of humor along with my job. I laughed out loud at the message from Mr. Seals, who'd called again and who'd finally been put through to my phone. He'd left a number but no message. I recognized the area code for the *District* of Columbia and not the country, Colombia, as I'd been led to believe by Susannah. A simple misunderstanding. Like turkey on the Fourth of July. Someone else would have to help Mr. Seals with his restaurant.

I was getting off pretty easy for someone who had accused the managing partner of murder while hiding the fact that she had resigned and stolen her resignation letter from a crime scene. Or what I thought had been a crime scene. I wasn't even sure about that anymore. According to David Knight, the firm had established to its satisfaction that Daniel Blake's death had been an accident. As much as I wanted to attribute his conviction to the usual legal bravado, it had a ring of truth to it. And the last message on my voice mail seemed like confirmation.

"This is a message for Amy Brown. It's Susannah Jones. I've been thinking about it. If you want to know what really happened to the old man, come to the Sterling Tower, 234 West Ferry Road, The Docklands at 12:00 today. Thursday. Wait for me at the lifts."

The platform at Bank station was not crowded. By 11:30 a.m., rush hour was history. It had taken me an hour to exit the office. Helen who was around after all had stopped me on my way out to bug me about clearing out my office. I had made up a story that I was off to find something to wear for the party. She seemed relieved that I finally had my priorities right.

I clutched my ticket for the London Docklands Light Railway and gasped as a modern train car came around the corner. "Light" railway was not a misnomer for the bright car simply sparkled in contrast to the dingy Underground train that I had just left. My companions were well-dressed businessmen to whom this journey did not seem like an adventure. My destination was one of the buildings in the Docklands that until now had only ever appeared to me as tall panels of twinkling lights in the distance, seen only on the infrequent visits to Steven's office. His office windows had a great view of the London business district that had popped up in the late '80s only to be sunk by bankruptcy in the early '90s. The rail car passed through the East End, then past an enormous stretch of empty lots. The view was a graphic display of the slump of the commercial real estate market.

The train made a series of quick stops and I exited at West India Quay. I looked around and up. I couldn't fight the feeling that I was Dorothy plunged into the English version of the Emerald City—surrounded by oversized, modern buildings plunked down in a watery version of Oz. The sidewalks were not paved with yellow brick but were a lot cleaner than those I had left behind in Mayfair. I wandered through the station and past the docks until I reached West Ferry Road and the address Susannah had left on my voice mail. I smiled at the guard while I made the obvious motion of checking my watch so that he would see that I was waiting for someone. It wasn't long before hordes of young women, identically clad in platform shoes and no stockings, suddenly began pouring out of the elevator banks.

I scanned the faces of the crowd concerned that I'd miss her. But I needn't have worried. I could've spotted

Susannah Jones at any distance, in any crowd. She wore guilt, an emotion with which I was intimately familiar, like a tattoo across her forehead. "Susannah?" Before she could speak, I put out my hand and said, "It's me, Amy Brown." She jutted her chin out in a poor attempt at the defiance I'd heard during our earlier telephone calls.

We walked out the door, and I battled to keep up. Susannah's hangdog expression belied a nervous energy that propelled her out the door and down a side alley. She wiped at her nose while she simultaneously popped a cigarette into her mouth. We stood still only for the second that it took her to light it. I glanced down at my extended stomach, certain that she'd put it out once she realized my condition, but that was assuming a level of concern for me that appeared to be beyond her.

Susannah inhaled her cigarette in our short walk to the Cat and Candle. The walls of the pub, purpose built for the '90s, were painted white and the floors were spotless, but for the butt Susannah stepped on as we made our way to an empty table. Her eyes caught mine as I turned and looked over my shoulder to the chalkboard with the day's specials. I saw not the tough girl I'd coaxed information from, or even the one I vaguely remembered—she'd actually stood up to Mr. Blake's tirades pretty well—but a defeated spirit.

"Tell me what you want, and I'll order it. It's on me. It's the least I can do for bugging you with all my telephone calls."

She grunted. "I'll have the ploughman and a pint."

I ordered two ploughman lunches. I needed the calcium and even the English couldn't ruin bread and cheese. I refrained from ordering a glass of milk and chose instead a bag of potato chips to go with Susannah's beer and my soft drink. We would need something to keep our hands busy while we waited for our meals, and from the look on Susannah's face, we would not be making idle chatter. I carried the drinks over and made the return trip for my food. I finally took my coat off, and expected her to comment on my new figure but her preoccupation was so deep she never did notice.

Before I could ask what she meant in her message, Susannah's chin began to quiver and her act of defiance disappeared. She didn't make a sound but tears ran down her face.

"I'm sorry. I didn't mean to upset you but you said that you knew. . . ." I reached inside my briefcase for tissues, knowing that I wouldn't find any. I handed her a paper napkin from the table. She wiped her face, and spoke, "It was me that killed him. I bought the chocolates, just like he asked. I told the girl at the shop 'no nuts'—I'm not an idiot—I know about allergies—me mum can't be near cats, they just take her breath away—I know I told her to be careful about the nuts—but I, I was running late—I'd met me girlfriends at the pub for lunch—we'd had a pint, just one pint a piece with, I don't know, fish pie or lasagna, something to eat—I wasn't that hungry—just desperate for a fag, a smoke, and a chance to be away from the old man. I was halfway back to the office before I realized I hadn't run his errands—he wanted the chocolates from Darlington's on Oxford Street. It was the biggest store so it would have the best selection he said. The little shop down the corner wasn't good enough for him. I know I said 'no nuts' but I sort of drifted off about halfway through the selection—all I could think of was that I had to make sure I was back in time to have a little visit to the ladies'—brush me teeth, rinse with that minty stuff—I'd been warned he'd really scream if he smelled lager on me, plus he'd be wanting to know where the chocolates was."

She spoke in one long run-on sentence with tears running down her cheeks. No sobbing, no runny nose. Just water springing from her eyes as she shared her story in a flat monotone voice. She paused only when the barmaid placed our two plates of cheese and bread on the table.

"He was so busy that he didn't even come looking for me."

"And did you leave the little note about the nuts?" I asked, swallowing my own tears and reeling from her revelation.

This brought forth a new wave of tears and a nod of her head. "I wanted him to know that I'd followed his orders. The police never mentioned it so I figured that it got thrown out in the trash. I decided to keep me mouth shut. How did you find out about the note?"

Like David Knight had said, I had my own secrets. "I found it in Mr. Blake's papers. When did you buy the candy?"

"It was probably around half one by the time I put it on his desk."

"You just left a note with the candy on his desk?"

"Yeah, I waited till he was on the phone. I didn't want to get into it with him. He didn't look up."

"Did he open it right away?" I asked another question, pained by the answers but still intent on knowing every detail, all the while biting back the words, "You should have been more careful!" That I'd lost my job as an indirect result of her carelessness was unimportant. Daniel Blake had died.

"Like I said he was on the phone. I don't know. I think so. Lookit." She looked at me directly. "I'd been warned by the agency so I thought I knew what to expect. Nuffink could really prepare you for him though. My assignment was up that day and I was happy to be on my way. I couldn't stand him. But I would never have hurt, physically hurt him, or anyone, on purpose. I'd do anything to live that day over again." I looked into her eyes and saw my watery reflection. I touched her arm and said, "I believe you."

She wiped her face again and drank from her pint glass, and after a few minutes said in a stronger voice, "Even if I'd wanted to hurt him there were so many other ways. Do you know that he made me set an alarm so I could bring him his medicine? Or that one day I came in and found him on the floor? He'd tripped over the phone cord or something and couldn't get up. I felt like a bloody nursemaid."

I'd no idea he'd become so frail. "I didn't know."

"But you've got to believe me. It's like I told the others. I wouldn't have done him in with that candy. That's just sick. And who'd be that stupid?" She pushed her cheese around the plate and fiddled with a cigarette she'd pulled from her pack. She looked away from the table and said to herself, "It weren't even for him."

"What do you mean?"

She continued fingering the cigarette as if the nicotine could work its soothing effect by osmosis. "The candy. It's not like he'd said something. But he didn't have to. I'd seen him come back once before with a bag from Darlington's tucked under his arm. He tried to hide it from me. Who buys a box of fancy chocolates for himself? No, I knew what he was on about." She blew her nose on the napkin and then said, "The old man had a dolly bird."

If I had had problems envisioning Daniel Blake with a life outside of the office, I was flummoxed at the idea of him having a lover. It was like imagining my parents, or worse, my grandparents, having a sex life. Who buys a box of fancy chocolates for himself, indeed. Even Mr. Blake hadn't been that egotistical, had he? But that was easier to contemplate than Mr. Blake and an unknown woman, or even the only one I knew who lamented not having married him. My knowledge of English slang may have been limited—was a "dolly bird" a lover or paid company?—but I was happy to remain ignorant. It was one mystery that I was content to have buried with him.

Not that there was any other mystery to clear up now that Susannah had told me about buying the chocolates and leaving the yellow sticker. We'd exchanged uncomfortable good-byes—I'd been too shocked to provide any comforting reassurances—before I headed in a stupor back to the station where a sign warned of delays. Seeking solace in routine, I tossed two coins into a pay telephone booth and waited for Nikki to answer my extension.

"Amy Brown's line."

"Nikki, it's me. I'm delayed here. I'm going to go home to change and go straight to the party so I'll see you tomorrow." I hadn't told Nikki about the accelerated maternity leave. I'd break the news to her tomorrow. "Did Steven call?"

"Not that I'm aware of, but your message light is on. I'm in your office. I'll hang up so you can check and I'll see you tomorrow."

"Great. Bye." I dialed again and listened impatiently through the series of instructions and listened to my one message.

"Amy. Polly Lawrence. I'm assuming you'll fill me in what happened last night when we meet. You hung up be-

fore I could tell you that the analysis is back on the candy. I, um, well, I was wrong . . ."

I heard a train roll in to the station below but let it depart without me while I strained to hear her. A smarty pants admitting a mistake? This had to be good.

". . . Not a really big mistake, the box did say 'Made in England.' Call it a natural mistake . . ."

Polly's mistakes sounded more painful than Polly's pedagogy. I mentally sped her, and the next train, along and fed the phone another coin.

"Anyhow, that's irrelevant. What is relevant is, we can forget about the vegetable fat scenario. There wasn't any. Vegetable fat, I mean. Just pure cocoa butter. And here's where I made my mistake."

I fished in the bottom of my bag for another coin half listening to Polly read percentages after percentages.

"The numbers just don't add up. I could go on and on."

And I was afraid that she would. I heard another train pull into the platform as I considered whether I could catch it.

"The point is, and here's where I was wrong, it's not even chocolate."

I may have taken leave of my senses—David Knight

would attest to that—but taste was not one of them. This drama of our own making had really gone too far. Polly had obviously spent too much time sniffing her aerosol samples.

"As for the nuts . . ."

Dealing with a smarty pants the only way I knew how, I hung up the phone. I would call her later to fill her in on the missing pieces of the puzzle. My need to hear that I hadn't seriously tilted the hands of fate against Mr. Blake by eating the pieces that had been nut free and leaving him with pieces with nuts had diminished with Susannah's confession. Guilt was a relative emotion and Susannah certainly had me beat.

CHAPTER 30

Her Majesty had been blessed with a clear night that felt more like Indian summer than autumn. The caterers had set up outside and guests mingled in the garden of Ted's house in Regent's Park. I wondered what deal Helen had struck to get Ted to agree to have the party at his place.

"And what did you say your name was again?"

"Amy, Amy Brown." I pointed to my nametag, but it was hanging obscenely across what had previously been the divide between my shoulder and my stomach.

"And whose wife are you?"

I had been cornered by a guest as soon as I had arrived and the conversation seemed strangely familiar to the one I'd had weeks ago with the caterer.

"I'm not anybody's wife." Helen had been adamant. Spouses were not invited.

"Oh, I do beg your pardon. Young women are doing their own thing these days. Now in my day. . . ."

"No, that's not what I meant. I'm married but just not to anyone here. You see, I'm one of the lawyers." Or at least I would be for another day. I tried explaining my presence at the party but my inquisitor had wandered off to the buffet table alarmed by my wantonness.

Everyone from DW3 was in the party spirit. Helen, her part in the celebrations nearly over, beamed as guests offered their congratulations. The only thing missing from the picture was a groom. Kimberly had attached herself to a group of partners from New York. It would be futile to try to join that conversation. Gideon, who stood alone, looked forlorn, and he'd clearly had a few glasses of champagne. I wanted to commiserate with him but didn't think he'd be happy knowing I'd been listening in on his misery. I walked toward him and we were joined by Walter Hughes and some of his associates. We chatted about the party, and the food and drinks. I refrained from commenting on the sliced but very nearly shredded salmon.

Even in the aftermath of disaster, I felt oddly content. Susannah's confession had provided the closure I needed to end my grieving. I looked around at my colleagues and wondered. Would little Robbie Hughes be expelled for merely following in his father's footsteps? Would Kimberly ever make enough money to satisfy her lifestyle? Would Ted delay his alimony payments while falsely maintaining that he had the best divorce lawyer in the world? DW3 was a soap opera, all right, and most, if not all, of the cast would survive another season. There was something reassuring about finding out that your office colleagues might figuratively, but not literally, stab you in the back. And who would have seriously thought that anyone at DW3 could be a murderer? Unlike Polly, I didn't need to answer my own rhetorical questions. If anyone had had a motive to kill Mr. Blake, it would have only been me.

Lost in my thoughts, keeping the prospect of a future confrontation with Steven at bay, I hardly noticed when Joshua Hall patted me on the shoulder and motioned that I follow him away from the group. He was the last person, after David Knight, that I wanted to see.

"Are you here to revel in my downfall?"

"No. I'm not like that. I looked for you earlier at the office but your secretary said you were out. I came to apologize."

"You mean that if you'd just told me that it was you and not Kimberly having the affair with David, or if you'd told me that you'd interviewed Susannah Jones, then maybe I would not have jumped to conclusions and made a fool of myself. Or lost my job in the process."

"Something like that."

"Tell me, why did you ask me to dinner?"

"I did need information. But that's not why I asked you to dinner. I asked you to dinner because, well, I felt a little sorry for you. Here you were this plucky pregnant woman trying to build a career based on babysitting the firm's biggest monster. It was, I don't know, admirable."

"Pathetic is more like it. Thanks a million. I could have used a few words of encouragement last night."

"That's all I wanted to say. That, plus I'm sorry."

"You keep saying that you're sorry. What do you have to be sorry about?"

"Well, I was the one who moved the fire extinguisher. From the kitchen door that Sunday."

"Really?"

"I didn't realize until the next morning that it was used to keep the kitchen door propped open. I took it out—I needed something heavy to prop my own office door open and it seemed like it wasn't serving any useful purpose in the kitchen, it wasn't like anyone was cooking and the door seemed to stay open on its own if you pushed it hard enough. Anyhow, I came in early the next morning and went in to find the kitchen door closed and your briefcase inside. I looked all over for you. You weren't in your office or the basement. I saw you leave as I was coming up the stairs and, well, I'm no detective . . ."

"Neither, apparently, am I."

". . . but I could tell that you had had a really rough night. I guess that was my fault. I'm sorry."

"Great. Another mystery solved. Are you also going to tell me that you accidentally rolled the library shelves and broke into your own car? Or helped yourself to some candy in my briefcase?"

"Excuse me?"

"Never mind. Thanks for telling me. About the kitchen, that is."

"So I guess this is goodbye."

"Not quite. I'll be in tomorrow. To pack up my office."

"Then I guess I'll say goodbye later."

"Right. Later." I started to do an about face but he grabbed me by the arm and said, "There's just something I have to ask you. Did you really think that someone would have had a good reason to kill Blake?"

"I didn't say it had to be a *good* reason."

"But what you were suggesting last night, you seemed convinced that someone actually killed Blake with those chocolates. You must have had your reasons. I don't need to know those."

"Look, I spoke to the temp. . . ."

"But I'm not asking how. I'm asking a different question. Why? What could have motivated someone to kill him? Or to get him out of the way?"

"I suppose any strong emotion—anger, fear, greed, hatred." A day ago, it would have been a longer list—real estate, making partner, pornography. But I didn't think Josh would understand. He hadn't been privy to the inside view of DW3 that I'd had.

"Love?"

"I suppose. Like unrequited love, or rejected love. Mother love."

"Or secret love?"

"Haven't I already agreed that David and you did not kill Mr. Blake?"

"But what about what David said? That everyone has secrets."

"What are you suggesting?"

"I'm not suggesting anything."

"If there's something you're not telling me, something about David, something that he told you or that you suspect . . ."

"No, no, it's nothing like that. I trust David. He could never hurt, let alone, kill, anyone. I'm not even talking about murder. Just forget I said anything."

"Who has a secret love, Josh?" Had Susannah been right about Daniel Blake's love life?

"No, it's nothing."

"If there's something you know or that you're suspicious of, don't make the same mistake I did. Don't keep it to yourself. Go to the police. Tell David."

"I'm sure it's nothing. Just ignore me. Forget that I said anything."

"Fine. Now, I think it's time we went back to the party." I knew I wouldn't be checking up on the possible secret loves of the staff at DW3. I didn't care if Helen still carried the torch for Mr. Blake or if Ted married wife number five. And I really didn't want to know what Hughes got up to behind closed doors in the pursuit of love if the state of the men's room was any indication. I'd learned my lesson again. Humility.

In my case, it felt more like humiliation. Humiliated for thinking that I had been so clever in unmasking David

Knight as a murderer, that I could be a better detective than I was a lawyer. That some overheard telephone conversations, a stray fax, a zealot, a box of chocolates, and a missing fifteen minute conversation from a lawyer's non-billable hours could add up to murder. My misplaced affection for an ogre of a boss had blinded me to my usual inability to perform simple arithmetic. I had been efficient and effective. And wrong.

I'd had enough lessons in humility.

Or so I thought. I stared at myself in the mirror in the guest room at Ted's house. The woman in the mirror was unrecognizable. She looked like a priest, dressed in a long sleeved deep red velvet dress, with fabric so generous it must have been intended for some liturgical celebration where they had measured the altar instead of the pastor. But it was me, and the dress—loose in all the right places—chest, tummy, and backside—but proportionately as big in all the wrong places—was mine. No one with any taste would claim it. My arms were lost in the folds of fabric and the sleeves came way past my fingers. Huge patch pockets big enough for a baby and a white lace dog collar were the only decoration. The fashion police would arrest me for wearing velvet in mid-October, but the real crime had been the price of alterations, which I had refused to pay. I had rolled the sleeves before I'd left for the party and had had to excuse myself when I realized that they'd come undone and that I'd scooped up a few hors d'ouevres on my last visit to the buffet table.

I'd bought the dress during my one and only pregnancy shopping trip with Steven, before I'd known the attendance at this party would be my final appearance before being banished from Winter, Worthington. Steven had agreed to accompany me on a forced march through the maternity stores of Oxford Street only after I had threatened to tell his parents that their first grandchild would *not* be named Goldman. He had unenthusiastically kept his end of the bargain by standing guard outside the dressing room.

"Can't you wear something you already have?" Steven had asked.

"Steven, I've told you, nothing I have fits anymore and I can't wear a T-shirt and leggings to a cocktail party."

"What about this? This looks big enough." He had held out a dress that could have clothed an entire nursery school class. The pattern, clowns and balloons, was more appropriate for that age group.

"Why don't you just suggest a circus tent, Steven?"

"What, do you mean . . ."

"Don't say it, don't even think it."

". . . a night out in the Big Top?"

"Do they think that just because I'm having a child means I have to dress like one?"

"What about this one?" Steven had realized that his being "helpful" would grant him a release sooner than he deserved.

"I might as well stick an apple in my mouth and go as the main course. At least the tablecloth would probably fit. Or I could print 'Welcome and Congratulations' across my chest and go as the Goodyear blimp. The possibilities are endless. I'm tired. I give up."

"Don't start crying. It will all be over soon. You look beautiful." Singing the last bit, he crooned, "I love you just the way you are."

"You are not endearing yourself to me. He left his wife you know. She was probably pregnant, too."

He'd finally grabbed the dress I was now wearing and had said, "This looks like it would cover you."

And I, in my ignorance of the humiliation to come, had replied, "I don't want to be 'covered,' Steven. I want to make a good impression. It won't be just my work colleagues. Ambassador Harrington will be there, the head of the Law Society."

Well, that was then and this was now. The closest I'd come to talking to anyone important had been the man who'd mistaken me for a fallen woman. And in his own way, he was right. The humiliating tumble I'd taken just wasn't gender specific. I looked at myself in the mirror one last time and scrutinized the giant red choir robe wrapped around me. There was no end to the possible uses for this dress. I could use it for the skirt on the Christmas tree. Or donate it to Rockefeller Center.

"Amy. Are you still in there?" Kimberly's voice came through the door followed by faint knocking.

"Yes. I'll be right out."

"I saw you go in and got worried when you didn't come out."

I dried my hands and opened the door to find her admiring herself in a gold tinted compact.

"I was afraid you'd fallen. Velvet—that is velvet, isn't it?"

"I think so," I said warily.

"Velvet can get so heavy. If you'd fallen in that dress, I don't think we'd have been able to lift you without a forklift!" She giggled into her hand. "Just kidding. I'll bet you'll be glad when this baby comes and you get your figure back." She stepped back to appraise me. "Shorten it a bit and you can wear that dress next year."

What was I thinking? I could use the dress to smother Kimberly. Like the opportunities for humiliation, the possibilities were endless.

CHAPTER 31

"Ladies and gentlemen, if I could have your attention."
David Knight walked to a small platform with a microphone
at the end of the garden and began introducing the firm's
distinguished guests. Ambassador Harrington was making
his way to the podium when Ted came up behind me and
whispered, "Do you think we could step inside and go over
the Declan fax?"

"But the speech."

"I've known Chewy Harrington for years. Long enough
to know why he's called Chewy. He and Walter. . . ."

"Yes?"

"On second thought, it's probably not a story I should
be telling in mixed company. The only thing the ambassador loves more than the sound of his own voice is ap-
plause. He's too stupid to understand that the clapping is
from relief and not adulation." Ted looked at his watch and
said, "He'll be at least another thirty, forty minutes. They'll
never miss us."

Ted had obviously not talked to David and the full
weight of his charm and his hand on my arm made me feel
like I was a part of something important with him that I
would miss very much.

"Sorry to take you away from your friends." He pointed
in the general direction of Josh Hall, the perpetually-in-

motion Walter and Kimberly.

"Don't worry, they're not my friends," I protested.

"Did I hit a sore spot?"

"No, don't mind me. I'm just not very good at these big parties. My feet hurt and I feel like a centerpiece in this dress."

"You look fine. More than fine. Radiant. You won't report me for that comment, will you?"

"Of course not." I smiled for the first time all evening.

As we entered the house, Ted directed me toward the stairs. "Let's go into my study. We'll be more comfortable and I can see the podium from there. We can make our way back when David takes the stage again."

He was right. I could see the back of the crowd from a window. The view became increasingly impressive as we walked up a grand center staircase.

"How many stairs?"

"Oh, I don't know. I've never counted."

"We have exactly sixty-eight stairs to our front door. Or so anyone who has to climb them with suitcases tells me. It's sort of a family joke." But Ted didn't seem to be listening. "Are these your children?" I lifted a framed photograph from the desk in the small study we had entered.

"Yes."

"They're beautiful." Ted with his children looked like a Benetton ad for world piece and global harmony. "Who's who?"

After a brief run-down on his first through fourth family, Ted asked whether I minded if he smoked. He excused himself to find a light while I continued looking at his pictures. The room was a gallery of family photographs. An older man and a woman whom I took to be Ted's mother. The resemblance was remarkable. A very young and handsome Ted and two other men with their arms around each other and a trophy. And a picture of an elderly man in judicial robes, a beautiful young woman, and two handsome men, one of whom was also in the trophy picture, and the other, Ted. I peered at the inscription and read, "To Teddy and Charles—the best law clerks a judge could ever have—take good care of my secretary—Henry" and then turned to see Ted when I smelled cigar smoke. He crossed the room to where I was standing, and said, "Here, I'll take that." He put the photograph back on the shelf and touched my shoulder. "Perhaps we should get started. Why don't you take a seat over there?" He pointed to a leather sofa near the door.

But I wasn't eager to work. Declan's future prosperity meant nothing to me now and Ted's company and compliments were preferable to another encounter with my soon-to-be former office mates. I lingered near the photographs. Pointing to a frame, I asked, "What a wonderful picture. Is that your mother?"

"Yes. My mother and Sir Gordon."

"She's lovely. They make quite a pair."

"Thank you."

"And the picture there," I pointed to the shelf above, "is that the judge you clerked for?"

"Yes. I clerked for Judge Tustin for two years after law school before I joined the firm."

"Didn't I just read somewhere that he's dead? Oh, yes, Helen said something about it. It must have been just after I came back to work. Let me see. I don't remember. You know what they say about pregnant women—shrinking brains. Who's the young woman?"

"Oh, that's Paige." Ted looked out the window as I remained rooted to the spot. "My first wife." He turned back and faced me. "I see that Harrington has moved away from the podium—Helen must have laid down the law on the length of his speech—and that the head of the Law Society has started speaking. Do you have your copy of the memo handy?"

"Wasn't she a secretary at Winter, Worthington for awhile?"

"Yes, she was. We probably should get started, Amy."

"Did she work for you there?"

"Yes, she worked for me. And Lawrence Worthington."

Sir Gordon, Judge Henry Tustin, Lawrence Worthington and Paige. Teddy had just reconstructed an invitation list, or the decipherable names on what I thought had been Mr. Blake's invitation list, without the help of Christmas cards or Helen's badgering. An ominous thought was making its way into my brain. I ignored Ted's request that we turn our attention to the memo and, with as much nonchalance as my sweating palms allowed, I asked, "And the young man?"

"That's the judge's other clerk. Charlie. We were good friends, drinking buddies. We must have closed every bar in Washington at some point." He unfolded a crumpled copy of a memo on the desk. "Enough of my rogues' gallery. Shall we look at this memo?"

"I'm sorry, Ted. Could you excuse me? Nature calls. Another affliction of pregnancy. I'll be right back."

I hurried out of the room before Ted could insist that we review the Declan United papers and walked down the hall to the first room I could find which, lucky for me, actually was a bathroom. The room had the same pristine look that I had seen in the ground floor guest room, only this one was even more spacious. Fresh flowers, monogrammed linens, expensive toiletries. Not a bad place to hide while I considered the people in the pictures and Mr. Blake's handwritten list that I had mistaken for party invitations. One relative, one dead, one friend, one screaming for alimony down the phone. And Lawrence Worthington. A retired partner. A named partner. Happy, smiling faces in Teddy Cunningham's library. Had they been involved in some conspiracy that Mr. Blake had found out about? Or just a harmless coincidence?

I doused my face with cold water. Amy, it's the excitement from the party, I told myself, the idea of unemployment and an additional mouth to feed, the cigar smoke, that are making you lose your mind. I wiped my face on the hand towel and looked around the room. Robert Theodore Cunningham, III, may have been the poster child for Winter, Worthington & Walker but he was clearly not above a little petty theft. The scalloped soap, heavy with the scent of French perfume, bore the imprint of a restaurant known as a DW3 favorite. The soap dish, in its first life, an ashtray, was an advertisement for a men's club in Mayfair. The white terry cloth robe on the back of the door still bore the tag that implored guests to buy it from the sports shop at a New York health club. The linens that I had taken for a sign of expensive and personalized luxury were probably as authentic as Helen Matthews-Smith's English accent. The stylized "C" entwined with the "R," were also the initials for a familiar hotel chain. And a tiny, embroidered crown—the emblem for Royal Crest Hotels, purveyor of beds fit for a king and complimentary boxes of Darlington chocolates—was one too many coincidences for me.

After coming face to face with proof that at least one partner at DW3 had stayed at a Royal Crest hotel, I spent several minutes in the bathroom considering how to avoid another conversation with Teddy Cunningham. The windows in the bathroom were too high for me to see anything other than treetops even when I stood on the toilet with the seat down. Jumping from a two-story height was out of the question and shimmying down a drainpipe using my dress, the towels, even the robe, as a rope, didn't appeal. I doubted if they made a drainpipe that could support a pregnant woman. And the windows looked to be so small that I couldn't have squeezed through them even if I hadn't been pregnant.

I thought about just staying in the bathroom forever or until someone—anyone other than Teddy—noticed that I was missing. Kimberly's talent for zeroing in at my most awkward moments meant she could be knocking on the door at any moment. The room was pleasant enough, and a vast improvement over the men's room at the office. But the lock on the door was merely decorative. If Ted did have something to hide, then I didn't want to be trapped with him in a room with an endless supply of water. I believed those stories about drowning in a teacup. And even if Ted turned out to be nothing other than a wealthy kleptomaniac who happened to know the same people Mr. Blake had known—I had jumped to the wrong conclusions before—sooner or later he was going to wonder what was taking me so long. The man had had four wives but even I knew that I had now been gone long enough to have powdered my nose and painted the Sistine Chapel. I opened the door and started walking towards the staircase.

"Going somewhere?"

"Oh, Helen, you scared me. I didn't see you standing there. I was just reviewing a document with Ted when suddenly I didn't feel well. I've been in the ladies' room."

"I saw you leaving with him." Her disapproval was palatable. "David is going back to the podium any minute and will be announcing the names of our distinguished English lawyers. That includes you. At least for another twenty-four hours."

The news of my dismissal was out. Refusing to be drawn into an argument with Helen, I smiled sweetly and said, "I know. But I'm very sorry, I really think that I must be going. I'm feeling a bit shaky. Ted's just down the hall. Could you make my apologies? It's been a lovely party, Helen. You really missed your calling."

I could hear her protests as I hurried out the door. Before she had time to realize just how idle her threats were—what could she possibly threaten that I hadn't already brought upon myself?—I was directing a cab back to the office. I had an urgent need to call Mr. Seals and Polly. And this time I had to make sure that there would be no misunderstandings.

CHAPTER 32

Helen would be serving copious quantities of champagne at the reception so I was confident that even the most conscientious of the young lawyers would not be returning to the office. I turned on the lights in reception and barely hesitated before walking back to the space I could continue to call mine for one more day. I shut my door and hoped that by having only my reading lamp on and not the overhead lights I could make my calls unnoticed and be gone in just a few minutes.

"You've reached the office of Polly Lawrence. Ms. Lawrence is. . . ."

Fed up with recordings, I pressed the receiver to disconnect. Confirmation from Polly that the chocolates on Blake's desk conformed to American and not European compositional requirements—what else could she have meant when she'd said "not chocolate?"—would have to wait. But my guess, that Susannah had been wrong not just about Mr. Seals' country of origin but also about his line of business, was confirmed as soon as a woman's voice with a slight Southern accent answered my next call with the greeting, "D.C. Bar, Records."

"Hello?"

"D.C. Bar, Records."

"Is this the D.C., I mean the District of Columbia, Bar?" I wanted to make sure that I was right. I'd been wrong about a lot of things lately.

"Yes." She made no effort to hide her exasperation. "That's what I said. How can I help you?"

"Are you sure?"

"Yes, I'm sure. There are some days I feel like I'm working at a zoo but this isn't one of them. Now do you want to speak to the D.C. Bar or don't you?"

"Well, yes, I guess I do. I'm sorry. I was given this number and I wasn't sure what I was calling. I'm calling from London and I'm trying to reach a Mr. Seals at what I thought was this number. Is it possible to speak to Mr. Seals?" I realized too late that, by identifying my location, I had triggered a response as aggravating as a London cabbie's interrogations.

"You're calling from London? You don't sound English. Are you a lawyer over there? Do you have to wear one of those wigs?"

"No, I'm not English. I'm American. And I don't wear a wig. It's already very late here . . ."

"What time is it there?"

"It's about 8:00 at night." The champagne would be stopping soon.

"Oh, so when you all are sleeping we all are still at work? I can never get that straight."

And they say that Americans are provincial. I rolled my eyes to the ceiling. "Sort of. We're five hours ahead."

"What day is it there?"

"It's the same day. I'm sorry but I really need to talk to Mr. Seals."

"What about the weather? Are you having fall there now

275

too, or is it the reverse?"

"It's just the same." I was being tested beyond even the usual Amy Brown limits of kindness.

"How long have you lived over there?"

"A few years now."

"Well, you still sound American."

"Thanks. I'll take that as a compliment."

"Have you ever seen the Queen?"

"No, I've never seen the Queen. About Mr. Seals . . ."

"What about one of those little princes?" She didn't pause for a breath. "I know it's a big city, London and all, but I gotta ask you. Do you know a Kyle Friendly? He's my cousin. He's over there studying."

"No, I can't say that I do. But it's a very big city."

"I just figured you being American and all . . ."

"Right, no, I understand. Since I am calling from London, I'm wondering if you could put me through to Mr. Seals?"

"Seals, Seals, oh, you must mean Jimmy Seals. He doesn't work in this department anymore. He's retired and working part time in Files. I'll just transfer you."

I laid my head down on my desk. Any hope of solving Mr. Blake's murder with one quick telephone call had just flown out the window with Kyle Friendly's cousin's touch of the dial. For the next ten excruciating minutes, I bounced through an electronic phone system like a pinball on sedatives. Pressing the button on the only option I hadn't tried, I prayed for a human voice to answer.

"Files."

"There is a god."

"I beg your pardon?"

"I'm sorry. I've been trying to reach Mr. Seals."

"This is Mr. Seals."

"Finally! Mr. Seals. I'm so happy to have found you. My name is Amy Brown. I'm calling from a law firm in London. I'm returning your call to Susannah Jones and Daniel Blake. You left a message and a number on my voice mail."

"That's right. About that number, I'm sorry about that. I can't receive outside calls on this phone and if I'd left the main number, well, you'd be caught up in that automated system."

"Yes, I was transferred to that."

"You could be punching numbers for days before you ever spoke to a living soul. Anyhow, you've found me. How is Mr. Blake?"

"How's Mr. Blake? Didn't our receptionist tell you?"

"He was the nicest man. We had a long chat about the changes we've seen in the legal profession. When I started working, we didn't have these computers. We knew everyone by name. I guess he felt the same way. Of course, there weren't so many lawyers then."

Great, a contemporary of Mr. Blake's. Another dinosaur among men. But a nice man? Maybe it hadn't been Mr. Blake who had called Mr. Seals.

"Mr. Seals, pardon me for interrupting, but I'm sorry to say that Mr. Blake's no longer with us."

"What, he's been fired? At his age? What is this world coming to? I thought they had laws to prevent that sort of thing."

"No, no, you've misunderstood. He's, Mr. Blake's dead, Mr. Seals. He died a few months ago. That's why no one returned your calls."

"I am so sorry to hear that. What a nice fella."

"Which is why I'm calling. I used to work with Mr. Blake and I'm following up on his files and telephone calls.

I was just wondering"—I pondered before I finished the question—"why were you calling?"

"Well, he'd called me a few months ago and we had a really nice chat. Guess they're changing the rules over there, making it easier for you American lawyers to be English lawyers. Said that he and his secretary were just filling out the forms and wanted to confirm some Bar numbers for your lawyers over there. We get those kind of questions all the time now. Can't be too careful."

"I realize that it's been some time, but I'm just wondering if you remember who he was checking up on?"

"No, I can't say that I do."

"Do you have the numbers, or better yet, the names, that you checked for him?"

"Probably somewhere in Records, but I don't work in that department anymore."

"Do you think that if I gave you a name you could check it for me?"

"Well, like I said, I don't really have access to those files anymore."

The line went silent as Mr. Seals and I contemplated how far either of us was willing to go to get the information I was now convinced that I needed. He finally asked, "Is it important?"

"It's very important."

"Didn't he get my fax?"

"I don't remember seeing a fax. Maybe it was sent to the wrong number."

"Maybe, maybe."

"That happens all the time overseas."

"You're right, it sure does. All those numbers, all those zeros. Now, when I used to work upstairs, we had the mail. Can always trust the mail. Of course, that was before you had to worry about the mailman. Being armed and all. This fax stuff . . ."

"Mr. Seals . . ."

"Sorry, I do go on. Why don't I do this? I'll look in the correspondence file and resend the fax that I sent to your Mr. Blake. Then, if that doesn't tell you what you need to know, you just call me and we'll figure something else out."

"Thanks very much, Mr. Seals. I really appreciate your help. I'll be waiting for the fax. Goodbye."

I had little to lose in following up my idea that Teddy Cunningham and his past were the key to Mr. Blake's death. After another failed attempt to reach Polly, I wandered down the dark corridor to Blake's former office hoping to find his dead files still there. When I turned on the light for a brief moment, I was disappointed to see the room had been emptied of everything except the unattractive furniture. I turned off the lights and headed for the only logical resting place—the basement. Maybe the archive room had lost its power to scare now that I knew that it probably hadn't been my imagination pushing the shelves.

Slipping past the security guard, I took the stairs as fast as my inappropriate outfit allowed until I was back in the cupboard that housed the archive files with the lights on. Careful to stay as close to the corridor and safety as possible, I quickly scanned the stacks until I found the latest additions to the shelves reserved for Daniel Blake. I frantically searched through them and was rewarded when the second box I found contained the files I had gladly left in their place for Helen to search for. I emptied the box onto the floor and scanned the draft application forms for the attorneys who had had aspirations to be English lawyers. Including an application form for the only one among us who had scoffed at our pursuit of this paper credential. In the space provided for Bar membership for Teddy Cunningham, someone had penciled in the words 'District of Columbia' and a number.

I grabbed the form and went back up the stairs for my vigil at the fax machine. Mr. Seals was more efficient than I had expected. When I returned to the machine, papers were rolling into the tray. Under a cover transmission page from the D.C. Bar, Mr. Seals had attached the names and Bar numbers for Walter Hughes and Charles Kent. The number on Teddy's application form was exactly the same number that Mr. Seals had written for Charles Kent. I thought back to Judge Tustin's inscription on the picture of the happy foursome—to Teddy and Charles. And Teddy Cunningham's earlier words to me about not becoming an English lawyer. What had they been? That he didn't need the validation?

I may have been humbled by my recent experience with David Knight but I hadn't been lobotomized. I wasn't a keen fan of the Internet—one of the few topics on which Mr. Blake and I had agreed—but it was a quick way to locate Charles Kent and confirm that Teddy was masquerading as Charles Kent or vice versa. Back in the safety of my office, I turned on my computer and typed in the numbers for the firm's online service provider. Once I tapped into the right directory, I would be able to locate any Charles Kent working in a law firm. Within minutes, I would be able to find a telephone number and address for him. I wasn't taking anything that Teddy Cunningham told me for granted. I typed in my four-letter password and waited impatiently for a connection.

"You could be waiting a very long time."

I jumped at the sound.

"I cancelled your password." A very drunk Helen—she'd made no effort to mask the odor this time—leaned over my desk. "I knew you were coming back here. I know how lawyers who've been fired think—going in to the office while the coast is clear and copying all the firm's files. Raiding the piggybank while the partners are out celebrating. I've seen every trick. Well, I'm several steps ahead of you, girlie."

I slid the application form and the paper on which I'd written the Bar numbers and the notes of my conversation with Mr. Seals under a pile of documents.

"As soon as David told me today that the lovely Ms. Brown would be starting maternity leave early and would not be returning after the blessed event I took immediate action. I cancelled your password for the computer. You can't do legal research, you can't copy computer files, you can't even send e-mail. I cancelled your library card, your health insurance, and your company credit cards. As far as Winter, Worthington & Walker is concerned, you, Amy Brown, no longer exist."

"You're right. Caught in the act."

"I should have you arrested. Or better yet, I should report you to David and the other partners."

I maneuvered my foot to tug on the phone cord. "Go ahead. Why wait? I'm sure that after a lovely dinner with his partners David Knight is just dying to hear from you. Here, I'll look up David's number for you. You can call him on my phone. Be my guest." I moved away from my desk and pushed her toward the dead phone. "Tell him that I've been raiding the files, stealing from the office, and that you caught me red-handed. Tell him whatever you want. Just make sure that while you're at it you tell him how you managed to allow one of the firm's best and brightest trick you into believing that he's a lawyer."

Of course, I still hadn't figured out how Teddy had tricked Winter, Worthington into believing that he was a lawyer or how it related to Mr. Blake's death. But Helen didn't know that.

What I did know was that suddenly I didn't have the energy to care. A weariness had crept into me in the last hour that made the crimson dress I was wearing feel like a suit of armor and my shoes like sandbags. Lethargy beyond physical exhaustion had seeped into my brain and I had to repeat my address to the taxi driver twice before I realized that the tired, slurred voice I heard was mine. It couldn't all be attributed to the fact that I was carrying what amounted to a little more than a Brit's annual consumption of chocolate around my waist. The upheaval of the past few months—resignation, death, unemployment—felt like an emotional bungee jump, a free fall where I knew the cords were not going to work. The task of exposing Teddy's crime—if there was one—felt insurmountable. Images of my bed were the only thing pushing me to place one foot in front of the other.

In anticipation of the Arctic blast that always greeted me upon opening the building door, I closed my eyes. The chilly air revived me a little but it was not the tonic I needed. The timer for the hall light felt cold to the touch but it was working. A brighter light from under my apartment door beckoned me to the warmth inside.

"Steven—I'm home." I shouted in the direction of the sound of running water down the hall. "I hope you're running that for me. I'm going to rest for just a second. I'm so tired, I can't move." I nudged my shoes off from my swollen feet and raised them onto a pillow at the end of the sofa and pulled knee-length stockings from my legs. I had lost the ability to pull on maternity panty hose a month ago. "I'm just going to close my eyes for a second. Don't let me sleep too long." I needed some more energy before I could consider telling Steven that I'd lost my job and what I had discovered tonight. I had drifted off to sleep when the telephone started ringing.

"Let the machine pick up. There's absolutely no one that I want to speak to."

If Helen had managed in her inebriated state to call David Knight, then she was a better office manager than DW3 deserved. I closed my eyes while my voice on the tape floated from the answering machine at the desk in the hall to my half-asleep ears.

"Amy and Steven aren't home right now. If you'd like to leave a message, please do so after the tone. Beep."

I listened for the beep and the pause before the person on the other end started speaking.

"Amy. It's me. You must still be out. I'm going out for a drink with some people from the bank. I should be home in about an hour. Love you, bye."

With the confusion of exhaustion and near sleep, I wondered, how could Steven be running water down the hall and leaving a message after the beep at the same time? I must be dreaming.

The touch of Teddy Cunningham's hand on my arm told me it wasn't a dream. It was a nightmare.

CHAPTER 33

"You were expecting someone else?"

"How did you get in here?"

"Details, details. Like nosy neighbors and locked doors. You should know me by now, Ms. Brown. I always leave the details to someone else. I'm a big picture man."

"What do you want?"

"Ms. Brown. Must you ask? I'm very disappointed. You've been so clever up to now. Sending that e-mail about the message lights, warning everyone to check for new messages. A golden opportunity for you to eavesdrop. Well, two can play at that game. Of course, I did refine the game a bit. That's what partners do. Sometimes it helps to erase the messages."

I felt my face burn at being caught out at my own little spying activity and a sense of doom descended when I realized what he could have learned from listening to my own messages. Had Polly left messages? D.C. Lawson, Susannah, Mr. Seals?

"And I worked so hard to throw you off the scent. I couldn't exactly charm the pants off of you—I've been told that I'm very charming but seducing the staff is frowned upon by management these days—and anyhow I draw the line at pregnant associates. Scaring you with the shelves was a diversionary tactic. Paying some punk to steal Blake's box back turned up trumps. I knew I had to keep you busy until you went off to have your baby. Keep you occupied and not pining away for your old boss. I could've handled the Declan United matter alone, but I knew that the way into your heart was through your head. To appeal to your mind. Just another form of flattery. Your weakness. Every woman has one. I find that to be the most fun. The most challenging. Finding just what makes a woman tick and then exploiting that weakness with a compliment. Yes, flattery has taken me just about everywhere. You were certainly ripe for the taking. Pathetic Ms. Amy Brown, toiling at Daniel's side, becoming an English lawyer. And finding you a secretary, that was a stroke of real genius."

"Nikki?" I asked weakly.

"She knows nothing. But the gratitude." He closed his eyes and grinned like the Cheshire cat.

"You killed him, didn't you?"

"Of course I killed him. The perfect crime—so fitting for a gluttonous, greedy, despicable old man—death by chocolate. Served him right for not minding his own business."

"And what business was that?"

"What, the cagey Ms. Brown hasn't figured it all out yet?"

"I guess I'm not so smart after all. Yesterday I thought David Knight had killed Mr. Blake. Tomorrow, who knows?"

I was hoping to get an opportunity to see tomorrow. I'd had lots of experience getting Mr. Blake to boast about himself and his accomplishments when I needed to deflect attention from a lost file, a typographical error or a missed deadline, anything likely to set him off. All it took was a little encouragement and self-effacement. I planned on keeping Ted talking long enough for Steven to return. He'd said an hour. Hadn't an hour gone by? But I knew that I had been wrenched from my dream-like state for barely five minutes.

"Now if you'll just be kind enough to get up off that sofa."

Teddy rose from the sofa and pulled a pistol from his pocket. I remained unnaturally calm while my eyes focused on the gun.

"Oh, don't worry about this." He drew imaginary circles in the air. "Just a little trinket from Sir Gordon's antique collection. I'm not going to shoot you if that's what you're afraid of. Not that it doesn't work, mind you. My esteemed stepfather insists that all his possessions be in good working order. Keeps the servants busy. I admire that about him. Letting others do the dirty work. No, this is just here to provide that added little push to get you to do what I want. Now, get up from there." He motioned with the gun for me to stand.

My earlier exhaustion was forgotten. I was wide awake now. I reluctantly swung my feet from their resting place and onto the floor. I felt around desperately with my sore feet for the shoes that only minutes ago I had happily discarded. Finding them was all that stood between me and panic.

"Leave the shoes. You won't be needing them."

The man whose predatory nature I had mistaken for charisma wrenched me to my feet and yanked me toward him. He pushed the gun into the small of my back and ordered me to walk from the room. I thought about all his beautiful children. What had their mothers seen in him?

"Where are we going?"

"In here." He pulled my hair with one hand and, with the gun in the other, we walked the length of the apartment until we reached Steven's bathroom. The room was steamy from the running water I had heard earlier. I faced a foggy mirror above the sink top while Ted looked over his shoulder to the bathtub behind us. "Take off those clothes. Damn, the water's drained. Bloody English plumbing!"

Steven's bathroom had a faulty tap and a loose plug. Would Steven explain to the police that I never took a bath in here? Could I rely on one little domestic detail unknown to Teddy to trip him?

Teddy let go of my hair while he bent to get closer to the bath behind me. I turned to face him and the gun that he held at arm's length while he opened the faucet. I held my arms up to my neck and pretended to fumble with the buttons at the back of my dress with one hand while, behind me, I felt along the sink counter with the other for something, anything, to delay the deadly soak Teddy had planned for me.

"It must have been really difficult," I shouted over the running water.

"It was difficult, but not that difficult."

Perfect, just the right mix of authority and obsequiousness, I thought.

"Once it was clear that he meant business, I started thinking about ways to get rid of him without drawing the wrong kind of attention. It had to look like an accident. A fall, or he forgot to take his heart medicine. I considered all the possibilities. And I knew, we all knew, about the nut allergy. I found out that his heart medicine could make his symptoms worse—it's amazing what one can learn from the Internet—I knew that it was the perfect way to get rid of him. And it helped to remove his vial of adrenaline from his desk until just after he'd died. Of course, unlike you, Ms. Brown, I put back what I steal from a crime scene.

"The candy sat there like a fucking time bomb. And I knew that sooner or later the old man would inhale the lot. I could keep feeding him bits of information, delay the exposure a few more days. Detestable old man eats nasty nuts, doesn't get to his medicine in time, and dies. And that was that. It was all so easy." He laughed to himself while the water rose steadily in the bath. "And do you know what was the hardest part?" He turned away from the bathtub to make sure that I had his full attention.

Recognizing my role in this tragedy as the incredulous but nonetheless impressed and self-effacing junior lawyer, I spoke the next line. "No, what was the hardest part?"

"Getting the fucking chocolates. I didn't want to run the risk, however slight, that someone might see me in a Darlington store in London asking for candy with nuts, so I had the brilliant idea to buy it while I was traveling. The only Darlington store in the U.S. that I knew about was too close to the New York office for comfort. And then I thought, why take the risk of being seen buying it when Royal Crest Hotels were giving it away for free? I started saving the boxes from the hotel. There were always pieces with nuts, just not a large number at any one time. Even a generous tip couldn't convince the maids to hand over more than a box at a time. I finally just found the staff linen closet and helped myself."

To chocolates and a house full of monogrammed hand towels, I thought. My free hand fell on a bar of soap. I pocketed it.

"And then switched them for the candy Blake had. But then you turned out to be more clever than anyone ever gave you credit for. You go and hire some cocoa nut. To analyze the chocolates. Who in God's name knows that American chocolate is not the same as European chocolate?

Who cares about the cocoa butter content of chocolate? That's not law, that's mental masturbation."

Now was not the time to come to Polly's defense. In the seconds that Teddy turned back to look at the bathtub, I moved both hands along the counter feeling for Steven's toiletries. Tears sprang to my eyes as I nicked the tips of first, my fingertips, and then the palm of my hand on a razor. I pulled the voluminous sleeve of my dress past my wrist to staunch the bleeding and with my other hand quickly grabbed the first bottle within reach.

Teddy, resting on the bathtub edge, spoke casually about his accomplishments while he dipped his hand in the water from time to time. He could have been drawing a bath for his children. I stood still, waiting for his next move.

"Blake would have relished throwing it up at me. You know how he could be. That I, Robert Theodore Cunningham, III, summa from Harvard College, magna from Harvard Law, could flunk the Bar exam. It was inconceivable. I was smarter than most of my instructors. I didn't need Bar examiners. Some holier than thou administrators telling me I wasn't a lawyer because I didn't score some measly five or six points."

I couldn't believe that anyone, even a lawyer, could kill someone because he'd flunked the Bar exam. Sure, it brought out the worst in everyone. You've gone to school for three years but you're nowhere until you pass the Bar exam. I'd had homicidal thoughts about the person who sat next to me on the day of the exam—his relentless sniffing had been like something out of an Edgar Allen Poe story. And there had been times when I had even wanted to kill myself. But I got over it.

"You should have seen him that week—he was shouting and spitting at me. By this time I had already started the plan in motion. He even told me that afternoon that he'd let you resign rather than let you get 'tarnished' by me. He'd already guessed. I knew it was just a matter of time before he had proof. He threatened public exposure if I didn't just resign and leave quietly. Me, leave? Me, admit that after all these years of practicing, carrying the flag for Winter, Worthington, that I'm not and never have been a licensed qualified attorney? Can you imagine the humiliation? I had no choice but to kill him."

The elusive "why." Not love, hatred, greed, anger or jealousy, but humiliation. Teddy and I had obviously gone to very different law schools. Ted's ego was even bigger than Mr. Blake's had been. I'd foolishly looked for clues among the private lives of my co-workers when the truth should have been obvious all along. What would be important enough to a lawyer to make him kill a lawyer? Being a lawyer, what else? Tears came to my eyes again. I knew the answer, but I had to ask. "What are you going to do?"

"Poor Ms. Brown. Can't we just picture her, trudging up all those stairs, heavily pregnant, so weary? She decides to have a nice relaxing bath but with all that extra weight and exhaustion she loses her balance as she's stepping into the bath. It's something about the change in a pregnant woman's center of gravity, isn't it? Tips the weight forward. So easy to get ahead of yourself, lose your balance, fall and hurt your head and drown in all this wonderful water. I'm familiar with all the risks. All those wives you know."

"Helen knows. I found the form that shows that you've been using Charles Kent's Bar membership as your own. She was calling David Knight when I left the office. And I never take a bath in here. This is Steven's bathroom. He'll know this wasn't an accident."

"Shut up, you lying bitch." He stood up from the bath

and slapped me hard across the cheek.

I resisted the urge to rub my face where Teddy had just struck me.

"Now take those clothes off."

"I can't," I said, sobbing now. "I can't reach the zipper."

"Turn around. This has to look right."

I closed my eyes while I turned around like an obedient child and allowed Teddy Cunningham, seducer and murderer, to unfasten the buttons and unzip my dress. He placed the gun on the sink as I had hoped. Undressing a woman, even for professionals like Teddy, was a two-handed operation. He was close enough for me to feel his breath on my neck and I trembled.

"Now take it off."

I turned to face him with my back to the door and my heavy velvet dress top falling across my shoulders. He reached for the gun just as I pulled the razor from my pocket. I dragged it deeply across his hand and bright red blood splattered across the countertop. In surprise and pain, he grabbed his hand and knocked the gun to the floor. The clatter of metal on the tiled floor was followed quickly by a popping sound that I didn't recognize. I gasped as something sharp and hot hit my bare foot.

Ignoring the pain, I ran from the room. Just as Teddy had planned, my neighbors hadn't come running at the sound of gunfire. I didn't look back as I left my apartment for the gloomy hallway. My home seemed too full of opportunities to become another one of Polly's statistics to linger there. I didn't pause to find the hallway timer but gathered the dress that Teddy had unfastened around my shoulders and felt for the banister as I raced down the stairs. I had made the turn to the third of four landings when I felt my feet buckle under me and, helpless to stop myself, sank to the floor.

★ ★ ★ ★ ★

Many years ago I had awakened from minor surgery in a refrigerated recovery room. I had struggled to rise from my horizontal position but pain and tight bedclothes had prevented any movement. From my limited perspective, the room looked white, austere, and forbidding and felt horribly cold. When I moved my mouth to speak, no words came out. When I managed to mumble something about the cold, no nurse came running. In my shivering disoriented state, I assumed that the operation had not been a success, that I had died and, in spite of a life lived playing by the rules, I had gone to Hell. Except that the stories I'd been told as a child about Hell being all fire and brimstone had been lies. Hell was eternity in a stainless steel freezer.

The sensation of being damned to ice cube purgatory had returned. My cheek rested on cold stone and I shivered as I lifted my head. It was moments before I remembered that I was not dead but if Teddy Cunningham had his way I soon would be.

I listened for him but heard nothing. Could you kill someone with a razor blade? Polly would know. The hallway remained black. I felt the baby kick and was reassured that my stomach had not taken the force of my fall. My right ankle throbbed and my left foot was sticky and wet. It was the only part of me that felt warm. I pulled on the folds of my massive red dress and tugged the skirt out from under me. It slipped off my shoulders and I clasped the long skirt around my legs. Encouraged by the silence—I must have cut him deeper than I had imagined—I stood up in order to continue my escape down the stairs. But nauseating pain from the pressure on my foot made me sit right back down again. If I was going to make it down the stairs, it was going to be bottom first.

The effort to scoot down the stairs was exhausting. I shook with cold and fear but my armpits were drenched with sweat. I tried to calculate the distance to the front door. Sixty-eight stairs divided by four landings. Numbers came tumbling into my head and I started counting backwards just to take my mind off the pain. Even with my poor mathematical skills I knew I had another dozen stairs to go. I was relieved when my hands felt the curved, worn grooved stairs of the last set of stairs before the door.

A sudden gust of cold air took my breath away. I was close enough to the front door to know that no one had entered and the sound of a hand banging on the unreliable timer three floors above me meant that Teddy was only about fifty-odd stairs away. Where was a dangerous vacuum cleaner when I needed it? I stopped my descent and moved as far away from the banister as I could get and then stopped when I finally heard his footsteps come nearer. I pulled my dress closer around me and huddled into the wall, hoping that in the darkness he would run past. I held my breath as the steps shook next to me and I heard him continue down the stairs. I listened for the front door and breathed out carefully when I heard the door handle turn.

The snap and sizzle of phosphorus on sandpaper broke the cold, dark silence on the stairs, and within seconds, Ted Cunningham's face was illuminated by match light. Standing just inches away on the stairs below me, he leaned toward me and laughed. "There you are. I hope you don't mind." He waved an arm wrapped in one of my white guest towels. It was soaked with red. Probably ruined. And unlike Teddy, I bought my own towels. "Your little escape means I'll just have to improvise. Ms. Brown takes an unfortunate tumble down the stairs."

Steven could still walk through the door. I felt as if I'd

spent a lifetime on the stairs. Maybe for once in our marriage, my husband would be early. Stalling for time and courage, I appealed once more to Teddy's ego and asked, "How did you know that Mr. Blake would have a box of chocolates on his desk?"

"That's the best part!"

But Ted didn't get to tell, and I didn't care about hearing, the best part. Laughing, he prepared to tell me one more detail that would convince me of his superiority. I leaned forward from my crouched position on the stairs above him and blew out the match. I heard him swear as he fumbled in his pockets while in the darkness I pulled myself up another step. The blue and white light of another match flickered as he teased it to stay lit. I gathered the folds of my enormous sleeves more closely around me as I pulled from my pocket the bottle—aftershave, air freshener, antiperspirant, I didn't know which—that I had taken from Steven's bathroom. And in the moment of strongest light, I aimed the nozzle at the golden boy wonder, the public face of Winter, Worthington & Walker, the fraud who would rather kill than be humbled, and, saying a silent prayer to the high priestess of product liability and consumers everywhere—Polly, forgive me—I ignored the 5cm warning DO NOT SPRAY DIRECTLY INTO FLAME.

CHAPTER 34

"Does everyone have a drink? Oh, that's right, Amy, you're still off the hard stuff." Polly, the perfect hostess, in contrast to her usual role as undesirable guest, circled the room with a tray loaded with champagne flutes and canapés. She had insisted on having the party at her house to celebrate the birth of my new son—like his mother, he'd arrived early—and the near return of my waistline. "Here, have a glass of sparkling water. What about him?"

"I don't think he'll be needing anything soon. I hope not. I just fed him before we arrived."

"And how is the little one doing?" Helen, not someone I would have ever believed to have an interest in babies, peered into the carryall at my side.

"He's great."

"And you?"

"I'm fine, just a little tired."

"I know this isn't the time or the place . . ."

"For what?" I looked around the room at the smiling faces of my colleagues and friends. "If this has anything to do with my office or the paperwork, I agree. It really isn't the time."

"No, it's nothing like that. I really just wanted to thank you. For putting an end to things."

"That's an unusual way of describing it. But what do you need to thank me for?"

"It was only a matter of time before I would have figured it out—I did think it funny that he wasn't interested in becoming an English lawyer—and then—who knows?—the next victim might have been me."

"My pleasure." I didn't feel like reminding her that I'd told her my discovery of Ted's duplicity. Alcohol had apparently induced amnesia. Still, I was happy that she recognized she owed me. "Gideon! I didn't know they let men into these things." I turned to see Gideon, the latest lawyer to defect from DW3, at my side, and asked, "How's your new job?"

"It's wonderful, I'm really enjoying the challenge. And what about the new chap? Have you met him, Amy?"

"No, I'm afraid I've been out of the loop." Prompted by the discovery that he'd been inflating his billable hours to levels beyond human endurance, Gideon had resigned. His suspicions that someone had been watching him had been right. His departure left DW3 without its required quota of homegrown English lawyers and David and Helen had had to hustle to fill the vacancy as quickly as possible. Lucy and Nikki—I saw them across the room with a still-tearful Louise—had described the whirlwind of interviews and offers that had followed. The process had been fast, but not so fast as to ignore certain details, like whether the candidate was really a qualified lawyer.

"I don't want to barge in. I really stopped by just to say hello to Amy. And to give my regards to this little fellow. I brought him a little something."

"Thanks, that's very sweet."

"I'll be going. Take care, Amy."

"Bye, Gideon, I'll miss you." I squeezed his arm affectionately and watched him walk away. "Can you just watch the baby a minute, Helen?"

"Oh, well, of course." Helen looked alarmed that her penance might be watching the baby.

"I'll be right back." I headed over to the table to set the gift Gideon had handed to me with others on the table. Dorthea Knight, recently separated from David, had miraculously recovered from her various ailments. She was now the picture of good health and was chatting with Barbara Hughes. They wished me well and I thanked them before they made their way over to coo at the baby.

"Amy." Kimberly stood next to me at the table, sipping her champagne.

"Hello, Kimberly. Partnership seems to suit you."

"As motherhood seems to suit you. Just look at you. Except for those little circles under your eyes and your hair—that really isn't your color—you're practically back to your old self."

Only in Kimberly's eyes was my natural hair color unsuitable. But nothing was going to burst my euphoric bubble. I ignored her last comment and asked, "Any celebrations planned?"

"Helen's coming up with something. Probably a joint do with Walter."

"With who?"

"Walter Hughes. Haven't you heard? The Hughes are moving back to Washington."

"Really?"

"Walter's snagged some big job. Ambassador Harrington's hands are all over it. It's a political appointment so he'll have to go through the usual vetting process but it sounds like it's in the bag. Could you imagine someone as cerebral as Walter having any skeletons in his closet?"

"No, no skeletons." Walter likes them with a bit more flesh.

"Amy!" Karen Sandler held out her arms to hug me.

"Karen, hi! Thanks for coming. Do you know Kimber . . ."

"Aren't you Kimberly?" Not waiting for me to finish introductions or for Kimberly to answer, Karen continued talking, "I believe you know my husband . . ."

I stifled my laughter—Karen was known to direct the animosity she usually reserved for the British at the same women her husband found attractive. I waited for the fireworks but Polly pulled me aside.

"Sorry to interrupt, but shouldn't you start opening presents?" Polly spoke softly, afraid to wake the baby.

"Sure."

I spent the rest of the afternoon opening baby blankets and rattles to an endless chorus of oohs and ahs. Steven's appearance was timed perfectly. He arrived just as the guests were leaving.

"Was it something I said? Here, give me these, I'll take them out to the car."

I handed gifts to Steven and Polly and I started clearing up while he carried the treasure trove to the car.

"How are you really doing?" Polly asked as the last guest left.

"I'm fine. Honestly." Being alone with anyone connected to DW3 meant that sooner or later I would be subjected to sincere and very serious questions about my state of mind.

"What did the doctor say about your foot?"

"Well, I won't be wearing any smart Italian pumps any time soon."

"And your hand?"

"That the bandages can come off soon and that it won't scar, but that it would be tender for awhile and that I should stay out of direct sunlight."

"This is England so that part shouldn't be a problem. Do you mind if I ask you one question? I mean, about Mr. Blake and all that happened."

"Sure."

"Are you sure you're sure? I wouldn't want to upset you."

"Polly, you won't upset me."

"All right, here goes. It's just the lawyer in me."

"Okay."

"How did he get away with it for so long?"

"You mean Teddy?" Of course she meant Teddy. I took a deep breath and began, "It certainly helped to have a secretary madly in love with him and a colleague who decided to drop out of the legal rat race. Paige, that was Teddy's first wife, ran Judge Tustin's office. By the time Teddy found out that he'd flunked the Bar exam, he was already sleeping with Paige. It wasn't difficult to convince her to fix the files and establish that he'd in fact passed the Bar. Of course, Ted had to marry, and then later, pay her to keep her quiet." I had mistaken Paige's demands for money as alimony and not for what it really had been—blackmail. "Paige—and Teddy—used Charles Kent's membership status, he'd gone inactive years before, for their own purposes. They, and later, just Teddy, paid Charles' Bar dues and other professional fees so there would always be receipts to show Helen and the firm."

"But what about after Teddy started working? Why didn't Winter, Worthington find out that he hadn't passed the Bar? And why wasn't he exposed when he moved overseas?"

This was more than one question from Polly but I didn't mind. For a change, I had the answers. "No one even checked. Teddy'd been out of law school for two years. The firm didn't even ask for a transcript. Happens all the time. Or at least it used to. His British passport came in handy in Hong Kong, London and the European Union. And he never officially moved or worked in Tokyo—he kept up the fiction that he was resident in Hong Kong and just traveling through Japan. The only posting where Cunningham really did need a work permit was Istanbul. He couldn't marry the entire immigration department, but he could pay them off. Eventually, he slipped off the firm's bureaucratic radar screen until Her Majesty and the firm's extravaganza. One of Blake's temporary secretaries, stupid girl, ran to Blake, of all people, when she couldn't find information on Teddy's Bar membership in the file. Mr. Blake was the last person to get involved in an administrative matter but he'd go to any length to annoy Helen. He apparently started asking Teddy some tough but probably innocent questions and the longer Teddy stalled the more suspicious Mr. Blake became. Blake kept pressing for information until Teddy had to act."

And without a cover page, I hadn't recognized the significance of the fax from the D.C. Bar that Saturday morning I had discovered Mr. Blake's body. I had left it for Tony and the trash.

"What a stroke of luck that that man from the D.C. Bar called back."

"Right. Mr. Seals."

"Without him . . ."

"Don't forget the Royal Crest towel!"

"And the towel, you might never have made the connection." By now, everyone had heard the story about the secretary who had mistaken the D.C. Bar for a Latino restaurant. "Why *had* he called?"

I smiled to myself. As a fellow expatriate American in

London, Polly would have appreciated the reason for Mr. Seals' call. How many times had I ended a conversation to another American with the words "If you ever make it to London, give me a call" safe in the knowledge that the call would never be made? Meaningless but no less sincere. Mr. Seals had defied the odds and had called to take up the invitation from the only American he knew in London. Daniel Blake's one act of uncharacteristic kindness—a hollow invitation to a stranger—hadn't redeemed him from a lifetime of bad deeds but it had led to the telephone call that had allowed me to find his killer. The irony was bittersweet. I looked away from Polly and said, "I don't know but I'm glad he did."

Polly was silent while the two of us contemplated the consequences of one old man's meddling. She placed the remaining piece of wrapping paper in the trash while I stuffed cards in a shopping bag.

"You know, you never asked me about the results of the research on the rest of the candy, whether it had nuts or not."

"I know. I mean, I don't want to know."

"Don't want to know what?"

"Steven. You're back."

"Are you ready to go?"

"Yes. We're finished here."

"Then just this last piece of cargo." He lifted the baby carrier and walked out the front door.

"I've got to go." I picked up the shopping bag and my coat. "Thanks so much for this wonderful party, Polly. It was really beautiful."

"It was my pleasure. Take good care of yourself. And keep in touch."

"I will. Goodbye." I waved from the car.

301

"How was the party?" Steven asked as we pulled into traffic.

"It was really nice."

"Who was there?"

"Oh, Polly, Karen, all the women from the office. Gideon stopped by. It was good to see everyone." I paused and thought that someone had been missing. "Steven," I said as I looked back at the sleeping infant, "he's out like a light. I think it's the motion of the car. Feel like taking a little drive? There's something I want to check. And I could use the peace and quiet."

"Sure. Where to?"

"1739 Hampstead Row."

CHAPTER 35

"Miss Brown. What a pleasant surprise."

"Please, call me Amy."

"Amy." Mei Leow nodded.

"I'm sorry to drop by uninvited. We were sort of in the neighborhood," I made a mental promise about keeping honest now that I didn't have a crime to solve, "and I didn't see you at the party although I asked Polly to invite you."

"Yes. I'm sorry. I should have called but I've been busy. Is that your husband in the car? Please, do come in, both of you, and bring the baby."

"If we're not intruding . . ." I motioned to Steven and within minutes we were following Mei through the hall until we emerged into a beautiful sun room filled with blue Chinese porcelain and furniture upholstered in yellow washed silk. I sat on the sofa with the baby carrier at my feet and Mei perched on a chair. Unlike the hall and entranceway, the room radiated warmth and personality.

"If you could excuse me, I need to check on some things in the car." Steven shot me a questioning look, as if to ask, "Amy, what are you up to now?" and then vanished.

"I don't think I've ever been in this room. It's beautiful."

"Thank you."

"It's your room, isn't it?"

303

"Well, I have always lived-in but the servants' rooms are . . ."

"But then they're all your rooms, aren't they? The whole house."

"Then you knew? About Daniel and me?"

"I guess a part of me always knew. Call it intuition. I should have guessed that day that I came here for his diary. But I was just blind to my own prejudices. Not about you being Chinese, but the two of you being old, er, older."

Funny how it only took a few minutes to remove a string of pearls, replace them with an apron and rubber gloves, and the mature lady of the house was transformed into the elderly housekeeper. I guess we all saw what we wanted to see. Teddy Cunningham certainly had looked the part of a real lawyer. I thought of a young secretary who had been granted a reprieve from a lifetime of guilt for a moment of inattention and recalled my disbelief at her suggestion that Mr. Blake had had a bird. I looked at the woman across from me. The description hadn't been too far off the mark.

"Have David Knight and Josh Hall sorted out the financial arrangements?"

"Yes, I closed on the house last week. Daniel had always intended that we live here after he retired. He'd started making the necessary arrangements with David and the bank. He even wanted to get married but I, well, you think you're going to live forever . . ."

"Those chocolates were intended for you, weren't they?" I asked gently.

Mei's eyes filled with tears. "Yes. He came home with them one Friday night a few months before he died. We'd had an argument—my temper was worse than his—and he wanted to give me a peace offering. He knew that I had a

304

sweet tooth—he called it my one and only weakness—and he said that a friend, I didn't know who, had recommended Darlington chocolates."

It wasn't that surprising to hear that Mr. Blake, months before his discovery of Teddy's fraud, had gone for advice to the one person at DW3 with the most experience in matters of the heart, or that Teddy had been happy to give advice to the lovelorn. Only later would the choice of chocolates become deadly.

"The chocolates became our Friday night ritual of sorts. Sometimes I'd buy them, sometimes he'd buy them."

"Weren't you frantic when he didn't come home that evening?"

"I wasn't here. I was still in Hong Kong. They were meant as a homecoming present. I'd been visiting relatives. My sister convinced me to stay on. I called Daniel that day to tell him not to expect me for another week. He had chided me. Said I was going to miss him and my special treat. I told him he should open them. Go ahead and eat them and to think of me with each bite." She choked on her words. She turned away for a moment while she regained her composure. "But today's not a day for sadness. It's a beautiful day. Daniel and I had several wonderful years together. I have many happy memories. And what about you? How are you doing? You seemed to have adjusted to motherhood very well. He seems like a perfect angel."

"Yes. An angel. At least he is right now."

"But?"

"But he's not always such an angel. He doesn't sleep through the night—hasn't since he came home from the hospital. And just when I think he's dozed off so I can finally get some sleep, off he goes. Crying. This pitiful crying. I swear he knows how to make just the right pitch to get me going. It makes me crazy. And he bites. And he's hungry all the time. If my body could handle it, he'd feed non-stop. It's like he considers these"—I pointed to my chest—"his very own property. He can be sweet, docile, after he's fed, naturally. But he wants to be held, entertained all the time—he just screams and demands my attention. And if someone comes into the room, tries to talk to him, or me, forget it. He'll have none of it. Only me, all the time."

I was on a roll. I was confiding feelings about motherhood that I hadn't even expressed to Steven.

"It's like living with a little dictator. I get up from my three hours of sleep and the rest of the day's schedule just revolves around him." The baby stirred, as if aware that we were talking about him. "He's awake now. It'll only be a few minutes before you see what I mean."

"Do you think I could hold him?"

"Well, he doesn't really like other people to hold him but sure. You can give it a go." I picked up the baby and handed him to Mei. He whimpered and I gritted my teeth and braced myself for a wail. But the wail didn't come. He settled into the cradle of Mei's arms—and looked straight up at her.

"It's been a long time since I've held a baby." She looked at me and then back at the baby.

I could only imagine that her thoughts were the same as mine. Screaming, crying, greedy, dictatorial, demanding, controlling. A new but familiar force in my life. It's not like I really believed in reincarnation, but I couldn't help thinking that Mr. Blake's spirit had just been waiting for my baby to be born. I'd been worried about being unprepared for motherhood when I'd already had years of on-the-job training.

"Where are we?" I looked out the car window and saw the DW3 office building flash past.

"You dozed off the minute we left Hampstead. Guess the baby gets the ability to sleep in the car from his mother."

"For a minute there I thought I was on my way to the office. I saw the building and thought . . ."

"I had to cut through here to avoid the traffic on Piccadilly. Are you going to miss the place?"

"No, I don't think so. Maybe just a little."

"So, no regrets?"

I had not regretted much that I'd done over the last few months. Listening in on my office mates' calls and reading their mail had been an invasion of their privacy but, I thought, forgivable. I certainly hadn't regretted torching Ted Cunningham's handsome face. I didn't think I even regretted the almost deadly confrontation with Cunningham, for, in that last illuminating moment, I had changed. No more sappy Amy Brown, easily intimidated by policemen, managing partners and office managers who had made her question her own state of mind. Just like Daniel Blake and Robert Theodore Cunningham, III, the new Amy Brown was going to do whatever it took to survive, to succeed, to win the case, to get her way. She would make and break the rules, follow her own directions, step on toes, make other people uncomfortable, maybe even lose her temper now and again. What else was a mother to do?

And I had already experienced one major victory. Steven and I had finally agreed on the baby's name. The usual bargaining method—husband concedes to wife during the throes of labor—had worked, along with third degree burns and a bullet wound. But I preferred to attribute his defeat to my new confidence.

"Amy, are you listening to me? I asked you if you had any regrets."

"Oh, sorry, I was listening for the baby. Are you sure he's breathing? He hasn't ever been this quiet before."

"Amy, he's fine. You didn't answer my question."

"You mean do I have any regrets about resigning for the second and last time so that I can stay at home with the baby?" David Knight had been very persuasive but I knew that I had made the right decision. Sixty-eight stairs and a stroller no longer seemed so daunting.

"Yes."

"No, no regrets."

But I did have one regret, an unspoken one. I looked back at Blake Goldman Brown—this baby would have three last names—asleep and for now as unlike the raging Daniel Benedict Blake on the day that he fired me as any living creature could be. But that image of the old man had been tempered by the look on Mei's face when she spoke of her happy memories, by the sound of disappointment in Mr. Seal's voice when I told him that a man with whom he'd shared a pleasant conversation was gone, and by the unexpected surprise of Ted's throwaway comment that Mr. Blake had fired me not in anger but to protect me. Maybe bereavement, like childbirth, had caused my body to produce some magical ingredient that made me forget the pain and aggravation caused by the deceased. All I knew was that the Daniel Blake I'd known and needed was fading from memory and was being replaced by an image of a benevolent pensioner carrying a box of Darlington chocolates. Which to me was a mixed blessing. The old Mr. Blake would have enjoyed jousting with the new Amy Brown. For that reason alone, my only regret—which I was sure that few who'd met the man would have ever understood—was that I hadn't eaten his entire box of chocolates.

The employees of Five Star hope you have enjoyed this book. All our books are made to last. Other Five Star books are available at your library, through selected bookstores, or directly from us.

For information about titles, please call:

(800) 223-1244

or visit our Web site at:

www.gale.com/fivestar

To share your comments, please write:

Publisher
Five Star
295 Kennedy Memorial Drive
Waterville, ME 04901